Sea of Liberty

KEVIN C. MILLS

Sea of Liberty
© 2014 Kevin C. Mills

ISBN: 978-1-938883-98-9

Designed and produced by
Maine Authors Publishing
Rockland, Maine
www.maineauthorspublishing.com

Printed in the United States of America

For all my ancestors that served the cause
of liberty, truth and justice.

"*The boisterous sea of liberty is never without a wave.*"

—Thomas Jefferson

CHAPTER ONE
Aboard the *Sparrow*, 1764

Some storms you see coming. You prepare in advance. You brace for them. You shore up the ship.

You're as ready as you can be for whatever nature offers.

Then there are storms you never anticipate. They blow in unexpectedly and wreak havoc. Their danger lies not only in their sudden intensity, but also in your vulnerability.

This is one of those storms. Luke Miller never sees it coming and barely has time to ready his crew.

Sailing for home from the West Indies, a sudden gale in the middle of summer is far from Luke's expectations. These types of storms blow regularly during the fall, but not this time of year.

One of the reasons Luke is pleased to be heading back to Portsmouth is that he'll miss out on some of the worst weather of the year at sea. Being a successful merchant mariner requires risk. Luke isn't opposed to taking such chances, but he isn't hell bent on facing the fickleness of nature in the fall and winter, either.

He's already established himself as a prominent captain in Portsmouth. Between his large home on the hill overlooking town, his wharf, his ships and a few other buildings he owns, Luke has been richly rewarded for his role in the growing shipping industry. Thanks to the wars with France, Portsmouth's shipping trade has begun to evolve. Luke is among a dozen other mariners who have sought a living on the high seas.

With his son Eli aboard to learn the trade from his father, Luke has no reason to press his luck or push his vessel into harm's way. But Luke is seasoned enough to know that sometimes trouble finds you, no matter how much you hope to avoid it.

There are no signs of such a storm as the day begins. Luke is driving the ship hard with a good breeze and making some progress on the westerlies. With a hold full of rum and sugar, he is anxious to arrive home and enjoy the rewards of another profitable journey.

The first sign is a sudden dip in temperatures. The tropical air the crew had gotten accustomed to is replaced with a cold, biting wind.

Luke notices it right away. He's a savvy enough sailor to know that temperature drops signal other changes. He can sense the subtlest shift in air, wind, and seas. He can often predict a storm coming hours before it actually arrives—but not on this day.

The temperature drops unexpectedly. The wind suddenly shifts and rises in intensity. The full force of the storm comes in an instant. A small shrill of a wind suddenly turns into a roaring rage.

Luke has never seen anything like it. He has spent much of the morning down below, letting Eli man the wheel while his first mate Ezra Budwick navigated. Luke was unusually weary in the morning. With clear skies and likely smooth sailing, he seized the opportunity to relinquish the helm to Eli.

He's only been topside an hour when he notices the change in temperature.

"You feel that?" he asks calmly, hiding his potential concern.

Eli and Budwick each glance around and shake their heads. It takes a moment before they each notice the sudden coolness, accompanied by a gust of wind that makes it more obvious.

"Ezra, you better rally the crew," Luke suggests. His first mate rushes into action, summoning crew members who were off shift and sleeping in their bunks. The others race to action, tightening up lines and clearing the deck of potential debris.

Before Budwick can get all hands on deck, the storm rushes in full bore. It comes with an eerie howl and frothing sea. The weather turns violent in an instant. The clear sky is replaced by a dreary gray that looms threateningly. With it come winds that pound the vessel and seas that shake the ship. The pelting rain comes from all directions on the fierce wind.

"Eli, you better get tethered," Luke tells his son.

"A tether?" he asks. "Do I really need a safety rope?"

"It's not a suggestion, it's an order," Luke says sternly.

Eli begrudgingly secures himself, knowing that Budwick will find great amusement at such an action. It is hard enough gaining respect as the eighteen-year-old young son of the captain, but being tethered only invites more ridicule from the mate.

From his place at the wheel, Eli watches the ship and crew go from a smooth sail to a violent fight for survival. The sea rises and washes over the rails. It reaches the point where many of the crew opt to tether themselves to the ship as well, just to be safe.

Eli has never seen sea conditions turn as badly as this. He's sailed numerous journeys with his father and battled through some challenging weather, but nothing this severe. He can see the fear in the eyes of the fellow crew. He feels his own stirring from deep within.

He sees no fear in his father's eyes. Eli watches Luke with amazement. The furious sea only provokes his father's tenacity. He sees a steely-eyed look of contempt from the captain, determined to sail through whatever the sea unleashes.

When a line on the mainsail boom breaks loose and begins to flail wildly, a crewman—Nathaniel Keating—attempts to gain control. His efforts land him sprawled on the deck as the line snaps unexpectedly and slashes across his face. Keating is knocked backward, landing in a heap on the deck with a bloody wound across his cheek. Another crew member rushes into action, but can't get close as he dodges the wind-whipped rope ready to slash the flesh of another.

"Hold the wheel firm, don't let her slide," Luke orders Eli. He leaves his post and rushes forward of the quarterdeck. He grabs a gaff hook and attempts to batter down the loose line and gain control.

He fails on numerous tries, dodging and ducking the elusive line. After narrowly avoiding the rope slicing its way above his head, he leaps up with the gaff hook and bats the errant line down. He holds it firmly to the deckboards. Before he has a chance to reel in the line or cut it loose completely, the ship rolls dramatically to starboard.

Luke flies off balance, and is nearly tossed over the rail. He lands hard against the side and reaches quickly to maintain some sort of grip to pull himself up. That's when another roll follows. A crashing wave comes surging across the vessel. It knocks all of the crew off their feet and even topples Eli. The wheel spins and the ship lurches.

Eli yanks on his tether to pull himself to his feet. He regains his grip on the wheel. As he glances over the deck, he sees no sign of his father. He looks more thoroughly, frantic. There is no sign of him. Luke has been washed overboard.

Eli quickly cuts loose his tether. He can see his father bobbing helplessly in the surf behind them. He rushes to the starboard rail, but is met by two members of the crew, including Budwick.

"No, Eli!" Budwick shouts, barely audible amidst the roar of the storm. "You cain't. There's nothin' you can do. You'll be lost as well."

Eli struggles for a moment, trying to break free from the hands that restrain him. Budwick and his fellow crewman hold firm. Eli is left standing frozen, unable to lend assistance, reeling at his impotence.

He looks out over the raging sea. He catches one more glimpse of his father, struggling in the cauldron of waves. Then, Luke slips out of sight.

He opens his mouth to call out to his father but no words come. He lets out a guttural, desperate, agonizing scream that can't even be heard above the volume of the storm.

Amidst the rollicking seas, Luke is gone.

CHAPTER TWO
Aboard the *Tempest*, 1773

D ead reckoning under such conditions just might get a sailor dead.

The *Tempest* has hauled out under the shadow of darkness. Only a scant number of lanterns provide light for Captain Ezra Budwick. His midnight escape from the West Indies is aided by his knowledge of the landscape, but precipitated by a hold filled with rum and molasses.

His potential for profit is great, if he can sneak away and make a hasty beat toward New England.

"When that ole bastard Buddy Bush learns he got swindled, he's gonna come lookin' for us," Budwick says. "We best be long gone before that happens."

He secured his cargo by slightly nefarious means. He played one buyer against the other and negotiated a lower price, convincing one gullible seller that his competition was willing to cut him a better deal. He knows Bush is too idiotic to know he's been had, but it is inevitable that even a man of his slight intellect will accidentally stumble across the fact that Jeremiah Hartwell, a seller on Barbados, wasn't offering a better price.

Rather than wait around for that to occur, Budwick loaded the cargo in a rush that late afternoon, amidst the harbor's usual activity. By the time nightfall arrived and the darkness obscured the intentions of Budwick and his crew, the *Tempest* had begun its escape.

There was just enough wind in the Harbor for the vessel to drift off a bit. By the time the ship reached the mouth of the cove, the crew set the sails with silent efficiency. In a matter of moments, the slight breeze was enough to carry Budwick and his cargo out to sea.

Eluding detection while hauling out was only the first foray into a difficult endeavor. Even if they are able to slip away unnoticed, they face a night of sailing into blackness and the weather is only worsening.

"Just our luck to be sailin' right into a screecher," Budwick says. "I knew this weren't gonna be easy."

It isn't like Budwick hasn't been through this before. He's been running cargo up and down the Atlantic seaboard for a decade. He's scrapped with pirates and matched wills with merchants more fearsome than Buddy Bush. For years, amidst the Seven Years War, he dodged the watchful eye of those combatants. Budwick has just about seen it all at sea. He's made a good living and managed to keep himself alive.

Budwick is a short, stout figure. He's shaped a bit like the barrels of molasses he's got stowed in his hold. The crumbs and stains on his shirt probably make him just as sticky, as well. Between his balding head and gray, almost white, beard and sideburns, he provides plenty of shine on a bright sunny day. His face is usually obscured by a black captain's hat. Its wide brim shades his often-sunburned face and his wild, glaring eyes.

But he's forgone the hat this evening. When the lantern light shines just right, his mate, Eli Miller, can see his bright red-cheeked face.

"I don't see any signs of anyone following us," Eli tells the captain. "I think we're away clean."

Eli is quite the contrast to his captain. He's a strapping young man, lean and muscular. He appears much younger than his prowess at sea implies. He has wavy, almost-curly blond hair and deep-set blue eyes. "I swear you're too purty to be a sailor," Budwick tells him on occasion.

Eli and Budwick go back years. The two sailed together with Eli's father, Luke. When he was lost at sea, both continued on in the seafaring trade.

"I'm more concerned about what's ahead than I am what's followin'," says Budwick. "I can't see jeepers of what's a comin', but it don't feel good."

As Budwick tries to keep the vessel on a north heading, a blustery wind is kicking up from the west. It provides the vessel a good brush of wind, but the waves are only getting wilder. The quiet calm that the *Tempest* slipped away under is now churning into a raging sea.

"These seas are lookin' meaner than ole Buddy Bush will be when he discovers he's been snookered," says Budwick.

Eli has little chance to agree. He rushes across the quarterdeck to shout instructions to the crew. He's got most hands on deck. Some are braving the weather up on the crosstrees in hopes of keeping the *Tempest* sailing hard.

As the weather worsens, the seas go from angry to downright furious. The ship is tossed about by large swells that lift the vessel momentarily and then drop it suddenly. The ship teeters with each passing wave. It is jostled about with little effort.

When one of the topgallants rips out, Eli sends crew members up to reel it in while others reduce the sails. Budwick eases the vessel through the savage conditions, trying to keep it from being blown too far out to sea.

It is a constant battle between man and nature. The fight against the raging sea turns mere seconds of grueling work into minutes and then hours. There's no time to be weary and no opportunity to rest.

After a four-hour fight, the storm finally begins to ease off and run its course. It has taken its power out on the *Tempest* and moved on. It leaves Budwick and his crew battered and beaten but still intact.

"It's gonna be a lot longer trip home," says Budwick. "I ain't got no idea in hell where we are."

The seas are subsiding slightly and the winds have ceased to blow with the same fury. It's a fresh breeze blowing now, one the crew hopes will maintain itself as their vessel works to adjust its course toward home.

The rotation for the crew is reset. Some head off for their bunks for a short rest. The others have a few more hours on deck to work, but their sleep is not far away.

As the sun begins to peak over the eastern horizon, it helps Budwick confirm his whereabouts. It also confirms that the *Tempest* is not alone in the spacious Atlantic.

"I'll be jiggered," says Budwick. "We got company."

Eli immediately grabs the spyglass for a look. The two-masted vessel well off their stern flies no flag to identify itself. Its dark hull and even darker sails cloak it in mystery.

"That cain't be Buddy Bush," Budwick exclaims. "He wouldn't have been able to find us out here if he rammed us with his bowsprit."

Eli lowers the spyglass and shakes his head.

"I can't make any identification," he tells the captain. "It looks suspicious."

He can confirm that it isn't Buddy Bush: He doesn't have a ship this large. It most likely isn't a British vessel, either. A Royal Navy cutter typically has just one mast with a square topsail yardarm and a long bowsprit. They'd have their colors displayed prominently on the bow.

A British brig would have guns that were apparent and a sail plan that was different than most sloops. This has neither. It is unlikely to be a French vessel; since the war, the French have left the American vessels alone for the most part. That leaves one option:

If it means harm, it has to be pirates.

Budwick takes a peek through the glass himself but reaches the same conclusion as his mate.

"I cain't tell neither," he says. "Only way to see who they are is to get closer, and I ain't gonna let that happen."

He gives the order, and Eli rouses the crew back into action. All the sails go back up. The torn-out top gallant is replaced. In a matter of moments, the *Tempest* is under full sail and riding the push of a steady breeze.

Now, they wait to see how well the vessel behind them can keep up.

Over the course of the next few hours, Budwick and Miller compare their speed to that of the vessel off their stern. It is a comparison that doesn't bode well for the *Tempest*. The mystery vessel is gaining slightly. Eventually, they'll be able to rob the *Tempest* of some of its wind. Once they get between Budwick and his source of power, it will be inevitable that they'll be able to approach.

Eli keeps his crew busy by tweaking the sails and trying to will every ounce of speed from the breezes, but Budwick already knows it won't be enough. He could ditch some of his load, be overtaken, or find another solution. The first two are not options in his mind. That leaves another option, which he hasn't found yet.

Eli returns to the quarterdeck, observing the closeness of the approaching vessel. He recognizes that they're not outrunning the predators and aren't likely to do so.

"Captain, it appears drastic measures may be needed," Eli says.

Budwick takes a quick look behind him, but already knows the answer to the question.

"It best be a quick one," he says.

Eli pauses for a moment and looks westward. The breeze has gotten colder, and it gives him an idea. They have been sailing up from the south with the warm air. When the cold seeps down from the north, it's going to create a weather system that just might be to their advantage.

"We're out to sea enough that maybe we don't see it," he explains. "My hunch is that the closer we get to shore, the more the fog will be herming up."

He waits to see the captain's reaction. Budwick looks to the west as well, then back at the mystery vessel.

"You're sayin' we could lose ourselves in a thick-a-vapor," he says.

Eli nods. He explains it won't be easy. If there is fog, as he expects, they may lose the ship. They could also put themselves in peril by straying too close to shore.

"No guarantees it will work," says Eli.

"But it may be our only choice," Budwick says.

Eli doesn't even need a vocal command. He reads his captain's face and understands the circumstances. The mate turns and shouts across the quarterdeck to his crew.

"Stand by about," he calls.

In an instant, the crew rushes to action. The captain gives the wheel a sudden jerk and the crew shifts the sails. The *Tempest* makes a quick tack to leeward. It is a maneuver that needs to be flawless and Budwick and his men manage a tack that is quite close to it.

The vessel turns sharply, but doesn't lose its speed. They'll have to battle into the wind a bit as they cut back toward the shore, but they hope the other vessel is caught so unaware that it buys them more time.

Once the *Tempest* makes its maneuver and is back sailing on the wind, Budwick and Eli glance back at the mystery vessel. They watch intently for any movement by their pursuer. If it stays its course, the chase may be over.

Both know better than to celebrate too soon, but when the mystery vessel doesn't move, it is a positive sign.

"Maybe they ain't givin' chase after all," says Budwick.

Eli watches through the glass. He sees movement on the deck but can't quite make out what is happening. Then the ship suddenly lurches. The sails swing as the ship tacks. The chase is still on.

"Their tacking," says Eli, watching every movement on their deck.

"They're slow, but they're coming after us."

Budwick mumbles a few curse words to himself and turns his attention to his own vessel. Any brief sense of relief that they may be clear of harm quickly dissipates. "Guess they want to continue this cat and mouse game," he shouts. "Well, I ain't no mouse."

Eli calls for the main sheet to be trimmed slightly and steps down off the quarterdeck to oversee the work on deck. He can't help but worry that his calculation might be wrong. If so, it could mean unspeakable consequences for him and the crew.

Even if he's correct, it is going to be a risky maneuver. Even if they manage to lose the other ship in the fog, they may very well lose course as well and wreck on something hidden. Regardless, the likelihood for disaster is greater than an escape.

Before he can refocus his attention on the sail handling of his vessel, a shout comes from the bow watch. A young sailor out of Boston, Rummy Spinnaker, is stationed there. He announces just what Eli wants to hear.

"Fog bank dead ahead," he says.

Eli steps to the larboard rail and peers forward. Well off the bow is a hovering mass of gray. Its mist beckons them and offers possible safety. It also cloaks mystery and danger to any that become consumed in its dense grip.

Who knows what they might encounter if they slip out of sight, but Eli just wants the chance. He looks back. The other vessel is sailing well to windward and is closing fast. If they get too close, the distance might not even be enough for the fog to hide them.

He turns and rushes back toward the quarterdeck. He grabs the spyglass and peers back at the mystery ship. He observes its crew standing at the ready. He can't tell how armed they may be, but that may not matter. He knows how unarmed his own crew is.

There are a few muskets aboard and the crew all has knives. The captain has a swivel cannon aft, but that's as much firepower as they can muster. Any boarding party would certainly be armed to the teeth. The vessel remains within a half mile. It has drawn close enough that Eli can see the anxious figures on deck, watching the chase intently.

Budwick is aiming the bowsprit dead center of the fog bank. He spots Eli watching the other ship and summons him to the wheel. His idea is to get into the fog bank, sail a bit, and make a quick maneuver to change course.

"We'll shout orders to tack one way, but we'll actually go the other," explains Budwick. "The sound tends to carry a mite in the fog. If they're close enough to hear us, it might throw them off. It could just work."

Eli rushes forward and explains the plan to the crew. He emphasizes the need for another flawless maneuver.

"Remember, don't do as we say," he stresses. "Do the opposite. We're not tacking to starboard. We're going the opposite direction."

As the bowsprit pokes through the mist of the fog, the vision off the bow begins to disappear. Steadily, the entire ship slips quietly through the grayness and is enveloped in the mist. In a matter of moments, Budwick and his crew can see absolutely nothing.

"Keep a sharp eye ahead," he instructs. "We don't know what is there."

As Budwick watches ahead intently, Eli minds the stern. He sees no sign of the mystery ship. As the minutes pass, he expects that vessel to be slipping into the fog as well. He looks at Budwick and nods, indicating the time might be right to make the move.

Eli rushes forward and gets the attention of the crew. He looks back at Budwick for the final signal. That's when Spinnaker calls from the bow. He calls for Eli quietly, his tone urgent. Eli heads for the bow. He can see the problem before Spinnaker can explain.

There, off the bow, not two hundred yards ahead, is a massive ledge. It rises up out of the sea. Its black shade, like an evil menace emerging from the deep, is the only reason it stands out in the mist. The water breaking over it hints at what lurks ahead.

Wasting no time, Eli gives the call, hoping it is not too late.

"Stand by about," he shouts.

Captain Budwick hears the orders and shouts his commands extra loudly.

"Starboard tack!" he commands. "Extra fast!"

The crew repeats the order in unison, shouting it with all their might. "Starboard tack!"

The crew quickly goes to work swinging the rigging and making a larboard tack. Budwick begins to turn the wheel. He's not aware of the breakers ahead, but Eli keeps a close eye. Spinnaker has even tried signaling. Eli waves to get Budwick's attention and signals for a hard turn of the wheel. He points forward and emphasizes that the ship must turn sharply.

Budwick understands what is needed. He leans into the turn of the wheel and forces the vessel to an extremely sharp larboard turn. For good measure, he shouts out a few extra meaningless orders.

"Harder to starboard!" he calls. "Starboard, I said. Hard to starboard."

He takes a quick glance behind him but sees nothing but fog. No sign of the other vessel. That's good, he thinks. He looks forward again and as his ship makes the drastic turn to larboard, he gets a view of the dark objects that lurk not far off the starboard bow.

"Godfrey mighty!" he says to himself. "That would have ended the chase right quick."

He's got the ship turned and sailing hard and fast into the wind. It isn't as strong as it was but still has a little gust to it. His sails luff as they battle against the breeze.

Eli scurries aft, knowing they won't stay on this tack for long. He expects new commands to come down from Budwick.

"That was a close one," Budwick says. "Glad you seen them breakers."

Eli explains it was the sharp eye of Spinnaker at the bow.

"We turned just in time," Eli replies. "Another minute and we'd be breaking upon them right now."

"Let's hope that damn ship ain't as lucky," Budwick says.

Both gaze around to see if there's any sign of the other vessel, or a faint view of land. There's nothing but gray all around. The mist is so thick that water is building up on the sails and deck. Budwick wipes his face, clearing the wetness from his eyes.

They've been sailing in the dark for hours, but at least the moon or starlight provide a slight glimpse of what is ahead. In the thick cover of fog, there is nothing to see but a wall of gray. And fearing what can't be seen makes it worse.

Budwick knows how close they came to doom, avoiding those breakers. He's still concerned trying to tack around amidst the vapor that engulfs him. He's anxious to sail his way out of it.

"Get them ready for another tack," says Budwick. "We're going to cut back to windward. Get the wind behind us, double back, and get out of this fog. Hopefully we get back out to sea before that bastard figgers out where we went."

Eli acknowledges the order and steps down from the quarterdeck. He offers a faint verbal command, one that only people on board can hear. Quietly, the crew goes to work to swing the vessel around once more. As Budwick gives the wheel another hard turn, the booms jostle from one side of the vessel to the other. The sails go flat for a moment, but once the turn is complete and the westerly breeze catches the other side of the canvas, the sails pop back into place. They flap into a stiff position as the winds fill them and send the vessel back on its way.

Budwick has the vessel turned and heading into the direction he wants. He hopes it is the right course. Being surrounded by nothing but gray air, it is easy to lose one's sense of direction. The last thing he wants to do is think he's turned and is sailing east when he's actually headed west and about to slam the vessel full bore into the coastline.

"You damn well better be right, Captain," he says to himself.

Of course, he's quite sure he's steering in the proper direction. If the wind had changed its pattern suddenly, that might have confused him and thrown off his readings, but he doesn't think it has. He's confident that he's maneuvered quite effectively back to a windward tack and has his vessel getting up to speed. Now he just needs the other vessel to make a mistake.

"That's some pretty good sailing, Captain," Eli says.

"Thanks, mate," he replies. "Let's just hope it rids us of our company."

Budwick steers the *Tempest* through the fog with the breeze blowing briskly from behind. The vessel has some good speed going and in a matter of moments, patches of blue can be seen through the gray. The fog is dissipating and a return to open-water sailing awaits them.

The vast open sea begins to show itself once again. Budwick can see the waves, the blue backdrop, and an array of clouds that dot the sky. They shed the fog like an old overcoat, discarded in their wake as the breeze pushes them cleanly through the water that now reflects a blue sheen.

"The breeze is a mite stronger out here," Eli says.

Budwick notices that, as well, and is glad to see it. He watches his sails holding firm as the wind provides a steady push.

"Sail like ya never sailed before," he says, coaxing his ship to find its maximum speed.

The fog bank quickly is left behind as the *Tempest* makes headway through the blue seas and back out into open ocean. Budwick keeps his eye forward, holding a steady course.

Eli stands at his side and watches keenly back toward the fog. As he stares intently, he thinks he sees a figure emerging from the mist. He blinks his eyes a few times to clear his vision before he looks again. There is no vessel in sight. He maintains watch steadily for any sign of the other ship. Nothing materializes.

Eventually, the fog bank slips out of sight. There's no sign of a vessel for miles and miles.

"Captain, it appears that we are alone once again," Eli says.

CHAPTER THREE
Aboard the *Tempest*, 1773

S tanding at the wheel, it inevitably all comes back to him: the wind, the rain, the heaving seas and the blowing spray. It isn't all that un-like the brief storm they encountered days ago upon escaping the West Indies.

Eli is at the helm. The day dawns anew, bringing blue skies, rol-licking seas, and a stiff breeze. After sailing on through the night, the *Tempest* continues making headway north.

But, as Eli gazes across the ship before him and twirls the wheel from hand to hand, he recalls that day nearly ten years ago. It was sum-mer weather, where the more violent storms were still a month or so away. It was a gale the crew of the *Sparrow* never expected or saw coming.

Captain Luke, Eli's father, was making good profits with his regular trips to the West Indies and an occasional venture across the Atlantic.

He had even overcome near disaster when he was captured by a French vessel in August of 1757. It was a story he proudly told his sons many times.

Eli learned everything he knows about the seafaring trade from those years with his father. Luke was never captured again. He proved elusive to pirates and both the French and British during the Seven Years War. The seasoned captain had known he was fortunate to survive that previous encounter with the French. The next time his ship was boarded, Luke told his son, he knew he wouldn't survive so easily. He made sure that wasn't to happen again.

And, it didn't. But the sudden storm that summer in 1764 brought with it consequences Luke had never expected, or had he? He had just written his will earlier that summer. Maybe the fifty-one-year-old sensed a looming destiny.

Now, nearly a decade later, a steely-faced Eli still looks over the rails of the vessel and swears he sees that desperate wave of the hand as his father succumbs to the ocean waves. The same guilt and helplessness overwhelms him every time. He still has nightmares about that moment. He sees or hears his father calling for help, but Eli only stands frozen, unable to lend assistance.

Eli knows that the crew was right in preventing his leap overboard in an attempt to save his father. He would have certainly been lost himself. Still, that was a selfish act he can't escape, no matter how sensible it was. He only hopes his father understood and could forgive him.

"Dead ahead," comes the shout from the watch on the bow. "Dead ahead."

Eli's focus quickly returns to the present moment. Yawly Moses is on bow watch and he waves frantically to catch the helm's attention.

Eli looks past Moses' waving arms and peers out over the horizon. He can see what Moses has sighted. He isn't quite sure what it is. He grabs the spyglass and looks to the distance. He almost can't believe his eyes.

Sailing miles away, almost hidden by the slight haze on the horizon, is a massive fleet of ships, all sailing across the Atlantic. Eli can't count the number of vessels if he tried. There are so many, and they all seem to blend together. No matter the numbers, it is a force he and his crew could never match.

"Rummy," calls Eli, summoning Spinnaker from the deck. "Go below and roust Captain Budwick."

Spinnaker responds with an, "Aye, sir" and rushes across the quarterdeck and down the companionway toward Budwick's quarters. Eli keeps one hand on the wheel; the other holds the glass to his eye, keeping watch of the fleet well off the bow. He hears the knock on Budwick's door and Spinnaker's voice as he awakens the captain.

Eli's sure that Budwick won't like being awoken, but when he sees why, he'll understand. The sound of movement below hints at Budwick's imminent return topside. Spinnaker rises up from the companionway first, getting a nod of approval from Eli.

A bleary-eyed Budwick steps out into the daylight, looking like a mole emerging from his darkened hole in the earth. Before he can grumble about being awoken, Eli gets his attention. He presents him the spyglass.

"You'll want to see this," he says.

Budwick takes the glass and holds it up to his eye. He pauses for a moment to clear his vision of morning debris. He puts the glass up again and gets his view.

"Holy hell," he exclaims. "It looks like the whole friggin' Royal Navy."

Budwick puts the glass down. He doesn't need a second look.

"I don't know what the hell that's all about, but we cain't go near it," he says.

The fleet of ships appears to be sailing west, toward Boston, they presume. Budwick determines their only recourse is to head east. It will make for a round-about route to Portsmouth, but one they must settle for.

Eli passes along the order to the crew. The ship's forward motion is quickly halted and the vessel begins to turn to the east.

"If we get pushed further east, who knows where we'll end up," says Budwick.

The ship completes it tack. It is a line Budwick will sail for a bit before tacking back toward the north slightly. He expects it will take them well up the coast, far away from Portsmouth, but hopefully out of harm's way.

Eli maintains a watchful eye of the fleet. It maintains its movement to the west. Wherever it is going, trouble is on the way.

"You suppose it's headed for Boston?" Budwick surmises. "It's the only thing that makes sense."

Eli keeps watching. Then he lowers the glass and nods in agreement. "Something must have happened," he says.

Tensions between the colonies and Great Britain have been delicate in recent years. When the Seven Years War ended, it provided greater opportunity for merchant mariners to follow the sea for profits. The seafaring trade became so prominent that it seemed obvious to the British that the colonies would soon seek its independence.

Britain's Board of Admiralty deployed a small army of customs and revenue officers to major ports of America. Those ships only patrolled the greater part of four miles from any port they were stationed. That allowed for a prevalent amount of smuggling.

The British have been imposing duties on colonial cargo vessels for years, dating as far back as the 1730s, but enforcement was lacking back then. Things became much stricter in the late 1760s, and the British have been rather heavy handed in their attempts to tax the colonies. It has prompted much unrest and conflict.

Boston has been the setting for much of the colonial disobedience. There has been a heavy concentration of seizures by customs officials there. It used to be that a merchant mariner might get a small fine for smuggling; now, the stricter customs officials will not only take a captain's vessel, but also his cargo and impose a stiffer fine, taking as much as a full year's profit.

As if that didn't rile the colonists enough, the British have tried to impose various other taxes. There was the Revenue Act, which gave the Royal Navy an active role in suppressing smugglers. That was in 1764; the proposed Sugar Act came a year later. It taxed paperwork of all kinds, including the playing cards that sailors considered mandatory supplies on board. The Mutiny Act ordered that British troops be fed and housed. The Townsend Act set taxes on goods produced in British colonies. The British proposals had most colonists infuriated, prompting great resentment and nearly leading to a depression of the British economy.

"It's almost like a down and dirty smuggler like myself cain't make an honest livin' no more," Budwick spouts off on any occasion where politics dominate the conversation.

The situation has only worsened, and the colonists' cry for rebellion is now at a fever pitch. John Hancock's sloop *Liberty* was seized by the Royal Navy. Then came the massacre of a handful of radical protesters by British thugs.

The response in the colonies has been severe. A Royal Navy cutter that had been used in suppressing smugglers was fired upon by rebels in Rhode Island. Another vessel was attacked in Providence and burned in the night. Hell is about to break loose in Boston. It's just seemed a matter of time before the spark will be ignited. Maybe now it has been.

CHAPTER FOUR
London, England, 1773

It is as if the sun and clouds jockey for position, one attempting supremacy over the other. One moment, the clouds fill the sky with murky gray. The color is forcibly burned away by the radiance of the sun, peeking through just enough to brighten the afternoon.

Thomas Kane pauses for a moment. He glances up at the clearing sky and shades his eyes for a moment.

"See, the sun is starting to appear," he declares. "I told you it would be a nice afternoon."

He stands in the middle of the yard. Nobody else is in sight. It is as if he's speaking to himself. He stops his momentary appraisal of the weather and continues his search. Hester is ducked behind a shrub, trying not to make a sound. Patrick has shimmied his way up a barren apple tree; the boy sits uncomfortably on a branch, trying to remain still and hidden by the bulk of the tree trunk. He'll peer around momentarily to catch a glimpse of his father searching the grounds.

"You think you can hide from me?" Kane says, slowly walking around the yard, trying to sense the slightest movement.

He steps quietly and deliberately. He makes little noise in the soft snow that covers the backyard, the last remnants of an unexpected spring dusting. He reaches down and shapes a handful of snow into a ball. He tosses it lightly in the brush of shrubs that line the right side of the property. The snowball breaks apart and scatters ice and snow through the branches. He stoops to gather more and shapes another ball of white powder. This one is hurled up into the trees, where it breaks apart and rains down, bringing more snow with it from the snow-covered limbs.

With his eyes focused on the collection of trees to the back of the yard, he stands silently. He searches for the slightest movement that might reveal the whereabouts of one of his children. He waits. Tempted to move and continue searching, he fights the urge and remains still. His patience pays off.

As Patrick leans to one side to gaze around the trunk of the tree, he sees his father standing not more than a few steps away. The boy suddenly lurches back to cower behind the tree, but his movement is enough to betray his cover.

His father notices the movement and knows he has one child found. He gathers more snow and steps a little closer to the tree.

"I wonder if anyone is hidden in the trees here," he calls out.

He tosses the snow into the tree and it prompts another shower from the quivering branches. Patrick tries to stay hidden, but when he ducks from the falling snow, his body is revealed. His father, in preparation of this very moment, fires a compacted ball of snow that splatters against his son's backside.

"Oww," comes Patrick's shout. Before his father can fire another snowball, his son swings down out of the tree and lands with a plop in the yard.

"Look what I have found hidden among the trees," his father boasts. "Now I have just one more to find."

He watches his son, and Patrick does just what his father expects. He instinctively glances toward the shrubs where his sister is hidden. It is only for a moment, but it is enough to alert their father. In an instant, another snowball has been formed and tossed in the direction of the shrubs.

A giggle comes from behind the shrub as Hester reveals herself.

"I believe some large critter is hidden behind that shrubbery," declares Kane. "Patrick, what do you say we arm ourselves with snow and try to defend against whatever lurks in there?"

Patrick, immediately turning on his sister, grabs a handful of snow and forms a loose snowball. "Let's get it," he says.

Both begin an exaggerated roar and stomp their way through the snow. That prompts Hester's retreat. She jumps out from behind the bush and scampers across the lawn. Patrick fires his snowball in a rush to meet his target, but he misses. He re-arms himself and dashes off in hot pursuit of his sister. Their father holds back a bit. He stays close enough to continue the chase, but allows his daughter to avoid him slightly.

She runs across the yard, screeching in both fear and delight as she senses a chance to escape. She reaches the backdoor of the house and stands there proudly. She knows she'll be able to dart into the house before either her brother or father can reach her. That's when a snowball thrown by her father smacks the side of the house with a large thud. Hester never saw it coming and jumps away, startled.

That prompts laughter from both her brother and father. The two of them gather up more snow and know they may have Hester trapped. As she reaches for the door, hoping for a last-second escape, the door swings out and her mother exits.

Margaret Kane barely emerges from the warmth of the house. She only swings the door open to peek outside. She's met by her daughter and the view of her son and father approaching, both armed with snow.

"Thomas Kane, don't you dare throw that snow," she says, cowering behind the door as Hester slithers in behind her to safety. She closes the door quickly to ward off any snow that might be thrown toward her. Patrick tosses one and hits the door. Thomas holds onto his. Margaret opens the door again, only slightly, enough to shout out to her husband.

"You have a visitor," she says, looking a bit concerned. "It's Haddington Pilcher. He needs to see you."

Kane flings his snow toward no specific target. It lands aimlessly in the snow. He signals to Patrick that no more snow will be thrown. Just a stern look is enough for his son to realize the game is over.

Kane steps into the house and walks through the hallway to meet his guest. He shakes off the snow and attempts to make himself presentable. He also transitions from his role as father to that of a Royal Naval captain. He knows Pilcher's presence likely means a new assignment.

His wife has already escorted his guest into the parlor, where he sits by the fire. Kane slips off his coat and leaves it on a hook in the front hallway. He changes his shoes and tosses his gloves on a table by the door. As he enters the parlor, he closes the doors securely behind him.

Pilcher is a commander in the Royal Navy. His visits to Kane's homestead are never social.

"Sorry to intrude on you today," he says as Kane sets himself down in a chair facing him.

"That's quite all right," Kane says. "Obviously, your visit is of some importance."

Before the two can begin discussions, Margaret knocks at the door and opens it. She enters the room carrying a tray of tea. She sets it on the table before them. Cups and a kettle of steaming tea are accompanied by a plate of pastries.

"Commander, you are welcome to stay with us for dinner," she says.

Pilcher helps himself to a cup of tea. "Thank you, but no," he says. "I will be brief and be on my way. Mrs. Pilcher is expecting my return soon."

As Margaret leaves the room, Kane pours himself some tea. It warms him nicely after being out in the cold with the children. A taste of the pastry is sweet and eases his hunger for the moment.

"I'm here to discuss the colonies," Pilcher begins. "We've gotten some news."

Kane sits back, relaxing slightly before turning his attention to Pilcher's message. "It can't be good news," he states. "Otherwise, you wouldn't be discussing it with me."

Pilcher almost laughs, but is not sure that Kane's comment was actually intended as humor. He nods to confirm Kane's suspicions. "We had three vessels attacked in Boston Harbor," he explains. "Rebels tossed all the contents overboard."

Kane barely says a word. His face turns stern, as if he's trying to contain any sign of anger. He remains quiet and lets Pilcher continue with the details.

Apparently a mob of protestors gathered in Boston two weeks before Christmas. The rabble rousing went from one act of contention to another.

"They say there were nearly 8,000 gathered," Pilcher states. "That Samuel Adams, he was the one who spoke to the crowd. Got them all stirred up."

As a result, Pilcher tells him, a mob of rebels dressed as native savages and attacked the ships in the night. They heaved the crates of tea into the harbor. They estimated that 350 crates were lost.

"It was all reaction to a skirmish that happened between colonials and a few British soldiers," says Pilcher. "A couple of the colonials were killed, by accident."

Kane nods some more as he listens intently. When Pilcher has completed his recounting of the details, he pauses, as if to hear Kane's reaction.

"You must be telling me all this for a reason?" Kane asks.

Pilcher explains that as retaliation, the Royal Navy has sent an armada of ships to Boston.

"We're closing off the harbor," he says. "We're making Boston pay and serving warning to others."

Kane sets his tea down and rises from his chair. He paces the parlor for a moment, stopping to gaze out the window. He senses what this meeting is leading toward.

"The Board of Admiralty wants you to command a fleet," Pilcher explains. "They expect more troubles in the colonies. They want you to…"

"Crush them," Kane says, interrupting Pilcher. He stands and faces his visitor. "They want me to silence this little uprising of ingrates," he says, with voice raised and anger bubbling out.

"I said long ago that we were only encouraging the colonies toward this," he continues. "We didn't enforce the law. Then suddenly, we start to tighten our grip. If we'd done this from the start, the rebels would be submissive by now."

Kane stressed to the Board more than a year ago that more control was needed in the colonies. If not, they'd only make a mockery of the British rule. That is exactly what they have done.

"If they want me over there to clean up this mess, I will do what I deem necessary," he states. "If the Board isn't going to give me free reign to do what is needed, they best find somebody else."

Pilcher understands and has already stressed to members of the Board that Kane is the right man to put in charge in the American seas. He has angered members of the Admiralty with his tactics in the past, but the colonies have become such a firestorm that a man as fierce as Kane might just be the right answer.

"They want this uprising put down," says Pilcher. "They know you are the right man to do just that. They give you full authority to handle it as you see fit."

CHAPTER FIVE
Aboard the *Tempest*, 1773

If there is any harbor Ezra Budwick can maneuver in amidst the darkness of night, it is Portsmouth. He's sailed in and out the mouth of the Piscataway River so often that he knows exactly where he must be and where he can't be.

"I can sail in there blindfolded," he boasts.

Eli is sure that his friend is waiting for somebody to challenge that assertion, just so that he can prove it. He sometimes even wonders if Budwick has already done such a feat, but knows he would have heard all about it if he had.

With a fleet of Royal Navy apparently headed for northern New England, Budwick took no chances with the final leg home. He stayed clear of any vessels until reaching the coast a few miles up, in the eastern district of Massachusetts.

Budwick hadn't initially gone straight for Portsmouth, not knowing what might be awaiting him. When he had reached the shoreline up the coast, he'd slowly doubled back toward his home port. He timed it so that he'd be entering the harbor in the dark. He hoped to slip in relatively unnoticed. Even if he couldn't eke his way into his own wharf, he knew a place to tuck away where he could drop the hook.

There is only a hint of moonlight shining down through the clouds. It illuminates his course a bit, but also makes him more visible to anyone keeping a keen eye out. As the vessel reaches the mouth of the river, he extinguishes all his lanterns and makes his silent approach.

All is quiet as he slips in through the two small islands that mark the entrance. Typically, he'd sail around Leach's Island and work his way through the narrows up past Blunts Island. He'll tack up into the main part of the harbor from there. It is a narrow approach and doing it in the dark is certainly a challenge, especially if there are any ships at anchor up there. Plus, Budwick knows if he's accosted by any vessel, he has little recourse. Taking a long route, up through the center of the river, around Leach's and Seavey Island, is a roundabout course, but Budwick knows it well. He is confident that he can escape again if need be.

The wind is very slight at this time of night. It barely pushes his vessel along. Fortunately, a strong current helps draw the ship into the river. As they drift past the easterly side of Leach's, there's little sign of activity. There are no ships on the move and none apparently on watch for anything mischievous.

"So far, so good," says Eli to the captain in a whisper.

Budwick just nods, almost afraid to agree and jinx their good fortune.

Eli can't help but let the thought of being home creep into his mind. He's been anxious to return after a few months at sea.

His wife Elizabeth is pregnant with their second son. He hadn't really wanted to be away during this time, but Budwick needed him on-board. It was a potential profit that was too hard to pass on. He'd also known that he wouldn't likely be sailing again anytime soon. That made a trip like this a necessity to supply his family with enough finances to hold them over for a while.

As the *Tempest* creeps around in between the islands and provides a distant glimpse of the inner harbor, Eli can see faint light from the town. His home is just a few blocks up from the harbor, property he inherited from his father. After his father was lost, Eli sold off some of Luke's wharf space and buildings to Budwick. What he had paid off were his father's debts. That allowed Eli to keep the family home. It has served his family well, especially since he has remained in the sea trade also.

This trip has been a nerve-wracking one for him. With his wife so close to giving birth, thoughts of her being alone have been difficult. Between outracing pirates and avoiding the Royal Navy and customs officers, Eli can't help but fear a trip wrought with such danger could ultimately interfere with him being there for his wife and children.

Eli was eighteen when he lost his father, and his siblings were quite grown as well. Luke's death wasn't easy for the family; the thought of his own young children being put in such a state is nearly unbearable. It is an idea that has haunted him for months.

Just as the ship approaches the harbor, Eli spots a vessel cloaked in the darkness. Only a few lanterns give it light and make it noticeable in the night. It is a new and dark presence in the harbor.

He points toward it without speaking. Budwick takes notice. It appears the vessel lies in wait, maybe to surprise a ship sneaking into the harbor just as the *Tempest* is doing now.

Budwick immediately ponders the idea of an escape. Turning to run would certain scream aloud his guilt. He's not even sure he'd be able to turn the ship around quickly enough to attempt a getaway. His only hope is to ease on past and hope to go unnoticed, or at least uninhibited.

Both Budwick and Eli hold their respective breaths as the *Tempest* rides the slight breeze and current toward their destination. They see no movement from what appears to be a British vessel with a small fleet of sloops anchored alongside. None of them make any move to intervene and the *Tempest* sails past without incident.

Eli considers them fortunate to get past without raising any suspicion. It still makes him wonder, though, if a confrontation is inevitable.

"That could cause us many problems," Eli says quietly, knowing that life along these shores may have changed dramatically.

As the vessel slips quietly into the harbor, Budwick orders the sails in. He sends crew out into rowboats to help tow the ship the final bit into its berth. Despite the commotion on the ship as it makes its final approach to the wharf, nobody seems to stir around them.

Arriving home safe and sound is always a relief for Eli. There's a weight that hangs upon every sailor. It is a fear that burdens from the first haul out until that last leg of any journey is complete. It isn't until the vessel enters its home waters that any mariner truly feels safe. With danger gone, the joys of home are theirs. Most all of them know a fellow sailor or two or three who never returned. Each successful journey is a small victory over the unpredictable life at sea.

Eli has never been so pleased to see the ship come alongside the wharf. As he steps over the gunwale and onto the dock, he's excited to be home safe. He looks back at the ship and glances out the channel and toward the open sea. He wonders if he'll ever see the world again beyond his home waters. He thinks of his expecting wife and his son and smiles, pondering the idea that he just might not follow the open sea again. He relishes such a thought.

CHAPTER SIX
Aboard the HMS *Lioness, 1773*

A few lanterns provide the only flickering light in the dark and enclosed quarters.

Kane reclines in a soft chair surrounded by the warmth of the candle. Despite the room's bleakness, Kane feels the glow around him.

He relaxes and takes deep breaths, finding peace within as he sips from his mug of cider. He relishes the sharp and sweet taste. Kane has never let alcohol touch his lips; the intense flavor of cider is about as tart as it gets for him.

He flips through the worn pages of his Bible. He picks out favorite verses and reads them softly to himself. Often, he reads the first line but knows the verses so well that his memory takes over. Rather than read them, he breathes the sacred words. It is a calming routine of his, a means of soothing his soul and focusing his heart.

Kane hasn't always been a man of God. Part of his dedication now to his faith are a result of his guilt for past transgressions. He fully knows he was more the Devil in his day and still may be. He struggles with the balance of a God-fearing man and being a law-abiding one. It was much easier when upholding the law wasn't dictated by his belief in God's word.

Reading from his Bible heals the anger Kane held for so long—anger that stemmed from the day his life changed as a young boy. Amidst a sunny and glorious summer day, Kane faced death for the first time.

While wrestling with his dog, Molly, the boy's recreation came to a sudden stop when a stranger arrived. Kane may have met the man before, but wasn't sure. Nattily dressed and quite important looking, he drew young Kane's attention right away.

The man passed him and smiled as he approached the house.

"Is your mother at home?" he asked politely.

Thomas could only nod sheepishly, ignoring the prodding of Molly for more attention. Instead, the boy watched intently as the man reached the house, knocked, and was greeted excitedly by his mother.

The two stepped into the house and closed the door. After only a few minutes, the man exited and went on his way. He smiled again, but his face looked saddened and hurt. Thomas never saw the man again.

When Thomas entered the house, he found his mother sitting in the front room. She was hunched over, face in her hands, sobbing. He had never seen his mother cry so.

The last time he had witnessed such emotion was the day his father left for duty in the war. He was a commissioned officer and was to lead a regiment in the New World. Britain was engaged in a lengthy conflict with the French and Indians in the colonies. More troops had been summoned and Barrington Kane was among those leaving for war.

Thomas had watched his father kiss his mother goodbye and walk away to join his regiment and begin his journey. Only a few letters had arrived from his father in the year since.

He stood watching his mother weep, unable to move. When she realized his presence, she asked him to sit next to her.

As he approached, his mother reached out and pulled him into her arms. Thomas was actually afraid for a moment. As he sat beside her, she wrapped him in her embrace and continued to sob.

"I just received very distressing news, my dear son," she said. "Your beloved father has been killed."

They are words still firmly implanted in Kane's mind. He can't help but recall that moment and feel that grief and heartbreak. Every memory of his father makes him relive that painful moment.

He later learned that it was his father's own men who led him to his death. While fighting in the Wilderness campaign of upstate New York, British soldiers betrayed their fellow troops. Barrington Kane and his men were ambushed by Indians and rebellious colonials in an attack that massacred much of the regiment.

The younger Kane not only felt the loss of the father that he idolized, but also witnessed the pain his mother endured. She was never the same, a bright and lovely spirit dampened by the tragedies of life. Experiencing so much hurt, Kane grew angry and let his hatred overwhelm him.

It wasn't until his own mother passed and he and Margaret were married that Kane began to find joy again. He felt the love of his wife, but was also consumed by the love of God. It was the healing his angry heart needed.

"Behold, I give unto you power to tread on serpents and scorpions, and over all the power of the enemy: and nothing shall by any means hurt you."

He leans back in his chair, quietly reciting the words from the book of Luke to himself. He feels such power in them, especially since he considered himself a bit of a serpent at one time in the wilting garden that was his life. There's a glorious feeling that makes his heart sing. He quietly hums a hymn to himself and relishes his blessings.

Kane never intended to be an officer. After the death of his father, being part of the British army was the least of his interest. What point was it to be part of an entity that would only betray you, he thought?

Yet, with his anger and lack of discipline growing up as a boy, it was military training that ultimately suited him best.

An uncle had paved the way for him to attend a military academy as soon as he was old enough. It was a fine way to get the boy an education. It also was a means to make this young rebellious teen hell bent on trouble someone else's problem. He had become too much for his mother to handle, especially as her grief evolved into a deep depression from which she never recovered.

Kane's military training shaped him and redirected his anger. He quickly became a young soldier with promise because he was smart, bitter, and ruthless. It was a combination that his superiors appreciated. They saw the Devil in him. They paved the way for his promotion up the ranks.

It wasn't until he found his wife Margaret that he found God. She was the daughter of a general. They met at a holiday gathering of military leaders. The young Kane had been invited along by a friend of his uncles. Margaret was one of the few women there his own age. After they danced a time or two, they stepped out on the balcony and talked.

"My father says wonderful things about you, Mr. Kane," she told him. "Will you be one of Britain's next great generals?"

Kane smiled sheepishly. It was a bit hard for him to step out of his icy demeanor and soften his personality.

"That is my hope," he replied. "However I may serve."

She made him feel different. He could feel his cold heart soften in her presence. He developed a desire for her and a longing for how she made him feel.

The love he had known, for his father, for his mother, and for himself, had become crushing heartbreak, but she showed him that he could love again. And as she introduced him to her faith and the love of God, Kane felt a rebirth.

Since then it has been a challenge for him to serve two kings. He yearns to serve God but also must serve his country and its laws. Sometimes he struggles with doing both.

It especially makes him feel isolated on his own ship. He commands it well. That's because most of the crew are scared to death of him. It is part of his commitment to law and order. He expects it from his men and tolerates nothing less from his ranks.

Yet, he struggles to be less than a commanding figure to them. He is uncomfortable with their language and ruffian ways. He'd disallow alcohol on board if he could but knows it is a way to keep his men satisfied.

So, Kane spends much time in his quarters, often alone. He reads from his Bible or shares his thoughts in letters to his beloved Margaret. It is a struggle to recall the joy of being with her when they're so far apart.

A forceful knock startles him and interrupts his chain of thought. Bosun mate Clive Henstridge opens the door before Kane even has the opportunity to summon him, irritating his superior, even though Kane has been expecting him.

Occasionally, Kane will have members of his crew in his quarters for food, drink, and conversation. It allows him to keep in touch with what is happening aboard but also allows for some other kind of communication.

Henstridge enters the Captain's quarters and sets himself down on a chair. He's brought a growler with him and immediately pops the cork and tips himself a drink.

He and Kane were students together at one time. He's a bit unkempt and somewhat brash. He's not exactly the type of company Kane usually keeps. But on board, he likes that different personality and appreciates what Henstridge brings to the crew in his tough and gruff demeanor.

While Kane sips from a cup of tea, Henstridge swigs mouthfuls from his bottle. Kane assumes the growler is full of rum but doesn't really care to know. Watching his friend chug that swill and smoke the most rancid of cigars used to make Kane want to retch, but he has since grown accustomed to Henstridge and his tastes. Being far away from home and enduring the lack of comforts aboard a ship, Kane can understand the need for one's pleasures.

Henstridge will often attempt to entice him into a taste of alcohol or a drag or two of his cigar, but Kane always politely declines.

On this night, there is no such offer. The two men settle into the captain's quarters and begin a conversation about the colonies and how Britain's rule is struggling to make a difference.

"The resistance is stronger than England knows, I'm afraid," says Kane. "It always has been."

Kane sits back in his chair sipping his tea while Henstridge rises and paces anxiously around the confined quarters. He has his growler in one hand and a lit cigar in the other. On occasion, his smoldering ashes fall off the cigar and onto the rug or the wooden floor of the quarters. Kane watches nervously, but Henstridge pays it no mind. When he does notice his ashes falling to the floor, he simply steps on them and stamps them out completely.

"I can't help but wonder if we'll be here far longer than we planned," says Henstridge. "I anticipated a better part of the year and then a return home."

Henstridge often complains about the slow pace of the war. What perturbs Kane most is that he'd just as soon let the colonies go about their way, but the law is the law. As much as he'd gladly let them all escape to a new land in the name of their freedom, their duty is owed to England. It is his job to enforce that.

Much of the British course of action along the coast has been a failure, he feels. The sea power has been used for coastal raids that were solely victories on paper. Most of the operations have been uncoordinated and little more than diversionary efforts. Little of what his British counterparts have done has actually made a difference in squashing the resistance.

Therefore, he has great disdain for this rise against British rule. They, like him, are sons of England, not sons of liberty. He takes his service seriously, especially when it affects how soon he'll be back home with his wife and children.

"Laws are passed and laws are enforced," he says. "There is no proper timeline for justice."

With those words, he understands this may be a lengthy process and a difficult fight for England. But he is also determined to do what must be done to alter such a reality.

Another sudden pounding at the door interrupts and irks Kane. Annoyed at being disturbed, Kane hesitates to answer.

"Captain," a voice calls quietly. "Captain Kane?"

Kane summons in the able-bodied seaman. The man has come to relay a message from the first mate.

"A ship has just entered the harbor," he reports. "It was easing past under the cover of darkness."

Kane thanks his crewman and sends him on his way.

"Wait," Kane calls out. "Did you happen to identify this ship?

The crewman stops and turns. He nods. "The *Tempest*," he replies, before continuing on his way.

After a quick stop over in the British-friendly port of Halifax, the HMS *Lioness* has continued its way down the coast. Kane will be patrolling these waters to crack down on the smuggling. After anchoring outside Portsmouth, Boston Harbor is due west and just a day away. .

Kane is tempted to give chase to what he assumes is a smuggler sneaking into port. He looks at Henstridge, who smiles at the thought of having a lawbreaker within reach. Or maybe it is just his drinking that has brightened his mood.

Kane sighs and gently closes his Bible. He holds it for a moment, almost feeling warmth from the words contained within. He sets it on the table where it will wait until another day.

"We won't pursue this one, not right now," Kane decides. "Their time will come."

He now turns his mind to Boston Harbor, the blockade, the law, and how he intends to enforce it.

He spots a sole beetle scurrying across the table a few steps away. Kane slowly rises and watches the beetle wander aimlessly across the table top. He stares intently before a sudden wave of his hand strikes like lightning. He slams his palm firmly on the face of the table, squashing the beetle beneath.

CHAPTER SEVEN
Portsmouth, New Hampshire, 1774

The winter months have taken a toll on Eli's house. It was an unwelcome sight to return home to find that his roof was leaking and many of the slats on the side of the house needed replacing.

Eli expected to have some work around the home, especially with a pregnant wife whose activity had become more and more restricted. Being away during some of the heartiest of winter months often has him returning home to find repairs that need attention. He just wasn't expecting the work to be this extensive.

Elizabeth has been well looked after while he was away. Eli's sister Maddie lives nearby and helped with whatever problems arose. Elizabeth has family not too far away, also. So, Eli never had concerns about his wife's safe keeping, but he is glad to be home to take that burden on himself. He just wishes so much of his time wasn't devoted to repairs.

He spent much of the day before replacing slats on the side of the house. The storms only tend to batter one side. While the westerly and northern sides of the house look as pristine as ever, the other two are worn and battered. Even after replacing some of the damage, he's not sure the façade looks any better.

He's focused on the roof today. He has identified problem areas and has been ripping them out and replacing the roof in sections. With the frequent spring rains, he hopes to avoid a home that leaks, creating the necessity for pots that dot the floor to catch the droplets that seep through.

"Pots are made for cooking, not catching," he often mumbles to himself when irritated by a leaky roof and intrusive weather.

He is so focused on his task that he barely notices the approach of

George Lathrop and Ezra Budwick. The two arrive in Lathrop's carriage and come to a halt in front of the Miller home. They climb out and gaze above the house, where Eli is sprawled out with his back to them. He works busily, oblivious to their presence. Or just ignoring.

"Well, look who is taking orders now, Captain Budwick," Lathrop says loudly. The sound of his voice catches Eli's attention. He stops his work and turns to face his visitors.

"I ain't never seen the mate workin' so hard," Budwick replies. "At least not when he's been under my command."

Eli crawls his way down the slope of the roof and climbs onto the ladder. He steps down quickly and lands onto the solid turf. He looks over at his two visitors.

"I've got the project started for you two," he says. "All the tools are up there. If you start now, you might be finished by dark."

Lathrop and Budwick chuckle, but don't budge. Eli approaches to greet them. He knows he should be working steadily through the day, but is glad to have the distraction.

"Come on into the house," he offers. "Elizabeth is upstairs resting. Have a seat in the parlor. I can heat up some tea if you'd like. I've got some stout to offer, as well."

Lathrop and Budwick follow Eli inside and step into the parlor. They initially decline a drink, but when Eli decides he could use some refreshment and goes for an ale, he brings back a pair of mugs for his guests.

"If you don't drink them, I will," he says.

The three sit together and sip their beverages before the conversation begins. Eli knows this isn't likely a social call. He's had conversations on and off with both Lathrop and Budwick over the past few weeks. When they completed their last trip, Eli had made it clear that he would not be sailing again anytime soon. Neither Budwick nor Lathrop truly believed him.

"If you're here to recruit me aboard, you're wasting your time," he tells them directly. "My decision is made. I'm not changing it."

Budwick shows disappointment, even though he expected to hear that same answer. Lathrop's reaction is slight, but he doesn't give in so easily.

"Eli, we need you," he explains. "We know we won't find any better mate around. We know how you feel, but we've got cargo all lined up. We'll be ready to sail in a matter of weeks. We wouldn't be here if we didn't truly need you. With the Royal Navy badgering every vessel up and down the coast and who knows what trouble lies beyond these shores, we want the best crew we can have."

It is a tempting argument. Eli can't help but feel as though he's abandoning his friends. He knows every journey becomes more hazardous as tensions rise. It is a dangerous time at sea, but also a potentially profitable one.

"One more trip, mate," says Budwick. "We'll make enough to keep you and your family happy for a long time."

Eli hesitates. He doesn't want to give his friends the impression that he is tempted, but realizes he is just that. He can't help but think about the extra money and the profits that would bolster his family's finances.

"We can even hold off until Elizabeth has the baby," says Lathrop. "Once that happens, you can sail. Maddie, myself, we'll all look after her. She'll be in good hands."

Eli takes a couple swigs of his ale. Both his friends look hopeful. He can see that they sense apprehension. He had vowed that his time at sea was done. After the last voyage, he declared that it was his last. His wife and son are his priority. With another child on the way, the last place he wants to be is at sea, especially in such tenuous times.

But his friends are persuasive. They know the yearning for the sea that still lingers inside. They understand the lure of the profits and know that nobody truly retires from the sea—at least not without second thoughts.

"A part of me is convinced to sign on again," he explains. The faces of Budwick and Lathrop brighten as they sense a conversion. "But I know I can't. It is tempting. The money would certainly be helpful, but a time comes to change direction. That is what I'm doing. I want to be here with Elizabeth and my boy. The sea life has been good but it has run its course."

His friends are disappointed. Budwick looks as though he understands; Lathrop shakes his head in disgust. Eli feels as though he's failed his friends and he's sorry for that.

Yet, he knows his loyalty lies elsewhere. As much as he sympathizes with his friends, his heart is here. His life is good. He misses the sea, but relishes the time he has with his wife and boy. With another child on the way, there is nothing he'd want to get in the way of the joy he has found here.

Sometimes the right choice is an easy one, even with temptation to lure your interests. Eli knows in his heart that he's making the proper decision.

He hears his son Joseph stomp his way down the stairs from the second floor. Having heard the voices, he enters the parlor to investigate.

"I'm hungry," he blurts out at sight of his father.

"Is Mother sleeping?" Eli asks his three-year-old.

Joseph just stands and nods, suddenly turning shy upon seeing the other men in the room, including the burly, wild-eyed Captain Budwick.

"Gentlemen, I appreciate you coming by to discuss this with me," Eli says. "I'd certainly like to help you out. I just don't feel as though I can at this time. If you'll excuse me, I have a son to feed and a roof to patch."

Lathrop and Budwick stand, sensing defeat. They head for the door. Eli offers his hand before being summoned by young Joseph in the kitchen.

"Think about it," Lathrop tells him, hoping one last word might persuade him, even though he's certain it won't. "If you change your mind, you know where to find us."

CHAPTER EIGHT
Aboard the *Sparrow* , 1774

Seated on the deck of his own ship, Jasper Spaulding has his hands bound behind him. Two of his crew are seated nearby—Oliver Thorndike and Eben Waterman. Their ship *Sparrow* was en route home from a trip to the West Indies. They had eluded various pirates, privateers, and British ships all the way home.

It wasn't until a few miles away from port that their route was interrupted by a small British fleet. Spaulding spotted the large frigate and thought he could outrun it to windward; what he didn't know was that a small collection of sloops were waiting for just such a move. His immediate attempt to flee signaled his guilt and invited their pursuit. Before he knew it, the *Sparrow* was surrounded by British guns ready to pummel him with cannon fire.

Now, a boarding party has commandeered the vessel, and much of their prize collection of rum, spices, and sugar has been off-loaded by British sailors. With each crate, Spaulding has watched his profits slip away. Now, he can only hope to salvage his ship after the British have flashed their authority.

The British have tightened their grip on trade violations. There have been custom rules for some time, but enforcement has been so lax, most sailors have scoffed at the idea of any trade laws. Spaulding had heard talk of the British seizing vessels and cargo, but most of what he'd heard was that sailors were attempting to run a gauntlet of British inspectors in Boston and surrounding ports, but nothing too far north. Being so close to home, Spaulding thought he was in the clear.

A trio of British guards stand over them, keeping watch with weapons at the ready in case of any attempted escape. Spaulding and his men can't really muster much of an attempt with their hands bound behind them. All they can do is sit and wait to see what fate may hold for them and their ship.

Spaulding has heard that some captains have not only lost their ship but have been fined severely, leaving them near ruin. He hopes the consequences he faces aren't so harsh.

The guards around them suddenly stand at attention. A silence quickly spreads across the ship, only to be filled by the thud of heavy boots. They clunk slowly and menacingly across the deck. Spaulding can't see, but hears the approaching footsteps.

A tall figure steps up before them and stops. He looks down to peer intently at the three prisoners.

"Captain Kane," says one of the guards. "This is the captain of the vessel and his crew."

Kane stares down at them with a fierce glare. He has boarded the vessel from his ship *Lioness* with the intent to deliver justice.

"We frown upon trade violations," he says sternly. "Now, do yourselves a favor and tell us who you were delivering to."

Spaulding sits silently. He has been sailing for his wife's father, Josiah Dix. Josiah helped outfit this vessel and financed the journey. Spaulding knows the repercussions that could follow if he reveals that Dix is his partner.

Annoyed by Spaulding's silence, Kane draws his saber and points the sharp tip of the blade at the captain's throat. The blade glistens in the fading sunlight, and the tip pricks the skin at the captain's neck.

"Let me repeat for the last time," says Kane. "Who were you delivering for?"

Spaulding gulps, the blade pressed against his neck. He clears his throat and attempts a slightly disingenuous explanation.

"I weren't deliverin' for nobody, sir," he says, trying to look humbled. "We bring cargo in on my own. Hope to find a buyer here in port."

Kane nods like he understands. He steps back and slides his saber into the sheath at his hip.

"I see," he says. He turns his back on Spaulding and his men. His voice rises with each word spoken. "I see. You take me for a fool. You break the law, and now you disrespect me and my authority."

Spaulding tries to offer a further explanation, but is cut short. Kane whirls around with a pistol drawn and pointed directly at Spaulding's head. The captain's face is dismayed, but only for an instant. Kane's pistol fires. The bullet rips through Spaulding's face. Pieces of his skull and splashes of blood are sent across the deck and onto his crew behind him. The captain's body topples over. It nearly lands in the lap of a stunned Waterman, who leans away from him and tries to shuffle backwards.

Kane lowers his smoldering pistol. He steps forward and looks intently at Thorndike and Waterman.

"Now, which of you would like to explain who you were delivering to?" Kane asks. "And I'm only asking you once."

It takes barely an instant before both blood-splattered men offer up the name of Josiah Dix. They not only give the name, but also his location. Their answer and cooperation makes Kane smile.

"Very well," he says, looking down at his boots. He notices specks of blood on them.

Kane holsters his pistol and begins to walk away. He summons one of the guards over. He picks up a loose cloth discarded on the deck and uses it to wipe his boots.

"Lieutenant," he begins. "We are done with these men. Take them below and secure them. Then abandon the vessel."

He tosses the cloth to the deck. His boots now shine like new again. He looks over the rest of the vessel and can see that most of the off-loading of cargo is complete. He begins to walk away as the lieutenant returns to his prisoners, but stops for one last bit of instruction.

"And before you go, be sure to burn the ship," he says.

Kane de-boards the *Sparrow* and is ferried back to his own vessel. He spends the evening enjoying a hot cup of tea from the aft deck while he watches the *Sparrow* go up in flames. Amidst the call of gulls and the rustle of the evening breeze, he can hear the screams of the prisoners as their ship is reduced to ashes.

CHAPTER NINE
Portsmouth, New Hampshire, 1774

Eli sets the cup of tea on the small table next to the bed and then sits next to his wife. Elizabeth looks weary. Their baby is due anytime now and she has been bedridden for days as the moment of birth draws closer.

Eli has been providing regular care for her, with a little help from their son Joseph. Now, the boy enters the room dragging a wool blanket that is three times his size. He drops it onto the bed and smiles at his mother.

"Thank you, my sweet boy," she says. "That will help keep me warm on this cold night."

The temperatures have taken quite a dip, as the early hints of summer have apparently come and gone. The New England spring is transitioning toward warmer temperatures, but is doing so slowly. Elizabeth picks up the tea cup and warms her hands, enjoying the aroma of the steam rising. It helps warm her bones almost immediately. She waits for it to cool before taking her first sip.

She looks at her husband, beaming beside her with a bright and content smile. It makes her giggle a little, forcing her to hold the teacup more steadily to keep from spilling.

"What makes you smile so?" she asks as she takes her first sip, savoring the flavor and the warmth.

That prompts an even wider smile. Eli reaches over and puts his hand on his wife. She's a sizable lump beneath the heavy bedding, but he still enjoys the touch of her.

"You just look so beautiful," he replies. "I'm excited about our new baby, and the family that we have growing."

"I'm glad it makes you happy," she says. "I'm anxious, too. I look forward to holding our new child, and being able to get out of this bed."

She sips her tea, enjoying the simple pleasure of it. She sees her husband still staring at her and smiling. She's glad to see the joy on his face and the love in his eyes. She has often missed that when he's been away.

"Don't you miss being at sea?" she asks. "You've given up so much just to be here with me."

Eli takes his wife's hand and holds it tight. He leans down and gently gives it a soft kiss.

"I'd much rather be here with you," he replies. "What I love most about being at sea is coming home to you."

Her mention of it does make him think, though. It is strange for Eli to be away from the seafaring life. Since he was a young boy, his life has revolved around following the sea. His friend Ezra has already set sail on a new journey. It is the first time in ages that Budwick has hauled out without Eli at his side. His brother-in-law, George, is still rather irritated with Eli's decision to stay ashore.

The thought makes Eli realize that he does miss it. It is a life that is so much a part of who he is; it is what he grew up preparing to do. He never knew anything else, or felt like he was meant to be anything else. Now, that has all changed.

He likes being here for his wife. He's looking forward to their new life with a new child. It's an exciting new beginning. He's unsure of how work will go trying to fish locally out of his coastal sloop, but it is a change he's ready to make.

He looks into his wife's blue eyes. She looks so lovely, despite appearing so weary. He has missed her when he's been away. It is exciting to think that he won't have to miss the love he shares with her. It will be a welcomed new chapter in their life to be able to have the kind of family that Eli never had as a boy.

"You will return to the sea," she says to him with a smile. "I know you can't stay away. It is part of your destiny. It has always called you, and it will again."

Eli's taken aback by her words, but he scoffs at such a notion. Like Ezra and George, she may have a hard time believing that he truly is ready to leave the seafaring life and all that comes with it. He has no intention of changing his mind, other than patrolling the local waters for whatever bounty he can find.

"I'm not leaving you, my dear," he says contently. "I'm not leaving our family. You are my calling now."

CHAPTER TEN
Portsmouth, New Hampshire, 1774

D aylight is slowly slipping away. With each passing moment, the faint sunlight is eclipsed by the approaching darkness. There are still a few boats maneuvering around the harbor, but soon the activity will cease. Another day will be done.

That's exactly what Eli is thinking to himself. With the sun struggling to keep its grip on the day, he knows his time to work is lessening. He can keep working into the night, utilizing the scant lighting from a few lanterns, but he is already sapped of his energy.

He's been working on refurbishing his vessel, Frances, for much of the day. He already spent the morning down below replacing rotting wood and fortifying the inside of the hull. The afternoon was filled with ripping out deck boards and slotting in new ones. With that task just about complete, he is ready to call it a day and leave the ship until the following morning.

He still has a walk through town before getting to his home. It's an uphill walk. The house his father owned sits on top of a hill that overlooks part of the town and some of the harbor. Luke's second wife still lives there, and shares the home with Eli. His sister Maddie recently moved out when she was married.

Eli is still a good month away from completing his work and having his ship ready for sail. His hope is to have it ready by early summer so he might generate some shipping business to get his career on track.

It has been four years since his father was lost at sea. Afterward, Eli continued serving on various vessels until he decided to go it alone. He purchased the Frances from his in-laws and decided to rebuild it and start up his own outfit out of his father's wharf, which he inherited.

He has spent much of the winter refurbishing and getting the vessel ready. After strengthening the hull and putting in new masts, he's been working on the structure below and now the deck.

He's pleased to see the progress he's made, but can't help but run through a list of projects that still need doing before he sails. At this point, he's been so wrapped up in the work on the vessel itself that he hasn't had opportunity to generate much business for when he does haul out. He hopes Maddie's in-laws can help in that regard.

With his tools picked up and stowed away, he steps onto the dock and gazes over his day's work. The orange glow of the full moon shines down enough on the deck to illuminate his progress. The fresh wood glistens as the moon's radiance dances across the deck. The trail of light stretches across the harbor, leaving a fiery path that glows across the water and off into the horizon.

The silence of the night is broken only on occasion, when some faint noise echoes across the harbor. Eli can't help but stand in awe of the beauty of this night and the peacefulness it has brought over the town. He's tired and anxious to get home to rest, but he can't tear himself from the majesty that shines above.

He suddenly hears the sound of footsteps on the dock nearby. The click clack of steps ring clearly in the quiet of the night. He can't make out the figure at first. Their clothing is dark and a hood covers the face. He remains calm, but focused on the person as they walk closer.

"Good evening," comes a voice from beneath the hood. It is the soft, sweet voice of a female. It is one that rings familiar in Eli's ears, but he can't place it. The figure steps closer and halts a few feet away. She gazes out across the harbor as well, admiring the same view that Eli had been engrossed in moments before.

"What an amazing sight," says the voice. Eli watches her intently as she slips the hood back from her face. The moonlight shines off her clear skin and hints at the identity. As she completely reveals herself, she turns to face him. Eli suddenly recognizes her. Her eyes are dark, but still glint slightly in the moonlight. She flashes a warm smile.

"Miss Douglass," Eli blurts out, as his mind recognizes the face and his mouth unleashes the thought almost instantaneously.

Elizabeth Douglass is the daughter of one of the local merchants. He operates a store down on the docks, and they have a fine home a short walk up the street in the village. Her father, Danforth Douglass, may be one of the most successful merchants in the harbor. Between his shipping business and store, he's been able to live quite comfortably. Though the in-laws of Eli's sister are quite successful, the Douglass family may be even more well off.

Elizabeth is the youngest of her family, still in her late teens. Eli is accustomed to seeing her along the docks. She'll deliver goods to vessels on occasion, or just be seen taking strolls along the shorefront.

"Aren't you out a bit late?" Eli asks, wondering what a young girl is doing walking the dark streets by herself.

Her smile brightens, almost amused at the question.

"My father doesn't like it when I go for walks at night," she explains. "But it is my favorite time. It is so different down here in the evening. Sometimes I walk down here even later, but tonight Father is out for a few hours. It was my best chance to sneak away. When I saw the moon rising up over the harbor, I couldn't resist."

Eli has known Elizabeth for many years. He still remembers her as the pre-teen who used to work around her father's store. Eli's father did business with Mr. Douglass quite often, and even hauled cargo for him on many occasions.

"Your father has good reason to be worried," Eli says. "A young pretty girl down here at night, all it takes is one drunken sailor out looking to cause trouble."

She laughs slightly, even though she knows such danger exists. "I steer clear of that part of the harbor," she says. "I try not to stay out too late or stray too far."

Eli nods, happy to hear that she is at least being cautious. "I was about to walk through the village toward home," he says. "If you'd like company..." As he pauses, trying to find the words to finish his thought, she answers without hesitation.

"I'd like that," she says. "I was about to turn for home but chose to walk along the docks and watch the light shimmer on the water."

Eli takes a quick look around his vessel and sees that he has not forgotten anything important. He waves slightly, inviting Elizabeth to follow him.

The two begin a stroll down the wooden boardwalk that connects many of the docks making up the inner harbor. There's not another soul to be seen or heard. An occasional voice from across the harbor or a dog's bark echoes through the night.

"It sure is quiet tonight," says Eli.

"That's what I like about it," says Elizabeth. "The peacefulness makes it so easy to get lost in your thoughts."

As they continue walking along the planks of the boardwalk, they both gaze off across the harbor. They watch the moonlight dance, and comment on various vessels they pass.

"My Uncle Martin used to own that," says Elizabeth, pointing to a sleek sloop nestled up against the dock, side by side with another vessel. "He sold it to Abner Scovill for a good price. He's putting that money into building a larger ship."

Looking over the sloop, she doesn't see the loose planking in the docks. As she steps upon the sagging piece of wood, it causes her to stumble forward. She loses her balance and nearly lands facedown. Eli grabs her arm and pulls her in to steady her.

Her quiet, quick shriek is immediately replaced by relief, startled but glad to have avoided a hard fall. She sets her feet back firmly and gains her balance.

"You all right?" *Eli questions, looking her over as he releases his grip.*

Elizabeth is a bit embarrassed for the moment, but glad it happened at night, and not during daylight in front of an audience who would have laughed at her clumsiness.

"Yes, thank you," she says. "I just took a bad step. Wasn't watching where I was going."

She looks up at Eli. He's tall and rugged, but it is a boyish face that peers down at her. It displays a look of concern until he determines that she is fine.

"Can't have you falling off the dock," he says, looking at her with a mischievous smile. "Don't think your father would let you out of the house ever again."

Elizabeth laughs at the thought, even though it is probably true. Just the sneaking out might be enough to keep her under his scrutiny for some time, but an accident or injury while walking might have brought about greater repercussions.

"At least I could tell him I wasn't walking alone," she says.

Eli chuckles quietly, almost under his breath. "But it might not speak *much to my credibility if you were to be hurt while in my company," he replies.*

Elizabeth laughs and reaches out to brush his arm with her hand.

"Oh, I would have defended you and told how you had tried to save and protect me." The two share a laugh. Eli extends his arm in her direction.

"Maybe you should grab hold, just in case," he says. "I can't have you falling in my presence. What father would ever trust me with his daughter, or what merchant trust me with his goods?"

Elizabeth takes his arm. She holds it loosely at first, but her grip tightens as a sense of comfort and security set in.

They stroll arm-in-arm past a few more docks before leaving the boardwalk and venturing into the village streets. There is some movement around town, but the two are able to navigate the streets in anonymity.

The Douglass family lives in a large estate at the head of the harbor. From the docks where Eli and Elizabeth entered the village streets, it is just a short walk past a few city blocks before a winding walkway takes them uphill toward the Douglass home.

The streets are quiet and empty as they pass an arrangement of houses that lead away from the harbor. Just a few hundred yards from the entrance to the Douglass home is a small village cemetery. Many of Portsmouth's early settlers are buried here, including some of Elizabeth's own ancestors.

An iron fence surrounds the small patch of hallowed ground. At the entrance is a pair of brick towers to which the large metal gates are attached. They are closed and locked tight. On most evenings, the darkness of the cemetery would shelter much of it from view in the night, but the full moon's glare shines just enough light to illuminate a small area at the entrance.

"I've always loved this little cemetery," she says as they pause to gaze through the iron fence. "It's a pretty little place."

Only some of the stones are visible in the darkness. Eli looks it over and feels an eeriness about it.

"It's a place I like to visit," he says, "but I wouldn't desire a permanent residence."

Elizabeth laughs and turns to face him. She leans back against the gate and looks up at him.

"You're not afraid of death are you, Captain?" she asks.

Eli thinks for a moment about his answer. He looks back through the iron bars. A shiver runs through his body.

"A sailor can't be afraid of death," he replies, with no hint of playfulness whatsoever. "I've already seen plenty of it and can always see it lurking."

It is more serious an answer than Elizabeth expected, but is one she realizes is likely coming from a sea captain. Trying to think of a means to change the subject, she suggests that maybe their walk is nearly complete.

"It might be best if I continue on alone," she says. "I'll sneak up the walkway and in the back door, just in case my father has arrived home early." That very well could be the case, since she has already been out much longer than she initially anticipated.

"I understand," Eli replies. "I hate to let you go. I have enjoyed our walk in the moonlight."

She leans back against the iron fence. When she looks back at him, the light from the moon reflects upon her face just enough to highlight her radiant smile. Her face beams with happiness, her eyes dancing. "The moon will be full again tomorrow," she says, flicking her eyebrows up for a brief instant. "We could pick up where we leave off tonight."

Eli steps closer and places his hands on the iron bars of the gate. He leans closer to her. The glow of moonlight shines a slight amount of light on her pretty face.

"That means we must leave off in a way worth continuing tomorrow," he says.

He pauses for a moment, freezing almost in time, waiting for any kind of signal. With nothing to dissuade him, he leans in toward Elizabeth and places his lips softly on hers. He leaves them there for a moment before pulling back. He stops momentarily, but feels her arms reach around him and pull him close. Still holding the bars of the gate, he leans in again. Pressing tightly against her and the gate, he kisses her passionately. He feels the cold chill of the iron bars but the warmth of the intensity between them.

The kiss seems to last for minutes, but still feels too short. When he pulls back, she slips away from the gate and away from his grasp. She flashes a brief smile that is barely seen in the darkness and begins up the road toward her home a short distance away.

"Till tomorrow night," she says as she disappears into the darkness, *just as she appeared earlier in the evening.*

A sudden twitch makes Eli's whole body jerk spastically. As he abruptly awakens from his restful sleep, Doctor Robert Krausse stands over him. The doctor watches Eli, observing whether the subtle poke he just gave him is enough to wake him fully.

"Eli," he says. "Wake up, Eli."

Eli rubs his face with his hands. He looks around for a hint of the time. The darkness that seeps in through the windows makes it clear that he has been sleeping since at least dusk.

He had very little sleep the previous day, as Elizabeth began her contractions. They came and went for much of the day. After getting very little rest the night before, the doctor sent him out of the room to rest in the parlor. Eli hadn't expected to sleep so soundly, or for so long.

He had been transported back in time to the first moments of his relationship with Elizabeth. It was a wonderful start to their romance. He almost wishes he could have slept a little while longer and relived the second evening, which was as memorable as the first. He had kissed his bride-to-be again that night as the skies flashed above them with the bright flicker of heat lightning and an occasional rumble of thunder in the distance.

"Eli," the doctor says again, this time with a sense of urgency. "The baby will be here soon. You better come with me."

CHAPTER ELEVEN
Portsmouth, New Hampshire 1774

He sits in the rocking chair holding his infant son. Eli beams proudly as newly born Eligood sleeps peacefully in his arms. He can see his own father's face in the crinkled eyes and wrinkly features. Eligood might even look a little like him, Eli tells himself.

Joseph comes by every so often to take a peek at his younger brother. He's been instructed to be quiet and not disturb his sibling. Joseph, who is now four, doesn't really look like the Miller clan. He resembles a Douglass. He has the dark hair and the long, narrow face. His eyes are deep set and his smile is subtle. He has the ears of a Miller, but that's not necessarily a good thing. It gives him something to rest a wide brim hat upon, but generously proportioned ears are something that seems handed down to each generation, whether they're wanted or not.

"When will he wake up?" Joseph asks with a whisper, barely containing a lowered voice. He seems to know that if he speaks loudly enough, he might awaken the baby, but he's not bold enough to try that.

"He'll be awake in good time," his father responds. "You go and play now, let him be. When he wakes, you'll know."

A disappointed Joseph storms off and stomps his way upstairs. He stops for a moment, pausing just enough to give his brother one last chance to wake up and summon him back. Dissuaded again, he continues up the stairs and quickly preoccupies himself with his toys.

Dr. Krausse steps out of the rear bedroom and peers down at a tired Eli and his resting son.

"You both look peaceful and in need of sleep," he says.

Eli just nods and takes a quick peek at his boy to be sure he isn't stirring. He raises his weary head and glances back at the doctor, almost hesitant to ask.

"So?" he inquires.

The doctor is fully aware of the meaning of the question. He regrets that he doesn't have much of an answer. He glances back into the bedroom, as if a sudden change has just occurred, giving him reason to deliver glorious news. Yet, the room remains silent. He can see Elizabeth sound asleep in the bed. Her sister-in-law Maddie is at the bedside. So is nurse Emilia Parker.

The vigil at her bedside is now around the clock. Complications following the birth have left Elizabeth clinging to life. The boy seems fine, but his mother may or may not survive long enough to see her son.

"There's no real change, Eli," he answers reluctantly. "I wish I could say there was."

Maddie exits the bedroom and approaches Eli as well. She suggests that she take the boy so Eli can get some sleep. He's barely closed his eyes in the last day, as he watched his son being born and then his wife slip into an unresponsive state.

"I can't," he says. "I can't leave Elizabeth until I know."

Both Maddie and the doctor nod their understanding. Maddie leans over and takes the boy anyway.

"Go sit with her, then," she suggests. "I'll take the baby."

Eli thanks her, then wearily stands and stumbles his way into the room. He sits down at the bedside and grasps his wife's hand. He had hoped to see something different from the last time he looked into her eyes, but he doesn't. Elizabeth's face is blank, her breathing labored. He yearns for some sign of improvement from his wife, yet he sees anything but.

His heart is full of love, but he feels it slowly breaking as every hour brings him closer to her slipping away. Her newborn baby cries in the other room. She hasn't had a chance to see her new son or hold him. Tears fall one at a time down Eli's cheek. He tries to hold them back, but emotion swells just below the surface. He's afraid to let it out, but his pain is too strong.

He maintains a grip of her hand as he leans back in the chair. He kisses her palm softly and remembers the tender kisses they've shared. Her twinkling eyes would sparkle back at him and a soft, rapturous smile would accompany every soft kiss between them. He longs to share that with her again, but fears he may not.

As helpless as he felt watching his father flail in the raging ocean waters to his death, Eli can't help but feel even more conflicted now. He can only sit and watch Elizabeth and the life they've shared drift away.

CHAPTER TWELVE
Gloucester, Massachusetts, 1774

The fire still smolders enough to light the room and provide heat. Josiah Dix stirs the embers just enough to rouse a few sparks and flames. He tosses another log and watches it burn. It should just be enough to keep the fire going a while longer.

The late spring thaw has quickly changed as the temperature dropped suddenly in recent days. He has warmed the house with the fire all evening, but thinks he may not need to keep it going through the night.

His wife, Nora, is in the kitchen cleaning up after dinner. He can hear her scrubbing pots and singing to herself. Her soft lilting voice is still clear, despite her advanced age. Josiah sits back in his chair and enjoys the comforts of his home and the beauty of her song as it echoes from the kitchen.

He sits with eyes closed and a warm contentment envelops him like a blanket. He listens to the singing—until it stops.

"Josiah dear, could you empty the wash basin?" Nora asks. "I hate to disturb you. You look so comfortable. But, I'm done with my chores in the kitchen."

Dix slowly rises out of his chair. He's glad to help his wife, but already dreads having to interrupt his brief sense of peace.

"You looked so content," Nora says as her husband follows her into the kitchen.

He puts his hand on her shoulder and runs it across her back. She turns to face him and flashes an appreciative smile.

"I was just reveling in your beautiful voice," he says, taking the moment to give her a loving kiss.

She almost hates to have the moment end as he continues on to the wash basin. He lifts it up off the stout wooden table and begins to carry it toward the door that exits the kitchen. Nora rushes ahead of him to unlatch the door and swing it open. She stands there holding it as he passes her and smiles.

Josiah walks the basin out to the side of the house. There's a small stream that flows alongside their property. He empties the water into the stream and shakes every last drop of water out of the basin before turning to return to the house. It is dark out, with little light to illuminate the property. Only the candles that flicker inside the house offer up any glow. The slight shimmers of radiance escape through doors and windows, bleeding into the blackness outside.

He walks slowly, making sure nothing is underfoot as he navigates the short distance back to the house. The door is ajar still. He expects Nora to be in the kitchen, but as he enters and closes the door, he finds the room empty.

"I thought you'd be in here singing for me," he says with a slight chuckle. He gets no answer. "Where did you go?" he calls. He exits the kitchen. He steps into the parlor. Josiah's heart drops. He utters an audible gasp when he discovers his wife sitting, tensed, in his favorite chair. Standing before her are three British officers. One of them has a gun pointed at her head.

"Mr. Dix, I presume," Kane says. "Sit down."

Josiah stands frozen in place. Almost paralyzed by fear but incensed by the intrusion, it takes a moment before he can react.

"What is the meaning of this?" he demands. "How dare you burst into my home like this."

Kane glares at Dix. He draws his saber and points it at Josiah's chest, just as he did to the man's son.

"I said sit down," Kane states. "You wouldn't want to force me to hurt your lovely wife. Your son's stupidity prompted a bullet in his head. Don't tempt the same fate for your wife."

Stunned at the news of his son's death, Dix hears his wife's sobs as she sits facing their child's murderer, a gun aimed at her face. Josiah is tempted to rush Kane, but the saber pointed at him dissuades such a notion. It is obvious that Kane can sense what Josiah is thinking.

"Don't be stupid, old man," he orders. "Sit down so we can talk."

Josiah steps over to a chair opposite his wife. He watches the officer standing to Nora's left with a gun pointed at the side of her head. Kane stands to Josiah's left, giving him full view of his wife.

"I want to talk to you about smuggling," says Kane. "We have laws and restrictions about that. Apparently, you and your son have ignored such things. Your son sold you out just before I put a bullet in his brain."

Josiah can't hide his emotion. His eyes well with tears and his body visibly shakes.

"I had to make a living," he answers. "Take my ship, take my money. I'll pay whatever penance I must. Just let my wife and me be."

Kane just laughs at Josiah's contrition. He looks over at the two officers who join him.

"I like how sorry they are after they are caught," he says.

He looks back at Dix sitting helpless in the chair, a frail and scared old man. Kane enjoys the fear that he has created.

"I don't need your money, Mr. Dix," Kane states. "And you don't have a ship any longer. It is just a smoldering, sinking hunk of wood as we speak."

Prior to their visit to the Dix homestead, Kane and his men stopped by the wharf that Dix owns. They not only set fire to the ship that was there but burned down the wharf as well. Dix's entire merchant business is now in ruin.

"What we want is an example," he says. "People need to know that they can't break our rules in such a way. They must understand that there are consequences for such action. We want your family to spread that message."

Josiah begins to nod. His expression is both apologetic and appreciative.

"We will, sir," he says. "Whatever you ask. I will be sure people are told."

Kane points his sword at Dix again. He glares into his eyes. "You won't be telling people," Kane informs before pointing the sword toward Nora. "Your wife will be the one spreading the message. She'll be the example of what happens to a family, a son, a husband, when you ignore British authority. The Widow Dix will be our shining example."

Josiah's face goes slack with terror. His wife shrieks and he tries to look into her eyes but only sees a flash. He groans violently as Kane's saber is plunged into his chest. Nora screams again as the life drains from Josiah's body. Kane withdraws the saber and is ready to sweep it viciously across the old man's throat, but he can see there is no need. Dix is dead.

Nora shrieks loudly and sobs into her hands. The officer beside her puts his pistol away. Kane signals for the officers to exit the house. He glances over at Nora one last time. He watches her misery intently. He almost can't tear himself away from it. When she realizes he is watching her, she looks up and stares at him. Her eyes are cold and filled with hatred. Kane just smiles. He turns his back and exits through the front door.

CHAPTER THIRTEEN
Aboard the *Gypsy*, 1774

The fog is as thick as Ezra Budwick has ever seen it, a shroud of gray that hangs down from the heavens and cloaks the night in mist and heavy air.

"Cain't see a damn blasted thing," he exclaims in frustration. "You don't see it so thick-a-fog down here like this. You'd think we was back in New England."

Instead, they are in the Caribbean, dodging pirates and smuggling as much rum and sugar as he can stuff in the hold of his sleek sloop *Gypsy*. He's avoided his old friend Buddy Bush in the West Indies on this return trip.

"He probably ain't forgot the last time I snookered him," Budwick tells his mate before opting to avoid that port.

Instead, he quietly eases his vessel into Barbados and finds business there. He has already delivered goods from the north to the Carolinas and to Puerto Rico. His last stop is one of the islands in the Caribbean before making a quick getaway toward the north.

He is tempted to sit tight in the harbor after filling his hold, but extra time in port provides more time for trouble.

"I feel a mite safer out in the open ocean than hunkered down here in the harbor," he says. "Besides, if my good friend Buddy gets wind of me laid up over here, he might bring his own mini militia in."

So, as he's done plenty of times before, Budwick sets off under the cover of darkness. This time, though, the fog is so thick and the air so heavy that his ship barely plunders along.

He doesn't admit it to his crew, but he actually feels a bit uncomfortable attempting such a getaway this time. His usual first mate, Eli

Miller, is no longer aboard. He's replaced him with Geoffrey Musgrave. Musgrave is an experienced enough sailor. He's sailed the international routes and risen up the ranks before the mast under some fine captains, but in Budwick's mind, he still isn't Eli Miller.

"He's probably as good as we's gonna find," Budwick had told George Lathrop prior to the voyage. "But, I trust Eli and I know what he brings to the ship. Don't mean I got anythin' against another man, but he don't bring what I've come to expect from Eli."

Eli brought not only a keen eye in such tenuous situations, but fine judgment. He wasn't afraid to share his opinion and challenge Budwick's strategy when necessary. Musgrave seems to just spout back whatever his captain tells him.

"I wish he'd disagree at least once in a while," Budwick mutters to himself after calling out an order and having Musgrave offer up a predictable, "Aye, sir," before following the commands. "I cain't be that right. I ain't that smart."

There's a tense silence on deck as the crew watches intently for any signs of trouble in the fog. It could come from another vessel or from a ledge that doesn't even have to be stealthily hidden. Musgrave has heard grumbling from crew on the forward deck.

"Who knows what the hell we're sailing into," says one, assuming he's out of earshot of the first mate. "This is supposed to be safer?"

Musgrave doesn't bother to report any griping he hears to the captain. He's had his own misgivings but has kept mum, fully knowing that a berth on board with Budwick could be a profitable one in the future. The last thing he wants to do is create a bad impression.

"Stand by!" comes the shout from Budwick at the wheel. Musgrave quickly relays that call.

The wind has shifted slightly, Budwick senses. He's been plotting a course toward the east but feels the light breeze in the night and billowing gently from off the ocean. It's going to edge his vessel more toward land, but he figures he's got room to maneuver. In time, he'll be able to tack back toward the open ocean and ride the westerlies steadily for New England.

The captain gives the call to maneuver and the crew rushes into action. The sails swing with one sweeping motion from one side to the other. Luffing sails are tightened. The vessel groans as it begins to move in a new direction. The breeze is pushing her, but only slightly.

"Come on," shouts Budwick. "You can give me somethin' better than this."

He begs the breeze to cooperate, but gets only a few gusts that fill his sails only to drop them, empty of any wind or momentum. The turning of the vessel has slowed and so has whatever momentum the ship was carrying.

"Godfrey mighty," he exclaims. "How the hell am I supposed to make a getaway if I cain't get nowhere?"

His thinking is interrupted by a loud explosion. It catches Budwick's attention immediately. He looks at his masts, fully expecting one of them to be cracking and tumbling over—even though he can't fathom why that would be. Instead, he sees a flash and another explosion.

His eyes suddenly widen and his jaw drops. Off the larboard rail is the dark shape of a vessel, well hidden in the gray night. The flash of its cannon is barely visible, but he hears the shouts and screams from the forward deck. The chaos hints at something wrong, and the fact that his vessel is dead in the water tells Budwick he's in trouble.

"Captain!" Musgraves shouts as he rushes toward the stern to update Budwick. "The bowsprit! It's..."

He never utters another word. A flurry of musket fire breaks out and Musgrave is hit square in the back of the head. The look of urgency that Budwick could see when Musgraves reported to him turns blank as his first mate drops dead in a heap on the deck. The captain watches his crew begin to surrender. The mystery ship has inched close enough to board.

"You think it's gonna be that damn easy?" Budwick shouts as he grabs a pistol for each hand. "Come get me, ya bastards!"

He steps defiantly along the aft deck, firing simultaneous shots from his pistols. He shoots with precision. Not a shot is wasted as he takes aim at each and every invader that crosses the gunwale and stalks his way. When his pistols run out of ammunition, he draws a saber and rushes forward, slashing and dashing about between attackers. It isn't until a shot burrows into his leg and knocks him down that he stops. Before he can muster the strength to stand or free his saber for a few defensive blows, he bears the brunt of a musket end to his skull.

CHAPTER FOURTEEN
Portsmouth, New Hampshire, 1774

The slam of each strike of the hammer echoes through the tight walls of the cramped wooden hull. Eli can only stand the sound that rings through his ship for so long. He'll hammer a nail or two and then stop, letting the echo subside.

He purchased this old fishing sloop a few years back, but never really did much with it. It was to be a vessel he'd use on occasion. Or maybe he'd just fix it up and sell it off to some fisherman or buyer with a better use for it. Instead, it sat along the docks hardly getting any care at all. It became a sign of all the things that needed care at home whenever he'd embark or return from another journey at sea.

It wasn't a priority. Between the house and caring for his pregnant wife and minding his son, Eli had his hands full. Now, life has changed. All the plans he had with Elizabeth and the boys died with her. Instead, he's starting over, trying to pick up the pieces of a shattered life.

Now that he's given up the merchant trade, he has the time and need to make use of this small vessel. His hopes are to get it seaworthy in quick order and get busy fishing. With the British blockade of Boston Harbor and their patrols along the coast, a small fishing operation might be a suitable means to make a living for the time being.

But there's work to be done before he hauls any nets or sells any catch. He's got a mast to replace and sails to mend. There are little repairs to do all about the ship. It can be a bit overwhelming when he thinks of it all, so he's focusing on just one task at a time.

So far, he's been fortifying spots in the hull from the inside, crawling into the depths of the bow. It's completely dark except for the lantern he's brought with him. He probably could use another light, but he doesn't have one. That's another thing he needs to do but keeps forgetting.

He hates crawling down into the dark recesses of the hull for this task. It's like being trapped, buried alive so to speak, in the darkness of his ship. At the same time, he feels like he could curl up and sneak a nap in the quietness there. The idea of slipping away into a restful peace is enticing. He can't recall the last time he experienced such a thing.

There are times he thinks it would be so much easier to just go back to sea; to sail away from his heartbreak and his fear of failure. But he knows he has a responsibility to his sons. He's determined to make a good life for them, even though he's unsure of his ability to do just that. And, beyond that, he knows no matter what he does or where he goes, there truly is no escape from his pain.

Instead, he pounds some more, cringing with the racket that it makes with each slam of the hammer head on nails he can barely see. He stops momentarily after one strike echoes loudly. He listens as though he heard something, a voice or movement on the ship. But he hears nothing else and lifts the hammer for another blow. Just as he strikes another nail with a few decisive strikes, he stops again, thinking he still hears something.

He wonders who or what could be boarding his ship—or why. Nothing realistic comes to mind. So, he sets another nail into a plank and taps it a few times before preparing to level a forceful blow. He raises the hammer and strikes it once. Before he can level another blow, he is interrupted.

"Eli," he hears from above. There are footsteps and creaking of the wood on the deck above. He does have a visitor, just as he suspected. "Eli, where are you? I can hear you down there."

Eli recognizes the voice as he extricates himself from the depths of the bow.

"I'm down here, far forward," he answers. "I'm coming up."

It takes a moment to extract himself and make his way back to the deck. He begrudgingly does so, knowing that he'll have to crawl back down to that tight spot into the bow again to finish the job.

He finds George Lathrop pacing the dock, giving the ship a once-over. Eli is sure his brother-in-law will scoff at the notion of getting this vessel back in sailing order to use for fishing. He's looked down his nose at the idea in the past.

"Sorry I didn't hear you, I was tucked up deep into the bow, putting in some planks," Eli says as steps out onto the deck, almost blinded by the bright sunlight. "What brings you down here? Something wrong with the boys?"

Lathrop quickly dismisses the notion. His wife is caring for Joseph and the baby as she often does. He actually hasn't been home or seen his family for hours.

"It's not about the boys," he responds.

"So, it must be something else important," Eli says, suspecting that his brother-in-law is here to pitch another trip on one of his merchant vessels. Since he and Budwick visited that day, he's been back numerous times to offer something similar. He took a bit of a break during Elizabeth's delivery and illness, but has since resumed. So much for the grieving process.

"If it is another job offer, I'm not interested," Eli tells him.

He can tell by Lathrop's reaction that that's exactly what he's here for, and he's not happy about being turned down before he's even had a chance to make his pitch. With each dismissal by Eli, Lathrop has gotten more and more exasperated.

"This is different," he says. "Will you at least hear me out?"

Eli nods, clearly sensing Lathrop's irritation. He decides to at least be accommodating and listen to the proposal before putting up a stubborn front.

Lathrop stops for a moment and then resumes his pacing. He seems almost reluctant or unsure how to proceed.

"I don't know whether you've noticed what is happening here and all along the coast," begins Lathrop. "New ships are being built. Vessels are being outfitted. The waterfront is becoming a front line of the war effort."

Lathrop pauses for a moment to see if his words spark any reaction from Eli. His brother-in-law listens intently, but shows no expression.

"There's talk that the Massachusetts Provincial Congress is going to outfit its own navy in the coming year," he continues. "The intent is to combat the British control of the seas, here and abroad."

This isn't exactly what Eli expected to hear. He assumed he'd get another stern talking to about the shipping trade and how he was failing to earn the living for which he was trained. Instead, Lathrop is now talking about the rebellion. Eli has never seen his brother-in-law as a son of liberty.

"How do you know all this?" Eli interrupts, despite knowing Lathrop won't appreciate being questioned.

Predictably irritated, Lathrop explains the many conversations he's had with fellow shipbuilders and even acquaintances with close ties to the Congress itself.

"The information is reliable," he says. "There is no doubt that a fleet of ships is being prepared. A war at sea is inevitable."

He has Eli's interest and curiosity peaked. Even if the Congress is preparing ships to combat the British, what does that have to do with Lathrop or him? He has a hunch as to what the answer to that may be. He's tempted to halt his brother-in-law right there, but is intrigued by Lathrop's sudden interest in the war effort. Or, what the war effort might do for him.

"It is a sign of things to come," says Lathrop.

He explains that he's going to outfit one of his vessels. He's going to turn it into a fighting ship and ready it for battle with the rest of the expected fleet.

"I want you to captain my ship," he says, making the offer that Eli has been expecting. Before Eli can utter a word, Lathrop throws up a hand to halt any response. "Before you say no, let me explain."

Lathrop goes on to summarize his strategy. With the British patrolling the seas and sending more vessels everyday, the only way to take back the seas and the merchant industry is by fighting back.

"We have to do it for our business, for our livelihood, but also for our independence," says Lathrop.

"George, since when do you care about independence?" Eli scoffs. "You just see an opportunity to make a profit."

"You can make a profit too, my friend," he counters. "It will do more than this wreck of a fishing sloop you have."

Eli can feel his brother-in-law's criticism masked by his job offer. He's been bitter about Eli's refusal to sail for him. It has prompted a questioning of Eli's judgment at every turn, making Eli even less interested in any business dealings with him. It is hard because he is so close to his sister Maddie, and needs her support like never before.

He can tell that Lathrop thinks his idea of fishing for a living is foolhardy, especially when one has the skills and experience to make far greater money in the international shipping trade.

"Profits don't mean a great deal to me," says Eli. "Not compared to my family."

Lathrop can barely contain himself as he sees he's getting nowhere in convincing Eli. "For God's sake Eli, those profits will benefit your family," he exclaims. "Your boys will need that money. You can provide for them far better than fishing."

Eli certainly knows that is true, but he is convinced there are other factors he needs to consider.

"I grew up sailing with my father, but still felt like I grew up without him after he was lost," Eli explains, almost choking back the words. "I don't want my boys to feel that way. They've already lost their mother. They can't be without both parents. I have to be here for them."

Lathrop realizes he can't argue that. He knows how hard it has been for Eli since Elizabeth died. Her loss was tragic enough, but to be left with a young son and an infant boy has made it incredibly difficult. Maddie has helped out significantly, caring for the boys nearly every day as Eli has worked on his vessel or done other jobs around the village for money. Lathrop knows he has little right to ask a father to abandon his sons, especially for the sake of profits.

"I can't begin to understand the struggles that you face or the pain you must feel," Lathrop says, suppressing his frustration with greater compassion. "I can't imagine leaving my boy like I'm asking of you."

He stops and pauses for a moment, emotional at the thought of leaving his young sons. Jack is eight years old and Abraham just turned five. They are the joys of his life. He can't imagine life without them. Before he can do away with his offer to Eli completely, he tacks in a different direction.

"One thing I worry about is, what kind of world are we creating or accepting for our sons?" Lathrop asks. "Are we willing to succumb to British rule and force our boys and their families to live under that oppression? Is that the legacy we want to leave for them?"

Lathrop is leery of getting into a philosophical debate about the war with Britain. He's not even quite sure where Eli stands in that regard. Both families are just two generations removed from ancestors who escaped Britain, sailing over from Wales to get a new start. Eli's father was actually born on the other side of the sea, but came to America as an infant.

"I want to fight the British tyranny," Lathrop says with defiance. "I want the independence our ancestors sought by coming here. It is the foundation they created for us. I want to build on that legacy. This is my way of being able to do that. It may earn me some profit, yes, but it will also help our efforts at sea against that menace. I can't do it alone. I need the right people to make it successful. I know you can do just that."

Eli is not sure whether Lathrop is sincere or not. He can imagine his brother-in-law concocting the whole independence argument for the sake of convincing him, but he also sees the truth in his point. It leaves him torn because he knows his boys need him, yet he also knows the country is at a crossroads with the war with Britain. America is at a point of no return. It is either fight and succeed, or fail and suffer the consequences forever.

"What about Ezra?" Eli asks. "Why don't you just get him to captain your ship? He's probably more suited for that than I."

Lathrop stops pacing and leans himself against a post on the wharf. He glances down at Eli but drops his head, avoiding his gaze. He's unsure how to answer the question and knows that the longer he takes, the more likely it is that Eli will suspect something. Lathrop takes a deep breath and sighs heavily.

"I didn't really want to have to tell you this," he begins. "I wasn't sure how you were going to find out, but Ezra is dead."

He pauses to let the news sink in. Eli just sighs and shakes his head. It is as though he almost expected such news someday.

Lathrop explains that Budwick had been captured and held prisoner. Originally, he was being held for a ransom but as time expired, various members of his crew escaped. Budwick may have been one of them. When they were caught soon after fleeing, they were executed. Budwick, being the captain, was chopped up and fed to the hogs.

"This is the kind of tyranny we are fighting," says Lathrop, implying British involvement of which he has no proof. "This is how they are ruling the seas, and now they are bringing that rule to our shores."

Eli doesn't even hear what George is saying now. Another person close to his heart is gone, and he is consumed with grief and ever-deepening loneliness.

CHAPTER FIFTEEN
Portsmouth, New Hampshire, 1774

Eli can't believe he misread the weather so badly.

He could sense the storm moving in. He even pondered the idea of not going out at all, but didn't want to miss a day of fishing.

Between poor weather, harassment from the British, or not getting off the dock because of sick boys, the fishing hasn't been as successful as he had hoped.

It's been such a struggle that he's feared a lecture from George telling him how he is wasting his time and money. That would inevitably lead to the suggestion that he captain one of George's vessels. George would hint at the disparity between his own success and Eli's lack thereof.

Eli can't think about all that now. He was just getting his nets overboard when the weather turned angry. It was a quick turn, too. Though Eli could sense something moving in, it seemed a good time away.

He had expected some weather, maybe some rain, a little wind and a few pesky waves running across the bay. But this has turned for the worse and it isn't looking like a simple squall that might be here one moment and gone the next.

This is the kind of storm that would have had him tied to the dock and maintaining a lengthy watch over his tie lines, had he stayed ashore. The last thing he wanted was be to be caught out in it and at its mercy, especially after opting to haul out today alone. He often brings a crew of one or two to help him.

What had been some gray clouds amidst murky skies have turned dark with a pelting rain. The subtle seas that had him bobbing along harmlessly have risen up with a violent might, churning up whitecaps that rage across the bay. The winds had been light with a few gusts that hinted at something stronger, but the approach of the storm quickly brought a forceful gale that howls above the sound of the heavy rain and ferocious seas.

Before Eli knew it, he was caught in a cauldron of bad weather. He's not only annoyed that he now has to battle this storm, but that he put himself in this position at all. He should have recognized the signs. His error has now not only put his vessel in jeopardy, but himself as well.

The bow is tossed up as it rides each crest, only to drop violently when it crashes off the wave into a deep trough that seems to swallow a portion of his boat with each new swell.

The icy rain stings his face. It clouds his vision and has him holding on desperately.

The southerly wind pushes him with a force that makes it difficult to steer. He has no choice but to ride the wind and waves toward the mouth of the river, where he hopes he can eventually gain some sort of control.

In most instances, the weather would dissipate enough to give him calmer seas once he reached the sheltering harbor, but the magnitude of this storm and the wind direction might not allow that.

So, he holds on and rides the wind and waves, knowing that other vessels and the havoc of the harbor will only make it more difficult.

He fears being pushed into another ship or capsizing as he tries to avoid ledges or some other obstacle. A larger vessel might give him some stability to work with, but this small one-masted ketch is at the mercy of the weather.

The waves are so powerful that each one wants to lift his vessel stern-first and spin it to one side or another. Any wave that turns him sideways only makes him vulnerable to another that could wash over him from the side. It could swamp him or simply roll him over.

He doesn't want to think about what happens if that occurs. It's a cold and icy swim in less than ideal waters, and Eli doesn't like to swim to begin with. He doubts he'd last very long in these stormy seas.

As the seas push him closer to the mouth of the river, he spots the breakers to the starboard side. The weather rushes him in that direction. If he misses it to the right, it will only drive him toward the island that marks the opening to the river.

If he doesn't miss the breakers, his vessel will surely be beaten to splinters. His only true option is to ease past the breakers to the left. That means steering the vessel to larboard side. As hard as he's tried to force the rudder to that direction, the vessel just hasn't responded.

He realizes he's running out of time and room. He has no choice but to drive the rudder as hard as he can and hold it. He forces the rudder so sternly he's afraid it might break under the strain. That would certainly mean the end. Still, he has no choice.

He leans into the rudder with all his force and wills his vessel around the breakers. With each wave that pushes him forward, he hopes one will aid his turn. No change is happening, but just as he draws close enough to see the breakers, through all the spray and refracting waves, the boat lurches to larboard.

He gives the rudder one more firm push that he thinks will surely snap his steering for good. Instead, his boat holds together and surges to that side of the ledges. One of the waves bouncing off the jagged rocks catches Eli and nudges him one last time away from danger.

In an instant, Eli is past the breakers and finds himself coming off the wave surge and into calmer seas.

He suddenly has a control over his vessel that he hasn't felt in some time. The weather is still raging behind him, but the intensity seems to have ceased as he ducks behind the island just enough to be in the lee of the storm.

He approaches the mouth of the river and can see the harbor just beyond. There seem to be very few ships, if any, under sail. It makes for a slightly easier approach to the harbor than he expected.

But a clear channel toward his wharf is quickly blocked by a small sloop that emerges from across the harbor. It looks similar to the many vessels that have accompanied the British ship *Lioness* that has been patrolling the coastline.

Eli has managed to avoid any confrontation with the British patrols, but here is one fast approaching. He isn't too concerned. It isn't like he has any catch to confiscate; he's done nothing illegal. That doesn't mean the British won't attempt to hassle him.

As he continues his way toward his wharf, the British sloop cuts in front of him and then tacks to sail past on Eli's larboard side. The sloop has a number of British sailors scrutinizing his vessel. A tall officer glares his way. Eli attempts to look both innocent and undeterred by the British flash of force.

He expects the sloop to order him to stop and attempt to board or search his vessel, but the British sail on past, giving him one more glare for good measure. Eli simply glares back.

By the time he reaches the dock, he's thankful for something to tie up to. He's relieved to be home safe, but frustrated with another wasted day of fishing. He hates the thought of going to Maddie's to pick up his boys.

Eli secures his boat and ties on an extra line just to be certain. He climbs out and looks past the vessel and out over the seas that still build to something meaner just beyond the entrance to the harbor.

He stands there and sighs, letting loose all his angst in one powerful breath.

Eli gathers up his composure and wearily trudges off down the dirt pathway that leads away from the dock and toward George and Maddie's house. He dreads meeting up with George. He knows he looks tired and battered after a wasteful day at sea. It will only prompt some form of comment from George.

When Eli arrives, Maddie answers the door. She appears relieved to see him.

"I was worried for you," she says. "George said the storm was something wicked out in the bay."

Eli wonders how George would know, but assumes some sailor passed along the details of the weather.

"It had some fearsome moments," Eli replies.

He notices that George is nowhere to be found and he doesn't bother asking for him. Instead, he looks for his boys and finds them quietly playing in the parlor. They are being watched by a young woman, about the age of Maddie and Eli.

"This is Faith," Maddie introduces. "She's been helping me with the boys."

Faith gazes at Eli and smiles. It's as if she knows him. Eli feels a warmth and friendliness in her face. As his boys rush over to greet him, Eli smiles back.

CHAPTER SIXTEEN
Portsmouth, New Hampshire, 1774

The aroma from the kitchen is one of comfort and warmth. It's a roasted air that wafts through the rest of the house. Even the boys notice it and anxiously await dinner.

The boys haven't been excited about anything Eli has cooked in quite some time. Their interest in his cooking usually only peaks when they're curious how badly he has burned something.

But on this night, there is the promise of a fine dinner, something Eli and the boys have only found on the few occasions they've taken a reprieve from Eli's limited culinary skills. That has typically been an evening at Maddie's, maybe a holiday meal or some other special occasion.

The boys have become accustomed to eating what they call 'grub.' It's an apt description, but the boys really don't know anything else. Eli had thought Joseph, his oldest, might recall his mother's cooking, but he doesn't. She was a wonderful cook. That might be why these blending of aromas are so heavenly. They remind Eli of those family times with Elizabeth.

It isn't just the smells he misses. It is the feeling of hominess. His wife filled their home with love and care; it has felt empty since her passing.

As Eli watches his boys quietly play, he knows he shouldn't be dwelling on Elizabeth at this moment. It is rather rude, he concludes.

Faith is in the kitchen working hard to make him a meal. To sit in the parlor and bemoan the untimely death of his wife is a bit disrespectful.

Faith comes out of the kitchen. Despite the effort it's taken to cook them a wonderful meal, she looks radiant in the glow of the warmth emanating from the kitchen. Eli notices how pretty she is. He likes having a woman in his home again.

"Dinner will be ready in a few minutes," she says sweetly.

Eli doesn't even have to speak to the boys. They hear her words and stop their play almost instantly and rush to the table. Eli laughs at their anticipation, but admits he's excited to eat as well.

This dinner was borne out of a chance meeting. Eli had been walking back from the harbor late one afternoon, taking a different route home than usual. This new path from the harbor led him right past the church, a few streets up from the docks. Eli had been a bit surprised to notice it. In all these years, he had never realized a church stood there before.

He wasn't sure whether that was a reflection upon his time away at sea or in his time away from God. Either could be reason enough, he surmised.

Outside the church that day were a couple of tables loaded with vegetables for sale. At first, Eli had little interest in the collection of carrots, parsnips, and zucchini. He barely even took notice of what the tables were selling. But as he walked by, he saw the woman behind the table. She looked familiar.

He paused for a moment and lingered long enough to try to recall her face, but he couldn't. His hesitation provided her the chance to notice him. She looked at him with the same familiarity, but quickly recognized him.

"Eli?" she said. "Aren't you Eli Miller, Maddie's brother?"

Eli had acknowledged that he was, even though he still struggled to recognize this woman. "I'm Faith, a friend of Maddie's," she explained. "We met last week when you came to get your boys."

In an instant, that night at Maddie's home had played out in his mind; there was that face. That was where he had seen her.

"Yes," he said. "I thought I recognized you."

He had stepped a little closer to the table to peruse the variety of vegetables. He hadn't even known what some of them were, let alone how you would cook them.

"These are all vegetables from our garden," she explained. "We sell them off each week."

Eli noticed the sizeable garden next to the church. It looked as though it might wield a decent crop. It might have been an acre of land, with a variety of different items planted there. He hadn't known enough to identify what was what in that space.

"I tend to the garden," Faith said. "Father, I mean *Pastor* Hamilton, says that we nourish the bodies in the garden and nourish the souls in the church."

Eli looked over the vegetables. He figured he might buy some carrots, he at least knows how to cook those. He and the boys found them somewhat likeable, as well. He started to dig out some money but realized all he had was a little change in his pocket. He didn't have nearly enough to buy anything.

"I'm sorry, Faith," he began. "I thought I might buy some things and take them home to the boys, but I seem to have left all my money at home."

She handed him a bag and suggested he fill it.

"Take what you'd like," she said with a smile. "You can just bring the money later."

Eli smiled and thanked her for her generosity.

"Do cooking instructions come with the vegetables?" he asked slyly. "My boys will be excited to have fresh vegetables, unless I burn them. Maybe they should just eat them raw."

Faith laughed shyly. She glanced back at Eli and offered a sweet smile. "I'm a rather fine cook," she said. It seemed as though she was trying to summon the courage to play along. "But I require some pleasant company for dinner."

Eli looked at her with a devilish smile hidden in an earnest face.

"My boys and I could make quite pleasant company, especially if someone other than myself is cooking the meal," he said.

Sure enough, a few days later, Faith arrived with a new crop of vegetables in hand, ready to cook. Eli had been on the water for a few short hours in the morning and had been working around the house all day. To have Faith there taking care of the dinner plans was a great help. Except, of course, that he still had to make himself and the boys presentable for the meal.

That evening, dressed in their most proper clothes, they gather around the dining room table as Faith brings out the meal. There are two kinds of vegetables, freshly baked bread, and roasted chicken. All of it smells so wonderful that Eli is almost unwilling to eat and allow the aroma to dissipate.

"Would you like to pray, or shall I?" Faith asks.

Eli pauses for a moment. He doesn't know what to say. He hasn't offered any kind of prayer in ages. It's been so long he's not so sure God would even know his voice.

Faith must recognize his hesitance, and offers to say grace herself.

She bows her head. Eli does so as well. The boys are a bit confused for a moment, but Eli motions with his hand for them to lower their heads.

"Heavenly Father, we thank you for this chance to share your goodness," she begins. "We take these seeds that you have sown and we grow them into great things to share. We thank you for this bounty and your grace. Like these crops, we are seeds for you to nurture and grow. We thank you for your ever-watchful guidance and care. Amen."

Eli waits for a moment to be sure Faith has finished. He offers up an "Amen" of his own. He looks across the table and sees two happy boys and a lovely Faith with a beautiful meal spread out before them. He smiles. His home feels full again.

CHAPTER SEVENTEEN
Portsmouth, New Hampshire, 1775

The ramshackle squadron of colonials was in full retreat. With a British battery of cannon fire coming from the warships anchored in Boston Harbor and the pursuit of a wave of Redcoats, what was left of Colonel Starks' troops from New Hampshire were hastily fleeing the battlefield on Breeds Hill.

Amaziah Goodwin could hear the musket balls screeching past him. The smattering of debris, dirt, and blood mixed into the smoke-filled air that was all around him and his fellow rebels. They had held the British at bay for much of the day, but from their position along the fence, they could see the Redcoats make slow progress as the battle wore on. Wave after wave of attacks had failed, but the British were wearing down the colonials and softening their weakest points.

When the Redcoats made a surge up the middle, between the hill and the fence, the rebel defenses couldn't hold. The British quickly made advancement. The redoubt was overwhelmed and the stand taken at the fences started to wither.

All that was left for the rebels to do was scurry to safety. Goodwin was already dazed and disoriented. More so because he knew he was lucky to still be alive. While firing upon the encroaching British troops from along the fence, a musket ball hit him square in the neck. The impact knocked him over. It was such a blunt impact that as Goodwin was toppled over onto his back, he thought for sure he was breathing his last.

"Oh, it hurt like a son of gun, but there weren't no blood," he explains

He felt an ache in his throat. It made him cough a bit as he tried to catch his wind. When he reached up to assess his wound, there was nothing there. He loosened the kerchief that was tied around his neck. It was a sweat-filled ring of fabric around his neck. As he loosened it, he found a musket ball wedged into the knot. The ball was stuck there, stopped by the fabric.

"I broke into the biggest grin, but nobody noticed," he recalls. "Everybody else was still busy fightin'."

With Eli sitting across from him and his proud wife Martha Goodwin listening in, Amaziah recounts his fight with the British at Breeds Hill. It proved to be a loss for the fledgling colonial army. The British ultimately captured the high ground that overlooks Boston Harbor and chased off the enemy troops, but it came with a heavy price for the Redcoats. The battlefield was strewn with British casualties, including Captain Pitcairn, one of their most respected and able leaders. It had been a victory that was reverberating all the way back to England.

"I just picked up my musket, dusted myself off, and rejoined the firing line," Goodwin explains.

He pulls out the musket ball from his pocket. It's his battlefield souvenir. He opens the collar of his shirt to reveal his neck.

"Not much left of the bruisin'," he says, almost disappointed that his scar is fading with time.

Eli listens with great curiosity. Faith sits by his side, when she isn't going back and forth from the kitchen to the parlor for more food or drink.

Eli's cousin revels in the telling of his battlefield tale. It is as though it is his proudest triumph, and the musket ball that likely should have killed him his greatest trophy. Martha even glows at the recitation of the details. Her face beams with pride even though a little good fortune is all that stood in the way of her being a widow.

Amaziah has more battles to fight. Colonel Stark's troops from New Hampshire are soon to muster off for what could be a prolonged battle with the British. What were simply small skirmishes to start have boiled over into that battle for Breeds Hill. Now, a full-fledged war between the fledgling colonies and Great Britain is imminent.

Eli sees friends and family becoming more involved in the war effort. Led by Amaziah, his Goodwin cousins are all prepared to march off to the next bloody battlefield. His brother-in-law George is proceeding with plans to outfit a privateer. George is still in search of a captain and crew, but he'll be actively involved, and likely making money, in the war effort soon.

Amaziah continues to dominate the conversation, recalling his own tales or telling somebody else's.

Eli tries to listen intently, but is growing weary of the talk of war and revolution. It all nags at Eli's conscience. He's been hampered by the British presence on the coast. Numerous times, his fishing sloop has been stopped and inspected by British vessels. Sometimes his catch has even been confiscated, all veiled by the threat of a harsher penalty. But penalty for what? He's simply been making a living and feeding his family.

It has created a tenuous working environment that he knows will only worsen. What will he do then? He wonders if he'll be thrust into the war effort regardless, only under less than ideal circumstances not of his own choosing.

He looks at Faith and her understanding eyes. He knows that she can tell he's deep in thought, but does she know what lingers in his mind? They've been together quite regularly since they met. She's a wonderful caretaker for the boys and a great gift of joy to Eli. But to get involved in a war? Now?

He has watched the tension with Great Britain escalate in recent months. First, there was the skirmish at Lexington and Concord. It was a sure sign that conflict was on the way. It seemed only a matter of time before more bloodshed followed.

Then came this fight at Breed's Hill and the firsthand account he has from his cousin. It makes this rebellion feel even closer to home now.

George Lathrop's expectation has proven true. The Massachusetts Provincial Congress did resolve to outfit a makeshift navy to counter British piracy. Fishing and cargo vessels have been converted into warships.

Lathrop's offer still lingers in his mind. He wonders if his brother-in-law is still waiting, expecting that he will ultimately agree to captain his ship. There's money to be made with him there. There's a cause to fight for. There's a responsibility to himself, to his family, and to his fledgling country.

Yet, the failure to save his own father still aches. The hurt from helplessly watching his wife die still pains him. The guilt of not being there to help his friend Ezra stirs misery in his soul.

What might this do to his relationship and future with Faith? The weight of responsibility and the fear of failing, it scares him.

He admires the fearlessness his cousin Amaziah displays in his war story. Eli also knows the price of that reckless abandon. It is a cost that he knows he must be willing to pay.

CHAPTER EIGHTEEN
Aboard the HMS *Lioness*, 1775

H e'd prefer to be writing a letter to his wife. Kane would much rather be focused on her and enjoying the thoughts of his family. Instead, he writes to Haddington Pilcher, his superior in the Royal Navy. He feels a need to discuss the progress of the war.

Kane misses his wife and children desperately. It has been a good two years since his departure. There appears to be no sign of a return to England in the near future either. It has been frustrating to be away for so long.

That's what prompts his letter to Pilcher. He is the man that initiated Kane's assignment to shores of the colonies. He is the man Kane trusts in this instance. Pilcher has the ear of the Board of Admiralty. Kane hopes that could help prompt some kind of change.

The plan was for Kane and his patrol to crack down on the smuggling in the colonies. It was all part of a strategy to smother the illegal shipping industry here. With that would come the withering of the rebellion and a return to order.

That outcome has not materialized. The British flexed its naval power with blockades of port cities. It has helped starve some of the local economies and made materials for the Patriot cause scarce. Still, the submission they had expected has failed to follow. If anything, the resolve in the colonies has only stiffened.

Kane sees the pitfalls of Britain's plans. It has focused on policing the Patriot uprising in various locations, but the force hasn't been great enough to pursue a conflict that runs up and down a lengthy coastline of the Atlantic.

Despite the immense British presence, it still underestimated not only the resolve of the rebellion but also the impact the local loyalists would have. The cause for liberty continues to grow and hopes of quickly squashing such fervor lessens each day.

Kane's role of patrolling the coastal waters and threatening the presence of smugglers has had very little impact. Smuggling continues everywhere. With the blockades and the need for various supplies in the colonies, vessels are finding ways to deliver goods. No act passed by British law and subsequent enforcement is dissuading them.

Kane has stopped his share and delivered his brand of brutal British justice. The threat of severe penalty and even death has only made a dent in the amount of smuggling that exists. The coastline is too vast and the British presence too limited to make progress.

On top of that, the rise of privateer vessels makes life for British ships that much more treacherous. Ships fitted out both privately and by the colonies create a greater danger. There's no telling what ships are armed with for weaponry now or what their intent may be.

So Kane is trying to emphasize to Pilcher a need for an adjustment in strategy. He can see his patrol is making little difference here. He might be better served in another role, maybe even patrolling the British waters. Either the British need to bolster its patrols here or defer to a new plan.

The rise in privateers has not only impacted these local waters but also threatened British shores. Numerous vessels have been struck and seized at home. While England has struggled to combat the uprising in the colonies, it has taken its focus away from protecting its own shores. Privateers are wreaking havoc there as a result. The fight for liberty has ridden waves all across the world.

As he writes, sharing his thoughts with Pilcher, he can't help but think about an assignment back home. What a joy it would be to see his family on occasion. His sacrifice for England's cause wouldn't come at such a price.

He can still recall the face and sadness of his wife as he left her. He can see his children's young, admiring faces as he departed. It reminds him of that moment in which he watched his own father leave – only to never see him again. It is a painful memory of loss that never leaves him. He fears his own family being scarred in similar fashion.

It took him years to purge the bitterness he felt inside at the loss of his father. Only a few memories of his boyhood experiences remain, but the hatred that consumed him following his father's death has long lingered. That anger still fuels the fire inside him.

Kane always wanted to be like his father. As a boy, he wanted to be brave and noble like the man he remembers that left that day to go to war. He's tried to be that man, but his father's death has shaped him more than his life ever did. Now he fears the legacy he leaves his own children.

It makes him loathe this uprising and its cause of liberty. It frustrates him to sacrifice so much and achieve, in his mind, so little. It makes him more determined to enforce England's rule and deliver justice to those that dare oppose. He is sworn to his cause but dislikes how it makes him feel. He sometimes wonders if it is all worth the cost, and he hates such an idea fermenting in his mind.

As he finishes the last few lines of his letter, he hears commotion up on deck. Before he is summoned, he rises from his desk and heads topside.

They've approached another smuggler. The threat of a barrage of weaponry proved too intimidating to thoughts of escape. The *Lioness* has pulled alongside with little resistance and secured itself to the other vessel. Members of Kane's crew have begun boarding while its captain pleads for mercy.

"I've done nothing wrong," the smuggler shouts, hoping someone will listen. "This is for my family."

He sees Kane peering down at him. The glare from above silences him in an instant. The man just gazes up at Kane with a pathetic look, full of guilt and desperation.

Kane pulls out his pistol and aims it at him. The captain returns a wide-eyed look of fear as he stares down the barrel of Kane's weapon.

Before the man has a chance to plead for his life, a fiery blast explodes from Kane's pistol. "That's for my family," he says.

The shot blows a hole in the middle of the man's chest and topples him backward. He lies on the deck, breathing what final breaths remain.

Kane looks over the rest of the vessel and watches his crew take command. "Confiscate what you can," he orders. "Leave the crew down below. Then burn the ship."

CHAPTER NINETEEN
Portsmouth, New Hampshire, 1775

Faith glances over at Eli and senses his detachment. He sits beside her in the wooden pew of the church, but he seems elsewhere. He's been that way lately.

It has been a happy time as their relationship has evolved. There was that initial dinner, then more time with him and the boys. Then came a walk on the beach under the moonlight. They walked hand in hand along the shore. Hardly a word was spoken, but there was a connection between their hearts.

Then mid-walk, halfway along the beach, Eli simply spun her towards him. He grabbed her with both hands and kissed her. They stood there alone in each other's arms as the water twinkled in the moonlight and the beach shimmered like a pathway of gold.

They've kept regular company since then. He's even taken to coming to church on a regular basis. It might be more out of respect for her father than his interest in church, but he's shown an effort to be a faithful parishioner.

Despite the bliss they share together, Faith can still feel Eli's pensive and burdened soul. She senses the struggle within him. The conflict between the colonies and Britain has increased; that has only heightened the conflict within Eli.

Faith has heard news that not long after the battles at Lexington and Concord, an episode occurred that has had ramifications up and down the coast. An armed cutter, the HMS *Margaretta,* was carrying four cannons and forty crewmen. It sailed into Machias, well up the coast, to obtain lumber to help fortify Boston.

A rebellion of locals commandeered a British supply ship and rammed the *Margaretta*. The captain and his crew were captured and hacked to death. The *Margaretta* was seized.

The man behind the assault, Jeremiah O'Brien, took the *Margaretta* and went in pursuit of British supply ships running between Nova Scotia and Boston.

The former general George Washington has taken command overall. Stymied by the continuous siege of Boston, he has summoned a privateer fleet. Eli's brother-in-law, George Lathrop, couldn't help but confront Eli with the news. Lathrop pulled out a newspaper with Washington's own words.

"Finding we are not likely to do much in the land way, I fitted out several privateers, or rather armed vessels, in behalf of the Continent."

Locally, Massachusetts lawmakers have continually received applications for privateer commissions and for "Letters of Marque and Reprisal," a permit for trade ships to mount heavy weapons. Lathrop applied and has been granted one such permit.

The Continental Congress has already begun discussion regarding financing the American fleet that Washington has deemed necessary.

The bloodshed is worsening. The war for liberty rages. For the longest time, the conflict with Britain was over taxes; small things that led to big disagreements, but the rebellion has grown steadily and liberty has become the new purpose.

As tensions and hostilities increase, so has Eli's turmoil. He doesn't discuss it, but Faith can see him struggle with his guilt.

He knows he could help serve the cause. Part of him probably desires to do just that. It is in his blood and in his roots. His experience as a mariner could be of great use. There is even the likelihood that he could share in the wealth of George Lathrop's privateer venture. There is ample reason and an even greater need for him in the war effort.

Yet, Faith knows that it is just as important that he remain home with his boys. It is his duty as a father to raise his sons, especially without their mother.

As a result, Eli struggles while being caught in between. There is guilt no matter the choice. He is trapped. Faith can see it, and knows no matter how their relationship progresses, he might never escape it.

He has suffered so much pain and loss in his life. Finding happiness has given him freedom from his past. Or has it?

Faith sees his joy, but can still see something else lingering. It is a discontent; a deep-seated regret. She knows it is more than guilt.

The war is calling him, but so is opportunity. He doesn't see it. She does, and she knows it is likely inevitable that the revolution will commit him to the cause.

Her father steps to the pulpit to speak. Faith reflects on the choices her father made in his life, choosing the ministry in a world that may or may not have wanted God's guidance. She thinks about that impact on her life and the choice she has made, one of service to others, sometimes at the expense of her own best interests.

"There is a spot here in town where five different roads intersect," Pastor Hamilton begins. "That's four chances to make the wrong decision and choose the wrong path. So, how do we know which route to take?"

Hamilton tells the story of Jesus calling the four fishermen to be his disciples by the Sea of Galilea. Peter and his brother Andrew and partners James and John had spent a disappointing night on the water. They'd had little luck trying to secure a catch.

Jesus told Peter to push off further and drop his nets for fish. Peter reminded Jesus that they had already spent an entire night fishing without success.

Peter agreed to try again. This time, he caught more fish than he could handle. He had to summon others to help him haul in his catch.

Peter then made a humble confession: "Go away from me, Lord, for I am a sinful man." He felt unworthy.

Jesus responded to Peter by saying, "Don't be afraid. From now on you will catch people." The four fishermen then left everything behind and chose to follow Jesus.

"When God calls us," Faith's father continues, "we must follow. It may not be an easy decision. God calls us to have faith and trust in him. It can be a challenge to believe in that calling, yet followers like the fishermen did just that."

Pastor Hamilton tells the congregation that it can be easy to give up. It is too tempting to lose hope. Sometimes, people give up just one effort too soon. Peter could have done that. Instead, he heeded God's calling.

"Life has many choices, and we are free to make the wrong choices or the correct ones," Hamilton says. "We need to take time along the route to ask God to give us guidance and wisdom.

"The fishermen had a choice to accept Jesus' call, or to remain as they were. In choosing to follow Jesus, it was like putting their hand in the hand of God, confident that God had a future in mind for them and that it was right for them."

Hamilton tells his congregation that it doesn't take wealth or prestige or the finest of educations to be called by God. In this instance, he sought the simplest of fishermen and led them to their destiny.

"This story affirms that the skills, training, and gifts of each of us can indeed be put to use for God and his kingdom," Hamilton concludes. "We may even be surprised that in the midst of our daily activities, we feel and hear in a new way the call of God upon our time, our energies. May our commitment to Jesus Christ be deepened each day as we walk with Him."

As Pastor Hamilton concludes the morning service with a prayer, Faith can't help but think of Eli and his destiny. She knows she must let him go. She can see it as his path. As difficult a choice as it is, she understands it is a calling greater than she or him. It is one he must face before his life moves forward.

She glances over at Eli. As her father steps down from the pulpit and the music for the final hymn begins to fill the church with glorious sound, Faith reaches over and touches his hand. He looks at Faith and is greeted by her smile. It hides her concern. Eli smiles back lovingly. It hides his conflict.

CHAPTER TWENTY
Portsmouth, New Hampshire, 1775

The sun is hot as it beats down over the garden. It warms the soil so much that Faith is constantly watering the plants. As the afternoon passes, the sun rotates enough that the church steeple will give her welcome shade. She often times her work in the garden to coincide with that relief.

But the dryness of the soil has prompted her to begin early. She's been toting buckets of water from the church well to the garden, where she waters each row methodically, hoping to bring relief from the drought they've seen of late.

Trekking back and forth in the hot sun is wearing her out quickly. She sits down on the church steps, using the water to quench her own thirst rather than that of the garden.

As she rests and catches her breath, she hears someone approaching behind her. She recognizes the voices as they get closer.

Suddenly, there is a flurry of commotion as Eli's two boys race from the church to the garden in search of her. Their frenzied pursuit is halted only for a moment, until they spot Faith sitting on the steps. Then, they rush to her at full speed, one struggling to keep up with the other, until they approach her with open arms and a hug.

Not far behind them, but at a slightly more moderate rate, comes Eli. He just follows the sound of his boys to locate Faith. By the time he spots her, he sees her engulfed in the arms of his two sons.

"We thought you might need some help in the garden," he says.

The labor soon begins again, but now Faith has helping hands to make lighter work. The four of them quickly get the entire garden watered. It almost appears more green and robust at the completion of their efforts.

Faith sends the boys out in search of vegetables ready to be picked. She's given them the task of seeking out the tomato plants and finding some worth harvesting.

She takes a respite and returns to the step beside Eli. They watch the two boys work together, advising them if they see them about to pick a tomato that isn't quite ready.

"You know how this garden began?" Faith asks.

Eli admits he doesn't. He wonders why Faith even brings it up.

"My mother started this garden," she explains. The garden was a good complement to her father's ministry. It also gave her mother a task around the church that she enjoyed. But just as the garden began to produce good crops, her mother took ill. She passed away rather suddenly soon thereafter, and the garden began to be neglected.

"It hurt my father so to see the garden in such a sorry state," she recalls. "I hated the sight of it, too. I think we'd both have gladly plowed it over and let wildflowers grow, but we also knew we could never do such a thing."

So, Faith dedicated her time to restoring the garden to full life again. She even expanded it into the full plot of land it is today. Her father would help her on occasion, when he wasn't consumed by the responsibilities of his ministry.

"I sacrificed a great deal of time and effort to restore this garden," she says. "It was something I felt I had to do, regardless of how challenging it was."

The boys bring over a sack full of picked tomatoes. Faith and Eli search through the bag to see if they picked any they shouldn't have. Most of the tomatoes in the bag are ripe and ready.

She gives them a quick lesson on picking carrots and sends them on their way. They busily work through the carrot patch, picking and choosing what are ready to pluck from the earth and which ones are not.

Faith returns to her seat beside Eli on the steps.

"My father needed my help here at the church, at home, in the garden," she explains. "I did all the things I felt a good, dutiful daughter should do. I was pleased to help and make a difference, but it changed the course of my life quite significantly."

Faith always thought she might go off to study, maybe even learn medicine or teach, but her life became consumed with taking care of her younger sister and her father, the home, the garden, the church.

"I think life isn't always what you plan or even want," she says. "Sometimes I think it is about your destiny."

Eli isn't quite sure where Faith is going with this conversation. One minute they were talking about tomatoes and carrots and now they're talking about destiny.

"What are you trying to tell me?" he asks.

Rather than continue on with the story, she gets to the purpose behind the telling.

"I think sometimes we have to do what we feel is right," she says. "We must do what we feel called to do."

She pauses for a moment, somewhat hesitant to say the words she knows she must.

"I think your place in the fight for liberty is inevitable," she says. "You have denied that choice for too long."

Eli is taken aback by her words. He is defensive initially, but truly isn't sure how he should feel.

"You want me to leave?" he asks. "You want me to go fight a war that we may or may not win?"

The weight of what she is saying strikes deep in her heart. She can hardly believe that she's telling Eli he must go.

"I'm saying that I know you feel a duty to that liberty," she says. "I know I must be prepared to let you do that. So, I am all right with such a decision if that is what you should choose."

Eli mulls over her words. He never expected her to say such things. He feels his duty to the cause of liberty, especially since he feels he could play a significant role. He also feels the guilt of wanting to leave his family and leave Faith. He's shouldered enough guilt in life; he really doesn't seek to add more.

"You're giving me freedom," he says.

Eli is nearly moved to tears at her strength and her devotion. It tears at him to witness such a selfless act. He's aware how it pains Faith to say such words. He feels selfish in the reflection of her sacrifice.

Tears stream down her face. She can barely contain her sobs. She hates the words she speaks but knows she must mean them.

"Yes. You must do what you feel is right," she says. "And I will support you. And I will be here for you."

CHAPTER TWENTY-ONE
Portsmouth, New Hampshire, 1775

Eli's ship bobs gently as the incoming tide makes it sway against the wharf. The vessel is slowly rounding into shape. Lathrop has been busy buying up guns and ammunition. It has been a challenge at times. Between the ships that Washington has outfitted and the various private endeavors cropping up along the coast, there's been a race to find available weaponry to arm the vessels. The wealthiest of business men and ship owners have won out, while the weapon manufacturers have already made their fortune.

Thanks to the proclamation from Congress that formally targets all British vessels as fair game for civilian and Continental warships, there is now a rush along the waterfronts to arm and outfit vessels. It has been a battle to obtain and outmaneuver other ships to secure the crew and weaponry that is needed.

It is actually the privately owned vessels that have fitted out their ships the best. The richest of owners have been able to afford the best in weaponry and have been able to pay their crews top dollar. Meanwhile, the government vessels have struggled and so have some of the smaller, less affluent ship owners.

Eli isn't sure where Lathrop falls in that mix. He assumes the man is a lesser version of the rich and driven ship owners, though Lathrop probably considers himself among the elite. Eli is not sure whether that has made a difference for him or not. He's outfitted the vessel fairly well. It could probably be a little more battle-ready, but under the circumstances, the ship is equipped with what it needs.

The crew is also rounding into shape. The pickings have been rather slim. The majority of the crew are not seasoned or even experienced soldiers. Going to sea with a rag-tag bunch is nothing new for any captain, but most of the times when Eli sailed with his father or Ezra and the crew was rather green, they weren't fighting a war.

Eli has been going over the vessel with various crew members, showing them the rigging, the weaponry, and trying to explain what their responsibilities will be. He knows most won't understand it all until they get out to sea and into action. As much as he'd like a few trial runs, he knows you just can't practice war.

He's let the half-dozen members of the crew go home. Now, he stands alone on this vessel that will be part of the war effort in a matter of weeks. As he contemplates the decision between leaving for home himself or staying to continue work, he hears steps coming toward him.

At first he assumes it is the night watch that Lathrop has on duty to keep an eye of the vessel. Instead, it is two figures—one of whom he presumes is Lathrop.

As they get closer, he can hear their voices. Lathrop is doing the talking, or in his usual manner, the selling. He spots Eli on board and waves enthusiastically.

"Eli!" he calls out as the two approach and step aboard. "Glad to find you here. I've got a new recruit to join the crew."

As the two men stroll down the length of the ship, Eli gets a better look at the man Lathrop is escorting aboard.

"This here is Eli Miller," introduces Lathrop. "He's the finest captain we've got around these parts. A well-seasoned sailor."

His recruit nods his head and offers a bit of a smirk as he looks over his potential captain.

"Eli," continues Lathrop. "This young man is a veteran sailor. He's been around the world. He's even been captured and escaped. He should make a fine addition to our crew."

Eli has bristled at Lathrop anytime he has brought a member of the crew to him, assuming he's got quite a find on his hands. Lathrop couldn't distinguish a qualified sailor from a slightly competent dock hand.

Though he's tried to make Lathrop understand that he doesn't want him signing on crew members without his approval, Lathrop is the owner and likes exercising that authority. This time, though, Eli won't stand for it.

"Thanks, George," Eli says, "but this man just won't do. We won't be needing his services."

Eli turns and begins to walk away. Lathrop is more surprised than the recruit, who just smiles at the development.

"Eli, wait," Lathrop says, leaving the recruit behind to chase after Eli. "Wait just one moment. This man is a qualified sailor. He's going to be a great asset to this vessel. We need men of his experience."

Eli stops for a moment. He looks back at the recruit. He stands there with a cocky grin, appearing unfazed at the debate before him. He may even be enjoying it.

"We don't need men like him," says Eli. "Sorry, George. I'm sure he can sign on with somebody else."

Eli starts to walk away again, but Lathrop grabs his arm. Reluctantly, Eli stops, knowing his ship owner won't give up this easily.

"I don't understand," says Lathrop, a bit agitated and still struggling with this turn of events. "What is wrong?"

Before Eli can provide an answer, the recruit takes a few steps toward the conversation.

"I think the captain has a slight problem with hiring his brother," he says.

Lathrop looks at him as if he doesn't understand. Then he looks back at Eli and sees the scowl, full of disgust and agitation.

"George, this is my brother Luke," explains Eli. "Let's make this simple: I don't want him on this ship."

Lathrop has heard stories of Eli and Maddie's younger brother, but neither sibling has ever talked about him much. All Lathrop knows is that Luke was always into trouble and has fallen out of favor with his family. Any attempt to discuss him with Maddie prompted the same irritated response he sees from Eli at this moment.

Luke followed the sea much like his father and brother, though he was anything but a respected sailor. His reputation included stories of him being a drunk, a thief, and not much of a sailor, or at least a very lazy one.

Then, local entrepreneur Samuel Snipe outfitted a vessel and put Captain Boyd Wesley in command. The venture was for a trip to the West Indies and the Mediterranean, strictly illegal under the Navigation Act. The journey was interrupted when the Algerians captured them.

The Algerians demanded ransom, even though it would be months until it could arrive. They sent the captain back home while holding his crew hostage. Wesley sailed immediately for home, fully knowing that his crew would be imprisoned in deplorable conditions, and if the ransom was not paid within the specific timeframe, the men would be left to starve to death.

Wesley arrived home and informed Snipe of the situation. The businessman assured his captain that the monetary sum would be sent, but he stalled as weeks turned into months. Family members of the crew begged him to pay the ransom, but he never did.

All the members of the crew were left for dead. All except for Luke Jr. Somehow, he had managed to escape.

Eli doesn't even know how his brother managed to elude the fate of his fellow crew. Most of the story, he has heard from other sailors. He has seen Luke once or twice since then, only enough to know that his petulant brother did manage to escape and return home. Eli has always wondered if his captors reached the same conclusion that he and his father had made of Luke Jr. long ago: That he was nothing but trouble and better left to his own dastardly means.

In his will, Eli's father had nearly written his youngest son out of it, declaring that Luke had not "behaved towards me as becomes the duty of a child." Because Eli's father felt his younger son should be left something, he was bequeathed ten pounds of silver and a suit of clothing and then told that he was "disinherited forever."

Between his own aggravation towards his brother and seeing the shame put upon his father by his brother's actions, Eli shared his father's view. He saw no need to consider Luke a member of his family.

"It's too bad you can't use a good sailor," says Luke with an air of disgust at his brother's rejection. "There's plenty of other berths to be had."

Lathrop fears that a fight now may break out between the two brothers. He sees a sneer on Luke's face and can already sense the anger from Eli. He steps between the two and tries to lead Luke off the vessel. Eli turns without saying a word and continues on toward the stern.

"We'll see you out there, my brother," Luke says with all the attitude he can muster. "Don't fall overboard. You won't have me there to save you."

CHAPTER TWENTY-TWO
Portsmouth, New Hampshire, 1775

Reverend Hamilton closes the door behind him and hears the echo flow through the empty sanctuary. He's been working in his office, adjacent to the rear of the church, but he can only sit in that stuffy room for so long, especially on a nice sunny day.

He's been writing his sermon for Sunday, but thought taking a quick walk around the church and garden might be just the break he needs. Walking and thinking is a good process for him. As his legs wander, so does his mind.

It frees his thinking a bit and allows him to refocus.

As he begins his walk through the sanctuary, he realizes he's not alone. Hunched over in one of the rear pews is a solitary figure. Hamilton can't quite identify him, even as he walks closer. His own steps echo through the room, announcing his approach.

"Good morning," he says as he draws near.

The man, with head down, runs his hands over his face and slowly looks up. It takes a moment for Hamilton to recognize the weary figure seated before him.

"Eli," he says. "I didn't expect to find you here. Are you all right?"

Eli remains quiet for a moment. He seems hesitant to share his thoughts. "I just needed to reflect," he explains. "Perhaps seek some guidance from God."

Reverend Hamilton steps into the pew and sets himself down next to Eli.

"Talk to me about it, if you like," he says.

Eli pauses and thinks about his words. He's not quite certain how to explain what he's feeling.

"It's fear," he admits. "I've been to sea many times. I've been to various ports around the world. I've seen violent storms. I've experienced tense moments. I've even escaped a few tricky situations. But I've never felt fear before."

He explains that as he is preparing to embark with his vessel, he's nervous. It doesn't feel right. He's confident in his ship and his crew. He has little worry about his own ability to lead. He believes he can captain that ship and carry out its purpose; he actually thinks he'll do quite well.

At the same time, he feels trepidation. Leaving his boys, leaving Faith, it is a tremendous weight on him. Going to sea and leaving loved ones behind is nothing new. He did so with little hesitation when his relationship with Elizabeth began.

He was away when Joseph was young; it was what he did. The consequences were what they were. He missed his family. They missed him. Just as he struggled as a boy with his father being away, it was a challenge for him to be away. But it came with the seafaring life.

He has since realized the cost. Now, he feels the choice and the weight of it.

"I know I'm doing what I feel is right and what must be done," he says. "But I'm fearful of what will change. There's so much I can't control and so much that will be different upon my return. And that's if I even return."

Reverend Hamilton thinks about Eli's situation. It is quite often that he meets a scared sailor about to go off to sea. He helps them seek comfort in God. Many of them develop their faith and cling to it during their voyages. Some sailors he counsels never return.

With Eli, it is different. He is a veteran of the seas, but he's sought a new life on land. Going back isn't so easy, especially in a time of war. And this man's decisions have a great impact on Hamilton's own daughter.

"Eli," he begins hesitantly. "I would suggest that you raise up these burdens to God. You must release yourself of your heavy heart. If you live on faith, you can trust God's guidance."

He's not sure Eli understands his point. He knows Eli has tried coming to church somewhat regularly, but he's done so out of obligation to Faith. He's not sure if a love of God has rooted itself in him.

"I'll pray with you if you'd like," he offers. Eli feels a bit uncomfortable at the thought, but then agrees.

The two bow their heads. There is a stillness and a silence inside the church.

"Heavenly Father," Hamilton begins. "We lift up Eli Miller to you this day. He is full of fear as he faces a new course in his life. We pray for his success and safety at sea. We pray for your watchful care of him and Faith and his boys. We pray for Eli's trust in you; that he can find solace in your love and might during these challenging times."

Hamilton pauses for a moment to give Eli an opportunity to pray himself, but no words are spoken.

"We thank you for your grace and your presence, Lord," concludes Hamilton. "Amen."

CHAPTER TWENTY-THREE
Portsmouth, New Hampshire, 1775

With each step, Eli savors the infusion of pure, clean salt air in his lungs. When at sea, he would hardly take the time to enjoy the scent of the salty sea breeze. He was so consumed by it, he barely noticed it.

Even when he's out sailing and fishing in local waters, he doesn't appreciate it as much. He smells the stench of bait and dying fish more than he does the scent of the ocean.

But on shore, he smells it. It is as though it is calling him, luring him back. Eli often sits on his porch, finding those few moments to relax. In comes a slight breeze, seemingly wafting up from the harbor to tempt him. Suddenly, he'll get a crisp whiff of the sea, and the sudden urge to follow it.

The ocean air prompted his regular walks on the beach. He wants to be closer to that air that smells and tastes so pure. He wants to breathe it in and feel that crispness in his lungs.

Eli finds solitude here. It brings him closer to his father, he feels. There's a quiet that blankets his soul and brings peace to his heart. He spent many walks here after Elizabeth died. He felt the lure of the sea then. He wanted to escape on the winds of the sea, hoping they'd take him away from his sorrow.

Instead, he was rooted here. At the time, he needed that support from family. He needed to grieve. He also needed to be strong for his boys. It was a painful process, but walking this beach gave him peace. It provided him a place from which to move forward.

He started talking to God here. He spoke to his father and even to Elizabeth. He'd talk to himself, all in an attempt to understand and find solace in his pain and his guilt.

At first, these were solitary walks, just himself and his thoughts. Gradually, he came to feel the presence of others. He found strength from his father and felt Elizabeth in his heart. As he talked to himself, he felt God's presence as well, something he had failed to recognize in his life, despite his mother's attempts to encourage his faith and worship.

He now brings the boys here on occasion. He'll watch them play in the sand and chase crabs, at least until one of them gets pinched by one they shouldn't have tormented.

And when he first became smitten with Faith, he brought her here. He walked with her on these shores. This is where he first kissed her.

He continues to enjoy the quiet walks here with Faith. He knows that she loves that time together, especially in the glow of dusk or under the shine of the full moon. There is a beauty in this setting that is meaningful for both of them.

With only a few days before Eli hauls out, the two of them share a final quiet stroll together. They barely acknowledge that this will be their last. Neither knows what to say with his departure so close.

Daylight is fading as a full moon gradually rises in the night sky. It is a quiet evening. Only the waves make noise as they roll in. One boisterous wave after another is sent in by the open ocean.

In the stillness, a number of thoughts flash through Eli's mind, things he wants to say and feelings he wants to share. It feels too much like a final goodbye, though, like those moments when he lost his father or Elizabeth forever. He doesn't want this to feel that way.

"There are so many things I feel the need to say before I go," he tells her.

Faith wants no part of it.

"We don't need to talk about you leaving," she answers. "We know it is coming."

As much as she knows it is the right decision for him, she struggles with his departure the closer it draws near.

"Why don't we talk about things we'll do when you return," she says. "It will give us something to look forward to."

Eli suppresses so many words he intended to share. He concludes that he'll write them in a letter and leave it for her the day he hauls out.

As they walk, he contemplates his return. He has no idea how long that will be. Might it be a year? Maybe it will be two. He truly doesn't know. The thought of never returning creeps into his thoughts, but he quickly dismisses it.

"I will look forward to when I return," he says. "I'll count down the days."

Faith can't help but well up. A tear or two slide down her cheek. She clears her throat in an attempt to compose herself.

"I will long for that day as well," she says, barely getting out the words before her voice cracks.

They continue to walk, feeling the softness of the sand at their feet. The small waves roll in and wash over the beach.

"I know what we can do when I return," Eli says.

He waits to see if Faith offers a guess or says anything, but she remains quiet. He stops and looks into her eyes and sees the tears stored there, ready to flow down her face.

"We'll get married when I return," he says with a smile.

Her face melts with emotion at his words. She doesn't even have to agree. Her expression tells Eli that she's willing.

"That's my promise to you," he says. "I'll be back. I'll be back for you. It will be a new beginning for us. It will be all that we dream of. I promise."

He grabs her and kisses her. Then, he wraps her in his arms. They stand there in an embrace in the shadows of the moon glow on the water.

As he stands there and holds Faith in his arms, he can smell the salt air and feel the warmth of her embrace. He enjoys the sweetness and tenderness of her lips. He cherishes the contentment of a heart filled with love.

But as he thinks about his promise and contemplates their future, he feels the sudden distance that is approaching. From this moment on, the void in his soul will grow. And so will the fear of failure.

CHAPTER TWENTY-FOUR
Aboard *Resolution*, 1776

The vessel has all the makings of a British supply ship.

It is too far away for Eli to tell for sure, even with his spy-glass. But, it is headed in the right direction and he's likely got the element of surprise on his side. It is the chance he's been waiting for. Even though he's not completely sure that a prized vessel may be there for his taking, he's ready for that gamble.

Eli has been sailing out of Portsmouth for two days. He's stayed inland a bit, knowing the bigger supply ships might be too large a foe to tangle with at this moment. His goal is to find a smaller ship trying to arrive under cover. Sailing closer to the shores enhances the opportunity to find a vessel that has already stopped at a port along the way and is continuing on toward Boston.

As he was sailing the inner channel, a good southwesterly breeze pushing him along, he spotted the other ship through the narrow passages between islands. He only had a moment to catch sight of it, but his quick assessment convinced him it was a worthwhile opportunity.

The orders were passed down quickly and the crew made a sudden about maneuver. Once the ship was turned around, trying to gain speed into the wind, preparation began for an assault.

First mate Skandar Mosely has instructed the crew, handing down orders to Ambrose Taylor and Jackson Montsweag. Now, he stands beside the wheel with the captain.

"I hope to get up to full speed here by that last island in the group," says Eli, pointing to one remaining island off the larboard side. They've been sailing parallel to their prize with this group of a dozen islands in between.

"Once we're on the opposite side of that land, the other ship should be in view. We'll have a bead on it. We'll identify it and, if I am correct, we'll be on them before they know what hit them."

Mosely has Merritt Connell at the bow ready to make any kind of identification. Eli has his spyglass at the ready, as well.

Mosely's rifle is loaded and in hand.

"Do I just scare the captain a mite or do I kill him?" asks the mate.

Eli ponders that question. The answer may very well be determined by what the other captain chooses to do.

"If I take him down, it will scare the rest of the crew witless," says Mosely.

Eli trusts his sharpshooter, but still isn't convinced that he can hit a target at his own whim, especially under these conditions. But he's anxious to see what kind of advantage Mosely's skill can bring.

"Just do what you have to do," says Eli.

As the ship eases past the island to its larboard, the open ocean beyond begins to come into full view. As it emerges, so does the sight of the prize. It is just a few lengths ahead. With Eli bearing down on it, he has the angle and the wind in his favor.

In fact, as he gets close enough to attack, he'll be stealing the wind away from what could become a vessel with little means of escape.

"Red flag," shouts Connell from the bow. That's the signal that it is a British vessel. Eli takes a quick look through his spyglass. He offers it to Mosely for his opinion.

"Looks like it's ours for the taking," Mosely says, confirming the conclusion Eli has reached. It is a British ship, and the chase is on.

"Prepare to attack!" shouts Eli. The order is passed from Mosely through the ranks to all members of the crew. They remain in wait for the proper moment.

Eli can sense the advantage. It is an unusual position for him. He's been accustomed to outrunning pirates, but has never been in pursuit himself. He realizes just how much he likes the thrill of it, especially when he knows he possesses the upper hand.

He'll surely overtake his prey and have a good angle for a barrage of cannon fire. The other ship has limited options. It can either surrender, be bombarded, or attempt a countermove. They likely won't be ready to fire back, so their best option will be to turn away. That might get them some distance if done right.

Eli feels the excitement, the anticipation of the chase.

"If we don't get them with cannon fire at first pass and give them a chance to turn off, we might lose them," he tells Mosely.

The British vessel suddenly sees the *Resolution* bearing down on them. They're caught by surprise to see this vessel coming at them so fast and so hard from off their stern. They are caught so unaware, there is almost little recourse for them. When Eli gets within earshot of his prey, he calls out for their surrender. When there is no response, he gives signal.

"Fire!"

A blast of cannon fire explodes toward the vessel and crashes through its wooden hull. Shards of wood and debris fly into the air as the crew scatters.

Eli watches for concession from his foe. Instead, he sees the captain of the British vessel order up the turn that Eli was expecting.

"Can you reach him?" asks Eli.

Mosely doesn't offer an answer. He raises his rifle, takes quick aim, and fires. In the flash, the other captain is hit, knocked forward into the wheel. He drops there as if he's dead while the boat veers out of control and the crew scrambles. Eli's men open fire and send another barrage of cannon fire.

And the battle is over.

The prey is now their prize. The crew offers up their surrender. Their vessel is stopped dead in the water. Eli pulls alongside and his crew boards their acquisition.

CHAPTER TWENTY-FIVE
Portsmouth, New Hampshire 1776

Voices grow louder as Faith continues walking. She isn't far from the house when she hears the rumble of chaos not far away.

Part of her wonders whether she should continue her journey to the church. She left the boys there this morning with her father while she did some seamstress work. She's caring for Eli's sons while George and Maddie are away for a few days. The boys have been living with the Lathrops, but still see Faith quite regularly.

She hears the increasing crowd noise and can't help but be curious as to what is going on.

The tension around town constantly makes her fearful. There's an edge in the air. Since the revolution progressed, the peacefulness around the harbor cloaks a much darker and more volatile reality.

Faith stays away from the politics of it all, but she feels the rebellion and angst in the air. There's often shouting going on or even a scuffle breaking out. It's like a slow simmer waiting to boil over.

As she gets closer to the harbor, the noise increases and people scurry past her to see what the commotion is. Faith is anxious to see for herself and wonders how close the church is to whatever is getting out of control.

When she rounds the corner to the street leading to the harbor, there's the mob of people. They've circled something and have turned unruly.

Faith attempts to see what is happening. The church is just down the street. The story of a crowd rioting outside a church in another colony comes to mind and strikes fear in her heart. That mob had determined the minister was a dissenter. Being branded a Tory these days typically leads to a beating or worse.

She fights her way through the crowd a bit, pushing her smaller self past elbows and arms that flail away with chants of, "Tar!" "Tar!" "Tar!"

When she finally gets into position to see what is happening, she finds a man being held by four others. They pull his arms and legs in different directions while restraining him. The man has been stripped of his clothing. He stands there pale and naked in the winter temperatures.

Another man stands over a pot of tar. He splashes the steaming liquid onto the captive man's back. He screams in agony as the heat sears his skin.

Faith recognizes the victim. He's Geoffrey Malcolm, a local tax collector. He's attended her father's church frequently and is known as a quiet and gentle man.

The man she knows, though, is not the one she sees surrounded by fellow members of their community. This is a terrified man crying out for help and mercy and getting neither.

The small pot of tar is lifted higher and dumped over the suffering soul. It oozes out of the pot and scorches the man's body as he screams in terror. Other men with satchels of feathers follow suit, emptying them all over the sticky tar. They cling to the poor man's body. He is released by his captors and dumped onto the ground in a crying, moaning heap.

The crowd cheers in celebration while others jeer him scornfully. Faith glances around in horror at the scene before her. She sees faces of people she knows: Fellow church members, people she grew up with, family friends. They all revel in the humiliation of the small man.

She begins to back away, unable to watch any longer. Her stomach is queasy at what she has witnessed. Tears run down her own face, consumed by the sadness that overwhelms her.

She fears what might happen next. Will they kill him? Will they turn on somebody else? She doesn't want to see. She gets herself away from the mob and scurries down the street.

She doesn't look back, trying to reach the church as fast as she can. She rushes through the church door and pulls it tight behind her.

She suddenly feels the sanctity of this house of worship. There's a quiet behind these doors. The mob rages outside; she can still hear their muffled anger and rage. But it feels safe and serene inside the sanctuary.

There's no sign of anybody. Her father and the boys must be out back or in another room. She's concerned about their whereabouts and wants to see them safe. But she feels the sudden relief for herself.

Sobbing, she collapses into the nearest pew, releasing the fear and sadness she felt at the sight of her fellow man being so cruel. It makes her hurt and scared of the world around her.

The sound of Faith's sorrow fills the sanctuary with mourning. A solitary cry multiplies and rings loudly around the walls of the church.

The sound alerts Pastor Hamilton. He steps from the back room to hear more clearly. He sees nobody in the church, but hears the sadness. He follows the sound. His footsteps on the wooden floor echo as well, but are lost in the tearful noise that fills the room.

As he approaches, Hamilton can see it is his daughter. His heart sinks to see her in such pain, though he knows nothing of its cause.

Faith suddenly stops her crying. She tries to hold back her sobs and sits upright. She collects herself when she realizes her father is standing there. She feels the weight of his gaze. For a moment, she is embarrassed.

He is about to speak but she suddenly rises from the pew and lurches forward, into his surprised arms. She begins to cry again while her father holds and comforts her.

Faith tries to speak, but her father doesn't understand her muffled words. He leads her back to the pew and sets her down. He continues to hold her tight, his arm wrapped around her. He looks into her face and sees the hurt and fear in his daughter's eyes. It creates an immediate fear in him.

"Geoffrey Malcolm," she says between sobs. She tries to continue but it just makes her cry more.

"What about Geoffrey Malcom?" her father asks.

Faith takes a deep breath and composes herself. Her sadness turns to anger as she thinks of the words to describe it.

"They tarred and feathered him," she says furiously.

Her father exudes a disgusted sigh. "Dear God," he mutters softly, shaking his head at the news.

"They stripped the poor man, humiliated him on the town streets," Faith explains. "What has he ever done to anyone?"

Both sit quietly for a moment. There's still noise outside. Both wonder what might be going on. Pastor Hamilton contemplates rushing out to help the poor man, but knows the likely repercussions. They could tar and feather him as well, or even do it to his church. He knows that fear should not dissuade him, but it does. He feels the sadness in his own heart for not doing what he knows is right.

"I'm sure he was attempting to collect some sort of tax," says her father. "That's what he does. He may have approached the wrong person this day."

The pastor sighs again. He knows how Malcolm has struggled with his profession. Doing the unsavory tasks of the British is unpleasant for him. He has told the pastor so in talks they have had. He has even contemplated leaving and finding another job. He chose to wait, to see if the rebellion ran its course.

"I don't like what is happening," says Faith. "It is barbaric. What is happening to this world?"

Hamilton holds his daughter tighter, feeling the comfort of her at his side.

"There are times we all reach a moment of conscience," he says. "That is where these colonies are now. We are past the point of no return. We're fighting for our liberty and it is a desperate time."

They mull over the consequences of that. The world around them is embroiled in anger and dissonance. That disorder is evident everywhere. The cost is great, and there's no guarantee of success.

"I see wives without husbands," says Faith. "I see children without fathers. I see women forced to work their own farms and survive on their own. I see suffering everywhere. Is this liberty? Is this what we sacrifice for?"

There are suddenly sounds from the back room. They startle Faith for a moment when she hears movement. Then, she sees the weary faces of young Joseph and Eligood. They had been sleeping the afternoon away in the back room while her father wrote his sermon.

They rush to her for a hug. Comforted by their love, she looks at their sweet innocent faces and smiles. She holds back her tears, both of joy and of fear.

"Let's go home, boys," she says.

Her father offers to walk with them, giving him the chance to keep watch over them, but also to look into the status of Geoffrey Malcolm.

As they exit the church, the street is quiet. A few people mingle about but otherwise, life has returned to normal. There is spilled tar and some feathers being tossed by the sea breeze. There are no other signs of what has just happened here.

As they walk up the street, the boys have no sense of what has oc-curred. They dart back and forth, expending all the energy they have re-stored with their naps. Faith watches them with joy, but strains to forget what she has witnessed.

CHAPTER TWENTY-SIX
Aboard *Resolution*, 1776

The chase is on once again.

Somewhere on the deep blue water is another British supply ship. They were travelling in pairs, but a storm and some needed repairs caused a separation. So, another prize is out there and Eli is in pursuit.

He has taken his last captured vessel and collection of prisoners to a nearby port, where he sold off what he could, and left the vessel behind and the prisoners in the hands of the locals.

With that captain dead, the rest of the prisoners no longer had fear of talking. They let it be known of the other ship, but had no idea as to its whereabouts. It was likely lagging behind, having been damaged in a storm and in need of a new spar. It was to be a quick stop of a day or two but enough to create some distance from the other vessel.

Eli and the crew are keeping watch for any vessel on the horizon. The crew is plenty attentive when a ship means money.

Eli is at the wheel and Mosely is at his side, keeping watch over the crew.

"I thought that attack went well," says Eli, who hadn't been sure what to expect with such a novice crew.

The skirmish wasn't much of a battle. That's how Eli hopes most of his actions go. With a smaller ship, speed, maneuverability, and quick strike capability are his assets. If he gets into a prolonged exchange of weaponry, it might prove to be his downfall.

"I was right pleased with that action," replies Mosely. "It went exactly according to plan and the crew did their jobs. Not bad for a first try."

The morale of the vessel is soaring after the capture. There were no casualties, not even a wounded sailor. The haul was meager, but they sold off the supplies and the ship and should make a decent earning. And there's plenty more out there. The fact that another vessel is known to be within their reach has the crew anxious and excited at the prospect of another prize.

There's no sign of any foreign vessel within their sights at the moment. There's a smattering of fishing vessels and a variety of coastal schooners, but none that look out of place. There are one or two vessels that look like they could be on the hunt for a prize as well.

"I wonder how many others know about this ship?" asks Eli.

"And I wonder how many others are out looking for it?"

Before Mosely has a chance to reply, there's the figure of a ship in the distance. It faintly appears on the horizon, the haze and island cover all blending together.

Mosely spots it and points, but doesn't have to say a word. Eli sees it too, and begins his pursuit. Mosely shouts out orders to the crew. The sighting of a potential prize only stirs up more excitement among the men.

Eli has good wind and a good angle to pursue. He thinks he'll be able to get close enough without raising awareness from his foe.

Their ship has come upon an island, and the hope is that the British vessel is on the other side. It would enable for a quick strike and an easy prize.

Mosely has his crew ready for a potential attack as they round the outer edge of the land. The back side of the island and open sea come into view.

What lies before them catches them by surprise. Sure enough, Eli was right. There is the other British supply ship. It is being towed by another privateer. Eli and crew tack off a bit as the victorious vessel parades by with the prize in tow.

He watches intently as the ship *Rampant* passes by. He waves to the captain, acknowledging his victory. The captain signals back, with a bit of bravado.

Eli begins to mull his next direction when he spots a figure on the bow of the *Rampant*. It is waving both arms vigorously. When the man catches Eli's attention, he offers a beaming smile. It's Luke, his brother.

Mosely notices it too, but says nothing. They both watch as the ship and its prize sail away.

"Let's head east," says Eli. "On to where the action is."

Mosely passes the word. The crew makes the transition from read-ied soldiers to sailors. They embark on a tacking maneuver that turns them in the opposite direction. Off they sail, further from home, and closer to the enemy.

CHAPTER TWENTY-SEVEN
Portsmouth, New Hampshire, 1776

The flow of people into the church is finally thinning. Most of the pews are full. Only a few spots between families and a few seats on the perimeter are available. Those are being claimed quickly. Most entering now can only find standing room somewhere in the back.

Faith has never seen so many people in the church. She's sure her father is pleased to see such a gathering, but it must also make him wonder where all these people are on most given Sundays.

The day has been declared a national day of prayer. The church has been offered up as a gathering place for those wishing to seek God's blessing.

The war hasn't been going well. For much of the past year, the Continental Army has suffered one defeat after another. It has meant that many a man and boy have died for little gain. As another year of fighting looms, prospects for success appear bleak.

Many of the people Faith sees around the sanctuary are women. They are the wives and daughters of men who have gone to war. Some are already widows. Some are left to wonder their fate. Faith realizes that she's one of those.

There is a smattering of older, feeble men and very young boys, but they're greatly outnumbered by the women.

One of those women sitting in a pew in front of Faith is Hattie Gibson. She has a husband fighting in the war. She has spent much of the past few months following him. She's been among the many women tagging along with the regiment as it moves from battle to battle.

It has been since spring that Faith and Hattie talked last. That was before either had watched their loved ones leave home. She looks frail and the weariness shows on her face. It appears she has returned home, not being able to keep up with the rigors of life at war.

Faith reaches over and touches Hattie's shoulder. She leans forward and welcomes her friend, whom she has known for years. Hattie and Faith grew up near each other and even attended school together as young girls. They've drifted apart as life has taken each on different journeys, but they see each other occasionally.

"It is nice to see you home again," says Faith. "You've had quite an experience, I'm sure."

Hattie looks pleased to see her old friend. She smiles with relief to see a familiar face.

"It has been difficult," she replies. "The men have been fighting hard, but it is such a challenge. Little food, tattered clothes, morale is down. I fear they are becoming overwhelmed."

Her firsthand account tightens a knot in Faith's stomach. Hearing how difficult life is on the field of battle, she can't help but wonder what hardships Eli might be facing at sea.

"I hope your husband is faring well," Faith says.

"He is," answers Hattie, her eyes welling with tears. "He was ill for some time. It made him very weak. He would fight when he could. He did so quite bravely. But I wish he were stronger and felt ready to endure the harsh winter."

Many a soldier has been lost to illness, while many others have struggled to survive the cold winters. The British have just been one of many sources of misery the army has faced.

"I hope these many prayers are what lift our soldier's spirits and strength in the coming months," says Hattie.

Faith and Hattie exchange smiles as the talking and movement in the church subsides. Faith sees her father step to the pulpit. He looks out over the community of people before him.

"War is nothing new to this world," begins Pastor Hamilton. He's glad to see so many hearts full of prayer and a community so united before God. It makes him optimistic that the colonies just might have a will that many don't realize. "The conflicts of the past have shaped what we are today. Just like this fight for liberty will define what we become as a nation."

Pastor Hamilton explains that despite the death and destruction, the turmoil and tragedy and the brutality and barbarism that rise from the evil nature of such conflicts, God's hand is at work.

"No earthly leader has absolute sovereignty in this world. Not General Washington and certainly not King George."

That prompts a rousing collection of cheers from the congregation, which Pastor Hamilton attempts to calm with the waving of his hands. The crowd settles and the pastor continues.

"They are all mortal," he preaches. "They shall all pass as their predecessors have passed. God is eternal."

He tells the congregation that God's agenda never changes as these conflicts come and go. It is a healing and saving agenda. Its purpose is to build up, not tear down and destroy.

He quotes Isaiah with the words, "He will rule his people with justice and integrity. Wolves will lie together in peace. Leopards will lie down with young goats. Calves and lion cubs will feed together and little children will take care of them…

"People of divergent interests and cultures can live together in peace, if rule is based on justice and integrity as God's agenda requires."

Pastor Hamilton pauses and looks out over his congregation. He can see the desire for peace in their hearts and a soothing in their souls. While the war wages on different fronts, he can see the toll taken on those left behind, fighting for their existence here amidst revolution. They all seek liberty, a freedom from England's rule and the repression from the evils of the world.

He bows his head and stands quietly as he leads the congregation into prayer.

"Our Heavenly Father, we gather here today to not only seek justice and integrity through you, but also the strength and conviction in our faith as this war impacts us all. There is much conflict in this world and a great sadness with its consequences. We are all sacrificing for a greater good and a future that serves your agenda. We seek your strength and guidance as we face these times with faith that is stronger than our fears and trust that is greater than our tragedies. War will come and go and shape our history, but you are our constant, the one foundation that we truly build our future upon. We ask for your watchful care for all through this conflict and pray that peace outlasts the wars we wage. Amen."

The congregation is quiet. Pastor Hamilton remains silent for a moment and then offers the people before him his own call to arms.

"Thank you for coming. Thank you for your prayers. Go in faith and armed in the trust of God's glory and power. Seek peace amongst us and hope that it is carried to the world."

Faith watches her father. He looks exhausted and exuberant at the same time. She knows the toll it takes on him to minister to a community in such need during these desperate times. But she's also never seen him stronger and more filled with God's power and conviction.

He's become a warrior in the fight for liberty, but armed with the truth rather than pistol or saber. It inspires her but also makes her fearful. She recognizes the struggles she faces in these times, and knows how difficult it can be to be filled with faith instead.

CHAPTER TWENTY-EIGHT
Aboard the HMS *Thunder*, 1777

The smell of the vessel has taken some adjustment. Despite the hulking size of the *Thunder*, the stench of dying and decaying prisoners inevitably seeps through various parts of the ship.

When Kane was first reassigned here, the smell would keep him awake in his quarters. No matter what he tried, he could never be rid of it, whether he tried washing down the prisoners or attempting to air out the ship. He's been on vessels with the overpowering stench of smelly sailors before but not like this.

His best solution was rubbing alcohol beneath his nose at night. He even grew to enjoy the smell of the alcohol and began developing a taste for it as well. He's also simply grown to tolerate the odor, even though a scant shot of liquor does help induce sleep.

Kane stands on the quarterdeck and observes the latest batch of prisoners being escorted onto the vessel. In a single file, the captives are paraded onboard and sent down below. They appear battered and broken. Kane can sense their vulnerability. He enjoys witnessing the defeat that displays on their sullen faces.

As the war escalates, so has the need for prisoner vessels and various prisons. The British have established prisons in both England and their stronghold in Nova Scotia. Kane was reassigned from his job patrolling the Eastern Seaboard to transferring prisoners. It wasn't exactly the new assignment he had in mind, but it is a needed aspect of the war effort.

The newly-passed Pirate Act has empowered the British navy in its fight against the rise in privateers. It was a controversial bill. It came at the suggestion of General Howe and introduced by Prime Minister

Frederick North to a lightly attended session at the House of Commons.

The bill allows for the detainment of persons charged with, or even suspected of, crimes of treason. It makes no difference between it being in North America or on the high seas overall. Any act against the British would be considered a crime and an act of piracy. The punishment could be as severe as death.

It was an unpopular proposal for some. It eliminated due process and the idea of prisoner exchanges. Its passage sparked debate between England's pro-and antiwar legions. Those against it saw it as a means of legalizing tyranny and oppression. For others, since it was an edict of the colonies, the act ultimately deemed the Continental Congress illegitimate. To Kane, it only encouraged his style of justice. His due process was his own.

The passage of the Pirate Act has not led to automatic executions, but it gives Kane the freedom to deliver punishment as he sees fit. It is why he assumes he was reassigned to this role.

The *Thunder* transports prisoners to Henley Prison in Halifax. He patrols the Eastern Seaboard, often following the British fleet. Prisoners captured by British forces are collected and relocated to prison. Some are eventually put on another vessel bound for England.

Various prisoners are chosen for prisoner exchange while Kane will select others in hopes of pressing them into service for England.

It's a distasteful option for many a loyal Patriot but earning a wage and living under the auspices of the British Navy is a far better option than rotting in prison. It makes wonderful propaganda when the British can display a former Patriot now serving the cause of England.

Kane has turned many sailors to the British side. Out of intimidation or fear of execution, not many dare refuse. Those few that dare decline often don't live to tell about it.

The *Thunder* is escorted by a small fleet of vessels that make a formidable group of ships to encounter. Kane likes the idea of being such an intimidating presence at sea.

He hopes one of these days he may command the transport back to England or even earn reassignment there. But his longing for home isn't getting him any closer to his family.

He gets letters from his wife and children periodically. He struggles with homesickness at times. Being at sea for so long makes him tired of the confined life on a ship. It makes him yearn for home all the more.

His family is doing quite well, but he misses them desperately. He feels incomplete without them. He can't help but think about how fast his children are growing. He'd give anything for a whiff of his wife's cooking, especially compared to the stench that comes out of the galley and the prison cells, both of which turn his stomach.

Still, he now feels a difference being made. As the collection of prisoners grow and the British prisons swell, Kane witnesses steady progress. The colonies are struggling and the brute force of the British appears to be succeeding.

Finally, he hopes, the will of the colonies is faltering. He can see it on the faces of the prisoners that shuffle past him. The lust for liberty is lacking when there's little food, clothing or hope of victory.

It pleases Kane to think that Britain's heavy fist might be finally pounding the Patriots into submission. Those that dare rise up against England's rule now pay their penance.

He realizes that he rather likes his new role in the war effort. He enjoys putting the captured and beaten colonials in their place. It makes him feel invincible and makes him sense that victory is inevitable.

CHAPTER TWENTY-NINE
Aboard *Resolution*, 1777

E li hears the gentle slap of the water against the hull of his vessel, a steady wave that comes every few moments and splashes over the wood of his ship. It echoes across a quiet night and hints at the gentle seas all around him.

It is peaceful inside his cabin down below. He can still hear the songs of the sea and the movement of crew on deck. Mosely or Jackson has the wheel as he rests. As much as he'd like to sleep, Eli hasn't been able to doze off. The adrenalin of the hunt and subsequent chase make it difficult to turn off the mind and shut down the body.

He's tried to fall off for a few relaxing moments of deep sleep, but instead he's tossed and turned more than the gentle seas on this late night.

He can still see the smirking face of his brother Luke, sailing past on that vessel with prize in tow.

It bothered him to see his brother there. It is an image that has lingered with him for months. As much as he'd thought he could just put his troublesome sibling behind him, there he was. His face, his smirk, the whole baggage of a relationship that has constantly failed reappears to torment him.

Eli can't remember exactly how it all went sour. He had his boy-hood scraps with his brother as a child. But they still were childhood pals, often doing everything together. That changed when Eli went off to sea with his father.

Luke was certain to follow the seas in his own good time, but when Eli joined his father, it not only separated the two boys but signaled the end of Eli's childhood. He became a man when he went to sea. He left behind a brother who was still a boy.

By the time Eli returned, it wasn't the same. Luke had begun to emerge in his own way, but the nature he had grown into was a rebellious one. Left to his own devices, Luke rushed his development and did so by whatever means were available to him.

Upon arriving home from the sea, Eli and his father found Luke already immersed in trouble. It was mostly petty crimes and a few skirmishes. As much as Luke had perfected getting into trouble, he had also developed an ability to avoid its punishment.

All Eli can recall now is what a scoundrel his brother was becoming at the time. No matter what he or his father attempted to change that direction, Luke simply rebelled and went his own way. It reached the point that Luke abandoned his parents and his brother and was fully immersed in a life of recklessness and rebellion.

He had stolen from his father. He'd been a regular drunkard involved in numerous fights. Ship after ship had dismissed him after some transgression or insolent attitude. His nasty disposition was only equaled by his contemptible actions.

Eli can't help but wonder sometimes what more he could have done. He, as well as his parents, had concluded they had done all they could or should to make up for the wicked ways of Luke. He was a lost cause.

Eli doesn't believe that has changed, but he still feels the helplessness that comes with the realization. It isn't unlike that feeling of watching his father drift off on the stormy seas as his ship sailed on without him.

Eli could have relented and allowed his brother to join his crew. He wonders how much that would have helped. Maybe it would have made a significant difference in their relationship. Instead, he dismissed him and any thought of allowing that to happen. He did so coldly, as well.

It is hard for him to not feel guilty over it now, but his thoughts still convince him that Luke would have been little help on board and, as always, more trouble than good. As he reaches that conclusion and feels the rightness of that decision, he begins to slowly slip into sleep, stepping from one realm to the other.

"Captain!" comes a voice from above.

Eli has become immersed in a deep sleep so quickly, he doesn't even hear the initial shout. That's rare for a captain like him, who is always on the edge of alertness.

"Captain!" shouts Montsweag once again. "Better get up here. Captain!"

Eli stirs as the final words pry him out of his sleep. He takes a moment to put on his boots and shake the weariness from his mind.

He's still groggy when he reaches the deck, but a serious look on his mate's face quickly gets the captain's attention.

Mosely simply points. Off the larboard rail and well in the distance is a small British fleet. There's a large vessel, almost as big as a warship. A few cutters and even some sloops are included.

Eli and his crew had captured two other prizes as they sailed east. One was another cargo vessel full of supplies. The other was a rogue sloop that had separated itself from the rest of its flotilla. It made for an easy capture and a bounty of extra weapons and ammunition.

As they've sailed further east, those opportunities have lessened. There are so many privateers patrolling the waters that it is a challenge to find a vessel ripe for Eli and his men.

As if that weren't making it hard enough, the British have bolstered the number of escorts around the most valuable of cargo ships. As Eli studies the oncoming collection of vessels, he can't help but wonder what an exciting challenge it might be to have another ship alongside him to aid in a daring attack.

But, he knows that's a foolhardy notion. It's the kind of thing Ezra would do. He laughs at that thought for a moment before concluding that that might have been the very scenario that got his friend killed.

He assumes that this small British fleet will stay together. It would be taking a risk for some of the small vessels to break off in pursuit of one ship. But it would be a fatal mistake if he were wrong.

He hates the thought of tacking and trying to sail away, but he knows he's better served to avoid conflict and fight another day.

"I don't think they'll pursue us," he says. "But we must take no chance."

He points to a series of islands. They're off the channel a bit and should provide an obstacle for Eli to put between him and the British ships.

"We'll tack off a mite toward sea and then take the outside of those islands," he orders.

He assumes command of the wheel and the rest of the ship jumps into action. Ropes are loosened and sails are shifted as a few quick maneuvers have the vessel turning out of the path of the oncoming British ships. It is a sharp turn for Eli, but he's counting on catching a push downwind that will help him accelerate toward the open sea, beyond the islands to the starboard side. It seems unlikely that any of the smaller ships will break off to challenge him if he's successful in that change of course.

He keeps a sharp eye out for patrols that might attempt to approach. He's also concerned about the presence of ledges as they tack around the island, making the maneuver more difficult than he had hoped.

As the ship tacks back into the wind, it loses its speed but the drift continues to push it closer toward the islands. Eli has little momentum to push him forward, so the current is acting as though it is just pulling him into the islands.

With his focus now on trying to clear the land, Mosely notices two sloops that have broken off from the small fleet.

"They're coming after us," he says. "Two of them."

Eli is sure they're just curious. Maybe they're hoping to reap a reward should Eli crash his vessel on the ledges. Regardless, he knows his crew needs to be prepared.

"Clear for action," he tells Mosely. "But we've got to make these islands first."

Land is his biggest threat at the moment, as he drifts ever closer to a point that juts out from one of the islands. He just might have enough clearance to eke past it and find open ocean. If he does that, he'll be able to put the pursuing sloops well behind him.

He eyes the land intently and hopes to spot no sign of ledges lurking on the outer edges of the point. He sees nothing threatening and finally is convinced he'll ease past the last without trouble.

The crew recognizes that, as well. They go from being battle ready to preparing for the next tack that should have them on their way once again.

"Captain!" comes a shout from the bow.

Eli immediately worries about a ledge that he might have missed and frantically looks about to see which way he might have to steer in a hurry. But it isn't a ledge; his eyes widen as he moves past the point of land only to see a completely unexpected sight.

"British ships!" comes the shout from bow watch. "Lots of 'em!"

Off in the distance is a collection of British vessels, but this group of ships is twice as large, maybe even three times, as the fleet they were running from.

"Godfrey mighty!" he exclaims.

Eli realizes he's running out of options. He can't move forward, he'll sail right into this group of ships. He'll never be able to sail across and around them, and trying to tack and sail back upwind wouldn't be a wise maneuver, either. The crew can see their predicament and waits for some kind of order.

"What are we gonna do, Eli?" asks Mosely, equally unsure of their options, other than engaging in a fight they likely won't win.

Just before he answers, Eli pauses. He has an idea, though he knows it may not work. It's a huge gamble, but it may be their best option. He concludes that he has no choice.

"There's space between those two islands, it might be just over fifty feet wide of water," Eli answers, pointing off the larboard bow. "We'll tack, get on the wind and sail through. They won't follow us there."

Eli knows it all sounds well and good. He doesn't mention the fact that he has no idea what he has for depth in between those islands. He could blow in there with a full head of sail and hit a ledge squarely. Even if they do squeeze through, who knows what lies on the other side.

Mosely looks at the space between the islands and then back at Eli. He says nothing, but his doubt is clear. Eli looks back unabashedly.

"Stand by," he calls, summoning the crew to prepare to tack.

As the ship turns, Eli feels the breeze fill his sail and push with momentum. The drift of the current certainly helps, as well. They gain some speed, and he focuses on navigating his way between the islands.

Mosely has sent extra crew ahead to scout for obstructions. Eli watches the water. He looks for all signs of shallows or lingering ledges. He sees none. The water looks blue and deep. The men on bow watch offer no signals of warning.

The current is strong, and it is a challenge to keep the ship steered on course. Eli can feel the drift that could take the vessel too far to one side, which could put it too close to one shore or the other. Without knowing which way he needs to go on the other side, it is difficult to know just how to approach. The wind and the current quickly assume control. Eli is left to manage as best he can. He steers with what little control the wind and waves allow.

As he drifts a little too closely to the larboard side, he does a quick turn of the wheel. He steers the bow out sharply, as if he's about to turn around. Then he twirls the wheel back around the other direction. The bow turns sharply, but also kicks the stern of the ship out significantly. It puts the vessel as centered as Eli can get it as it flows through the small channel and between the islands.

Eli has plenty of water and sees no sign of any ship tempted to follow. Ahead is another island straight off the bow, but it is all open ocean to the starboard side of it. He keeps the ship on course, headed straight downwind toward the open sea.

As he clears all islands and reemerges into the open sea, both groups of British ships have continued on. He's well behind them with plenty of wind.

"Looks like it's all open ocean now," says Mosely, relieved to have escaped such a predicament. "If you'd like to return below, I can take the wheel."

Eli is reminded of the rest he was getting and the sleep he had been awoken from. It would be nice to drift back into that peacefulness, but he's too wide awake now. He's got the wind, the waves, and a little bit of luck on his side.

CHAPTER THIRTY
Portsmouth, New Hampshire, 1777

T he radiance of the fireplace sends a warm glow around the house. The shadow of the flames flicker. They dance upon the walls of the room.

Faith is enjoying the coziness of the evening as the winter chill begins to set in. The boys are getting ready for sleep, and she thinks she may not be long behind them.

She glances around the room, but despite being warm and comfortable, she realizes she still feels like a stranger in somebody else's home.

Originally, the boys went to live with the Lathrops. It was hard for them. Being away from their home disrupted their routine. Living with George and Maddie was a challenge, for the boys as well as the adults.

The war effort has been a struggle for George's business efforts. The stress of the war and the family finances combined with a crowded home increased the tremendous pressure on George and his wife. The fact that the boys saw less of Faith didn't do them much good, either.

So, with financial issues getting worse, George and Maddie rented out their property and moved into Eli's spacious house. The hope was that it would allow them to avoid selling off their home and wharf. They also invited Faith to live there and help take care of the boys. Maddie was going to try to find work. Any help Faith could provide in caring for her boys as well as Eli's was a welcome addition.

It still feels awkward for Faith. She feels like a visitor and as she mulls that over, she can't help but think that she is. Even on nights like this when the Lathrops are away, leaving Faith alone with just Joseph and Eligood, it doesn't feel like her home. But it does for the boys, and that is important. It's the same house the boys were born in and grew up in. The same house Eli shared with another wife. It is his home and their home, but not hers.

She wonders when or if that feeling will ever change.

It is nothing truly out of the ordinary, Faith reminds herself. Much of her life has revolved around the needs of others. She's been consumed by their world and not her own.

When she was younger and her mother took ill, Faith was the one who did many of the chores around the house and helped care for her mother. The deadly fever lingered for quite some time. Her mother would seem to feel better and nearly be ready to leave her sick bed only to take a turn for the worse.

The doctor wasn't sure what the sickness was, some type of virus, he finally concluded. They thought of taking the pox of a sickened person and trying to immune her, but they opted not to. It would be of little help since she was already sick. And this, they thought, wasn't a pox that she had.

Their best hope was to let it run its course. Faith followed her mother's wishes and did her best to cook dinner for her father and younger sibling while also maintaining the house. She'd tend to her mother's needs, as well. It was a heavy burden for the teenager.

That lasted for a full month or two. When her mother finally succumbed to the illness, Faith's responsibilities only increased. She not only had to assume the household duties after her mother's death, but she helped her father at the church and with raising her sister.

Her mother had always been a wonderful partner to her husband in the ministry. She would handle many a task that served her husband and church well. That included choosing music each Sunday, playing the piano, organizing prayer groups, and maintaining the lawn and gardens surrounding the church.

When she died, she not only left a significant void in Faith's life, but also that of her father's and the church. Faith attempted to carry on her mother's work, taking on the challenges the woman faced each day.

Her childhood was short-lived, Faith realizes. She grew up rapidly, as life forced her to do. It has shaped the person that she is, but Faith can't help but wonder what she has forsaken as a result.

She's done that once again in her current course and role in life. With the uncertainties of war, she can't help but ponder where that all might lead. What kind of future exists for her when most of her days revolve around others?

While deep in thought and mulling over her own path, she hears the commotion of the boys coming into the room. They have changed into their nightclothes and are ready for sleep.

"All right, off to bed, you two," she says. She rises from the comfort of her chair and follows the boys into their room. They climb into the bed and lie beside each other. They snuggle in under the blankets.

The candles in the room flicker light across their innocent faces. Faith looks down at them and smiles. She loves these boys. But at the same time, she sees again that she's now fulfilling someone else's role.

"Let's say our prayers," she says.

The boys put their hands together, interlocking their fingers as they rest their hands on their little chests. They lie there peacefully. They close their eyes but can't help the temptation of opening them for a quick glance. Faith kneels down at their bedside. She bows her head and clasps her hands together.

"Dear God, we pray for our mother up in heaven," begins young Eligood. "We pray for our father too, who is away."

There's a short pause before Joseph takes his turn to speak.

"We pray for Faith," he says.

After being sure the boys are finished, Faith concludes the prayer.

"We pray for young Eligood and Joseph," she says. "We pray for your watchful care of them and this family. We pray for Eli's safe keeping and safe return. In Jesus' name, amen."

She opens her eyes and lifts her head. Eligood appears nearly ready to doze off. Joseph looks up at her, unexpectedly forlorn. Faith isn't sure, but thinks she sees a tear running down his cheek.

She reaches over to wipe it away and feels another slide down his skin. "What's the matter, Joseph?" she asks.

The boy remains quiet for a moment. He looks puzzled and unsure of what to say.

"I miss my mother," he says. "And I miss Father. When will he come back?"

It pains Faith to see the young boy longing for his parents so, especially knowing one of them isn't returning. She's unsure what to say about their father. They don't understand the full complexities of the war.

They just know he has gone to sea.

"I'm sure your father is just fine," she says. "He's thinking of you and missing you more and more every day. That's why he'll be home as soon as he possibly can."

She pauses for a moment and sees a little bit of a smile on Joseph's face. Eligood is sound asleep now.

"You just have to be patient and strong," she says. "God will bring him home."

She leans over and gives Joseph a kiss. She stands and kisses Eligood, as well. She blows out the candle, leaving the room in darkness. She returns to the dwindling glow of the fire. She tosses a few pieces of wood into the flames and returns to sit in her chair.

She takes a deep breath. Her heavy sigh eases her tension, but only for a moment. Her body quivers and shakes as her sobs begin. Tears run down her face. She at first reaches to wipe them away, but resists. She just lets them flow.

CHAPTER THIRTY-ONE
Aboard *Resolution*, 1777

T he sky begins to glow. It has a soft radiance at first, but soon
the horizon ignites with a fiery color. The intense shine spreads
through the clouds and illuminates the land and sky in the distance.

The stars above twinkle with an immense brightness, straining to
be seen behind a soft haze of clouds above.

Eli can't help but notice the explosion of color amidst the dark sea
and black-as-night silhouettes of the islands. He wonders if it could be a
ship on fire. Maybe it is one under attack, which would mean the victor
in the skirmish might seek more prey or be vulnerable.

He laughs at himself and his assumptions. His initial thought is
about an attack, one he might fall prey to, or one he might instigate. Both
show a different inclination than he had when sailing cargo around the
world or catching fish off Portsmouth shores.

War changes men, he realizes. He can see it in the people around
him.

George was a simple businessman, building a successful shipping
business. War turned him greedy. There was no cause to him. No revolution. It was a chance to make money and exploit the situation. It's an
endeavor that could make him wealthy beyond his hopes. It could also
ruin him.

For what cause? For what sacrifice?

Many others have done the same. War is an opportunity, not just a
fight, not just a rebellion or a quest for freedom.

Eli ponders his own motives; his own cause. His own search for
liberty.

He looks up at the sky. The masts stand straight and tall, reaching up into the darkness as though piercing the sky. The stars appear to shatter and scatter out through the galaxy.

He thinks about watching the stars as a boy. He'd stand on the porch of their home and gaze up with wonder at all the bright specks of light that illuminated the night.

The world seemed so bright and amazing back then, unlimited in its grandeur. The possibilities of life seemed awesome and powerful. There were no boundaries, just a magical world glistening with light and wonder.

The fire in the sky isn't what he first thought. There's no fire at all. The bright glow of the rising moon has ignited the sky and filled it with color, brightening the blackness. It isn't the color of war after all. It is a tapestry of peace, a piece of beauty amidst the world in conflict.

Life has been filled with conflict for Eli. Much of it has been within himself.

The sea is a constant danger and threat. He watched his father taken by the grasp of a harsh and unforgiving ocean.

Equally cruel, he watched his wife suffer. She gave life as her own slipped away. Eli was just as helpless.

His brother has been a constant source of frustration and aggravation, another sign of his own inadequacies.

There's Ezra and his capture, another drama that he was helpless to change. They all combine for a lifetime filled with dark days and disappointment.

He thinks of the love he had for his wife, and her loss. The renewal he feels with Faith, the pride in his children, these are the stars that shine. He smiles as he recalls the faces and feels peace with the love in his heart.

The moon continues to shine and illuminate the black sky and the dark sea below. Eli watches its radiance until the grayness of the clouds seep across the galaxy and consume the light above.

Eli takes a deep breath and exhales. He looks down over the deck of his ship. Sailors, soldiers, patrol and prepare. They await the action of the coming engagement. All is quiet. The ship lies still. The night is at peace, but a new day comes.

CHAPTER THIRTY-TWO
Portsmouth, New Hampshire, 1777

The news spread around town weeks ago. The Battle at Bennington has been fought. A great victory has been won over the British General John Burgoyne, but those left behind await the cost.

Burgoyne's troops have begun to move down from the north, threatening New Hampshire, Vermont, and New York. It is being said that Burgoyne hopes to split New England from the rest of the colonies. General Stark led a response that included hundreds of New Hampshire men.

Among those troops was Amaziah Goodwin. Goodwin was active in the attack on Trenton, and was also with Stark at the Battle of Princeton. His luck in combat has continued. When Stark returned to New Hampshire during the previous winter, Goodwin returned home as well. He had been wounded but they were meager injuries, just more battle scars to be proud of.

When Stark was passed over for promotion by Washington, the disgruntled officer chose his own course. He was determined to lead an attack on the approaching Burgoyne, vowing to do so in the service of New Hampshire and not the colonies. Goodwin elected to join the cause.

Part of life around town now is the steady flow of news. The Continental Army has suffered many defeats. Word of casualties arrives soon after. Absent members of the community are never returning home.

Faith hears the names. Some are people she knew. Others are families she now knows have been irrevocably changed. She waits and fears for news of Eli.

As hard as she tries to suppress her worries, she's surrounded by the war's consequences. She watches her father conduct more funerals.

What was a life built around promise and happiness is now overwhelmed by death and despair.

Even news of success brings sorrow. Trenton was a victory, but it came at a cost. Burgoyne was turned back by Starks and his troops' efforts, but the local force still lost dozens of men. Some of them are likely people Faith knew.

She sees no end in sight to the war. She can see no hint at how it will conclude. So much of her future and destiny lies out of her control.

What often gets her through each uncertain day is her dedication to the church and the work she does for a seamstress in town. Her efforts to care for the boys and provide them normalcy amidst a chaotic war-torn world is what drives her forward.

She sees herself filling the roles of others, but she realizes now that she finds purpose in that. She hopes her efforts and her service can make a difference, not only to the world around her, but also to herself.

As she prepares dinner, the boys are in the yard. She can hear them at play. Their joyous voices often lure her to the door, where she can gaze out and watch them. Their energy and happiness make her smile.

When she sees their attention turn to the front of the house, she suspects someone has come visiting. She didn't hear a carriage of any type, but that means little. The boys are curious, but make no movement toward the front of the house. After being diverted from their play momentarily, they return to their running and climbing of trees.

Then comes the knock at the door. Faith can't imagine who it might be. The uncertainty of an unannounced arrival always makes her heart skip a moment.

As she opens the door, she sees Martha Goodwin standing on the porch. She looks weary and sullen.

"Well, Martha, how wonderful it is to see you," says Faith, trying to be cheerful, while hiding any concern she might have as to why Martha is here.

Martha smiles and leans in to embrace Faith.

"Sorry to arrive so unexpectedly," she says. "I wanted to drop something by."

Faith welcomes her in and leads her into the parlor. She offers her some tea, but Martha declines, noting that she has other stops she wishes to make.

There's an awkward silence as the two women sit looking at each other. Faith offers an uncomfortable smile. Martha takes a deep breath and forces herself to speak her intent.

"I don't know whether you have heard," she begins. "It's Amaziah."

Faith fearfully suspected that it might have something to do with Martha's husband, but had hoped she was wrong.

"He fell at the Battle of Bennington," Martha continues. "We were given the news a few days ago. "

She pauses for a moment. Faith offers her condolences and an understanding glance, filled more with fear than consolation.

"We had hoped for the best when we heard of the success of General Stark and his troops," says Martha. "But my dear Amaziah was lost in battle."

The silence returns for a moment. Martha suddenly recalls the reason for her visit. She opens up a satchel and reaches inside. She pulls out a knife. She presents it to Faith in the open palm of her hand.

"This was my beloved Amaziah's," she says. "He wore it at Breeds Hill. It was a prized possession of his. I know he'd like Eli to have it, from one brave soldier to another."

Faith takes the knife and clutches it in both hands. She thanks Martha for thinking of Eli.

"I know this will mean a great deal to him," she says. "I look forward to giving it to him when he returns."

Her voice breaks as she finishes her words. She tries to hide her emotion, but isn't sure she does so with success. Martha just looks back at her and nods. Both women would gladly break down tears, but attempt to remain composed and strong.

"I look forward to that day for you," she says.

She reaches over and grasps Faith's hands, still with the knife enclosed in her grip.

"Let me pray with you," says Martha.

The two bow their heads. Suddenly, the silence isn't awkward. It is a peaceful quiet.

"Heavenly Father," Martha begins. "We lift up my darling Amaziah to you this day. We pray for your guidance as you lead him to glory. We also pray for our beloved Eli, his boys, and Faith. We ask for your watchful care. We pray for strength and peace and lift Eli's safe keeping up to you. We offer our faith to you for his safe return. Amen."

The boys enter the house. Their curiosity ultimately gets the best of them. They come to investigate the visitor and see what of interest there might be for them.

"They're growing up so fast," Martha says gleefully, suddenly realizing that she's not even talking to their mother.

The boys spot the knife that Faith has set on the table. They rush over to have a look. Faith advises that they can hold it gently, but must be careful.

"That was, I mean, is my husband Amaziah's knife," Martha explains.

The boys gawk at it in amazement.

"He's a great war hero," Faith explains. 'He wants your father to have that knife as a keepsake."

The boys are excited as they take turns holding the knife.

"You'll have to have your Great Aunt Martha tell you stories about Amaziah sometime," Faith says, "but she's got to be going. She has other visits to make."

Faith approaches Martha and gives her an emotional hug. They pause in each other's arms for a moment before heading for the door. Before Martha leaves, she embraces Faith one last moment briefly.

"My thoughts and prayers to you, Martha," Faith says.

Martha chokes back her tears and nods. She pauses for a moment and mutters a faint, "and mine to you, Faith," before she turns and hurries off.

Faith closes the door and looks back into the parlor, where her boys are still preoccupied with the knife and talking about being war heroes themselves.

CHAPTER THIRTY-THREE
Aboard *Resolution*, 1777

Eli isn't sure whether it is the dampness that he hates the most, or the inability to see. Too many times in his sailing life, he has felt overwhelmed by the cover of fog and damp air that comes and goes over the cool ocean waters.

Even as a young man, he'd feel the dampness in his bones. It would linger in his muscles as well as any clothing or bedding he'd have aboard. It meant for a great level of discomfort and cold.

Then there was the visibility. The thickest of fog leaves him feeling stuck in this pocket of dense air. It makes his dislike of this weather that much stronger.

He also doesn't like not being able to see what is out there, or what is coming. Whether it be commanding a privateer or sailing a merchant ship, there's always a level of danger that looms just beyond each horizon.

Being stuck in a thick-a-fog only enhances that danger, and makes him more concerned about what might lurk beyond the wall of sea smoke.

His old friend Ezra not only had eyesight that could spot a ship in any condition from a great distance, he could also smell a ship coming. Many a sailor scoffed at such a notion. Eli has told the story many times and been met with disbelief, but he saw his former captain and friend patrol his deck, sniffing the salt air. Ezra could smell the gunpowder or find the scent of a vessel as it approached without even seeing it. Eli witnessed it many times.

Once when Eli was at the wheel, he watched a ship approach from behind. He kept close watch of it and was sure it was no threat. Ezra was down below in his quarters getting some rest. The ship was well off his stern and unlikely to catch his vessel, but Ezra was still drawn topside saying, "I smell a ship." He looked the vessel over, realized himself that it was no threat, and returned to his quarters.

On another occasion while anchored in the fog, their ship was tucked away alone in a small cove. It seemed unlikely that any kind of dangerous vessel might find them there. But sure enough, somehow a pirate vessel discovered them and saw opportunity to trap them there.

Ezra had recognized the danger immediately. He'd been surveying the fog quite regularly, searching for any sign of impending trouble. Eli was right there when in midsentence, Ezra stopped talking, which was a quite a rare feat for Budwick as it was. He inhaled a deep breath and exhaled.

"The air has changed," he said.

Eli and the few crew around him knew nothing of what he meant. They smelled nothing themselves.

"Trouble's coming," he said. "I can smell it."

Eli thought nothing of it until Ezra ordered the crew to haul out and prepare for an engagement. It was a slow, prodding start from anchorage, but just as the ship started to move, the faint shadow of a vessel appeared in the distance.

A flash of cannon fire lit up the fog and the splash of a near-missed shot got everyone's attention. Ezra had the ship sail away from the oncoming vessel. His crew opened fire with a few musket rounds and before the attacking ship could get close enough to do damage, Ezra had navigated his vessel to a quick escape out of harm's way.

Whenever Eli is hunkered down in some kind of fog, he remembers that adventure. As he awoke this morning and saw some of the thickest vapor he's been consumed by, he couldn't help but be reminded. He has passed the word that the intention is to eke out of the wall of fog and hope for clearer seas out in the open ocean.

As he tells Mosely about Budwick's ability, he receives the typical scoff of a response. Though Eli has attempted to develop a similar knack by trying to smell the air and differentiate the scent, he's never had any success.

"So what do you smell this morning?" Mosely asks with great sarcasm. Eli thinks it curious that his mate, with an uncanny ability as a sharp-shooter, doesn't believe in the unlikely gift of somebody else.

Eli smells nothing this morning, but senses something. He's not sure what it might be. He is uneasy and doesn't know why. As he and his crew prepare to haul out, he's yet to understand that sense of trepidation.

He's left himself no choice but to attempt to move past it.

As his crew gets the anchor free of the ocean floor, Eli takes hold of the wheel and gives it a quick twist. It doesn't react quite right. As he turns the wheel from one side to the other, he sees that its control of the rudder is compromised. He still has some control of the vessel, but not as he should.

He immediately calls forward for the anchor to be let go. Before iron returns to the mud and the vessel comes to a halt, Eli has the base of the wheel torn apart to examine its parts.

Mosely comes astern and looks over the situation, as well. Before having to ask, one quick look tells him what he needs to know.

"It's the pin," says Eli. "Sheared right off."

The wheel base sets into a rotating mechanism. As the wheel turns clockwise or counter-clockwise, the base below moves in circles as well, to adjust the rudder. There are small pins that connect the two functions and allow for the turning. One of the pins has broken completely in half.

"How the hell does that happen?" asks a disbelieving Mosely.

Eli has no answer. No explanation for how it happened. No immediate solution as to how to fix it. His hunch is that George Lathrop may have cut costs in the building of the ship, but he admits, maybe he can't even put that on his brother-in-law. He wouldn't know enough about ships to skimp on purchasing parts, let alone a pin like this.

What makes the problem worse is that part of the broken pin is still in the foundation and can't be pried out.

"It's going to take some work to repair this," says Eli.

Mosely says he'll summon Asa Panterre. He's the ship engineer, a jack of all trades who boasts that he can fix anything. Panterre has sailed many a merchant ship and seen a multitude of problems and predicaments. Most he's been able to solve when he's had a hand at the solution.

Panterre quickly approaches the gutted wheel compartment and peruses the situation. He scratches the gruff hair on his chin, looking puzzled. On other vessels, it was suspected that fellow crew members would break things for amusement, just to see if Asa could fix them. He almost always did. But he doesn't appear confident as he looks over this problem.

"Jumpin' Jeezum," he exclaims. "Ain't never seen that before."

"Can you fix it?" asks Eli hopefully.

"Got to be a way to fix it," Panterre says. "Hell if I know what it is."

CHAPTER THIRTY-FOUR
Aboard *Resolution*, 1777

You can tell how well things are progressing from the cursing that is coming from back aft. There will be a few clinking of tools, a whack or two of a hammer, and then an exasperated profanity or two.

Not one to curse himself, Eli isn't sure what bothers him most: hearing the profanity that streams from Asa's mouth, or knowing that it indicates a lack of progress.

He's tempted to ask, but knows Asa likely isn't in the mood to explain. Eli is already sure that progress isn't being made. So, asking likely isn't going to tell him something he doesn't already know.

The entire morning is gone. It has been hours since the sheared pin was discovered, and a solution hasn't materialized. After ducking down into his cabin for a quick belt of rum, Eli returns topside.

He finds Asa standing, stretching out his body, and not cursing. Before he has a chance to ask, Asa offers up a report.

"I've almost got the pin out," he says. "Been trying to pry the damn thing. I've chiseled at it quite a bit but it ain't a-budgin that way. So, I've been drilling down into the middle. I've got a piece of iron down in there good and have been working it out. It's a slow goin' but it's moving. I might have the pin out in a bit."

Eli is relieved to hear that, but he knows that simply getting the pin out doesn't solve the problem. With a crowd gathering to hear the update, he waves the extraneous members of the crew away, leaving just him and Asa standing face to face.

"I'm gonna have to jury-rig it somehow," explains Asa. "Ain't got a clue how I'm gonna do it. Got to find something that can go in there and be solid and hold like that pin did."

Eli realizes that no matter what, the repair is only going to be temporary. It's going to mean docking somewhere to get it fixed right.

"I'll know more when I get something in there to replace the pin," says Asa. "Whatever it is probably ain't gonna last long. Might get us where we need to go for a new pin."

Asa sees the disappointment on the face of his captain. He leans back to stretch out his back one more time before returning to a tiresome crouch again to attack the sheared-off pin. Eli stands over him and watches, exasperated and tempted to curse, himself.

"Captain!" comes a voice from far forward. "Captain!!"

Before Eli can determine whose voice is calling him, he sees what is developing. Off in the distance, well immersed in the grayness of fog is the faint shadow of a ship. It is slowly moving closer and has Eli and vessel well cornered.

Suddenly, the pin is the least of his ship's worries. Mosely approaches. The rest of the deck stays close, waiting for orders. Eli knows he's got to act fast. Otherwise, his fate may be determined for him.

He looks at Mosely seriously. "Clear for action," he says. "Follow me."

With that, he begins to move back aft. Asa is working and cursing heartily at the wheel, unaware of any other drama on the ship. Eli pulls Mosely close and explains his plan.

"I want a line of guns, right here," he says, pointing to the middle of the quarterdeck. "Have some cannon fire ready to go, and I want two scout tenders in the water immediately. They can hold off until any action begins, but when it does I want them on the move. If there's an offensive move to be made, we're making it."

He looks at Mosely as if to ask if he understands. His mate nods and rushes into action to prepare the deck and crew for action. Eli ducks down into his cabin for a musket and a pistol.

When he returns topside, he sees the other vessel coming closer. He can see it more clearly as it drifts in through the fog. He has a good plan of attack, he thinks, but he just doesn't know whether he should instigate fire. Maybe this vessel means no harm. He mulls that over for a moment. Sometimes his head, his heart, and his stomach all provide differing hunches about a situation. In this case, they seem to be in agreement. He doesn't like the way this feels and knowing that his vessel is currently dead in the water, he sees no choice but to take the initiative to defend himself.

He looks down and sees the crew hustling to prepare on deck. They should be ready with the cannons at any moment. Mosely is on his way back aft. He has a handful of weaponry, as do a couple of sailors who follow him.

"Wait a few moments," he says. "When they get within range and you have them in your sights, open fire. After each shot, take another musket and do it again. Keep firing as you two reload as fast as you can. I want a rapid fire, no hesitation. Meanwhile, I want the cannons taking aim and firing as soon as you take your first shot."

Montsweag overhears the orders and passes them along to the deck. As the final sailor slips over the starboard rail and down into a pair of long boats, Montsweag tells the two crews to stay back. When the firing stops, they will attack.

He glances back at both Mosely and Eli and nods, indicating that his men are ready. The crew of the other ship comes into view. It is hard to tell, but they appear ready themselves, almost as if they plan to come broadside and board.

"We're not letting that happen," says Eli.

Mosely picks up a gun and takes aim. He looks at the approaching vessel and finds a figure near the wheel.

"Ready when you are, Captain," he says.

Eli waits and watches. He looks over his deck and sees his crew at the ready. He takes a moment to rethink his plan. Maybe he should hold off, he contemplates, looking at the other vessel, wishing for a sign to change his mind.

"Fire," he says simply. Mosely hears the order and pulls the trigger. His musket shatters the quiet of the late-morning fog. With it comes a barrage of cannon fire.

Mosely's first shot takes down the figure at the wheel. He quickly grabs another musket, picks out a target, and fires. He's on to another weapon while the two sailors scramble to keep up and reload the muskets.

One by one, the cannons explode and send destruction into the hull and rigging of the other vessel. After one round of fire, the shooting halts and the two rowboats move into position.

Mosely continues to drop crew of the vessel. As his rapid-fire barrage wreaks havoc on the other ship's personnel, they all scramble, too concerned about ducking for cover than firing back. Before they know it, the boarding parties are scurrying over the gunwales and taking control of the ship.

Mosely holds his fire, keeping his gun on a target and at the ready. The sighted sailor can see the musket fixed on him and offers up a surrender.

"It just might be our lucky day there, Asa," says Eli. "With any luck, this ship might have a pin in its wheel that would work."

Asa looks up and glances around as if he hasn't heard a thing. He sees the captured ship, rendered helpless by firepower and a raiding party.

"I've got the pin out," he says. "If they've got something like it, we're back in business."

CHAPTER THIRTY-FIVE
Aboard *Resolution*, 1777

With the vessel back fully functional, Eli has his crew gathered on deck. He stands above them back aft and looks them over as he prepares to speak.

For days, the *Resolution* has been at the dock. The vessel taken for a prize was towed into the nearest harbor. That was after it surrendered a make-shift pin that helped stabilize their own steering mechanism. Upon reaching a downeast harbor, Eli was able to find a boat builder who was able to shore up the new pin and secure the steering once again.

While ashore for repairs, Eli confirmed the passage of the Pirate Act by the British. It states that any sailor can be detained and charged for high treason if accused of acts of piracy.

Eli has never considered himself a pirate before. As he mulls over the news, he realizes that judged by British standards, he very well would be a pirate. Certainly he doesn't see it that way. Pirates are the people who stole and raided his vessels or other vessels in so many parts of the world. He has defended his life and cargo against such thievery, developing such a distaste for it that it makes him ill to think of returning to a world of such violence.

To Eli, this is a cause to believe in, a fight for freedom. That has been his justification. Surely others accused of piracy by the British are privateers in this solely for the money. Thinking it through, he realizes this is a motive he can't exactly exonerate himself from, either. But in his heart and mind, his cause is just. No new Pirate Act is going to dissuade him from doing what he sees as right.

"When I was ashore, I was talking with a regimental commander," says Eli. "We just got talking about his troops and where they were headed. But he said the latest news from the war is that the British have passed a Pirate Act."

Mosely chuckles a little at the thought.

"What the devil is a Pirate Act?" he asks, suddenly realizing it might not be a good thing.

Eli explains the new law of the seas. Vessels, like theirs, if captured by the British for raiding and destroying their fleet can be tried as pirates and the crew executed for the offense.

"It means we could be considered pirates and hanged for what we're doing," says Eli.

Mosely thinks about it for the moment.

"Heck fire, they probably were going to do that to us anyway," he says, thinking he might need to inform his crew of that development. "I guess it means one thing."

"What's that?" asks Eli.

"We don't get caught," replies Mosely.

Mosely summons the crew on deck. With them all gathered together, Eli makes his pitch. He knows he must make it clear to them of the risks they now face.

"We are now no more than pirates," Eli tells them. "We are criminals in the eyes of the British. It could certainly mean our lives. You must all consider this and determine for yourself whether you wish to continue."

He offers any man opportunity to return to the harbor, where they can find passage home. Otherwise, he is sailing onward.

"We're not just destined for the Nova Scotia coast," he declares, citing the British stronghold. "We will hit England in its heart."

His aim is the English Channel. With so many vessels committed to the colonies, Britain has failed to secure its own land properly. The English Channel is a ripe place to attack British cargo ships coming and going.

"I'm bound for England," he exclaims. "It will take six to eight weeks. Who's with me?"

There's a momentary pause as crew members think about their opportunity to leave the ship. A sudden wave of enthusiastic hands shoot up. The crew overwhelmingly proclaim their willingness to continue.

"To England," shouts Mosely, speaking for the entire crew.

Eli smiles, pleased at the determination of his men.

"To England," he replies as he retreats aft to the wheel.

CHAPTER THIRTY-SIX
Aboard *Resolution*, 1777

I t is amazing how a ship, slipping away from the dock and finding a clear breeze and an open sea, can brighten the moods on board.

The ship repairs are complete. The crew enjoyed some liberty ashore. Many managed to get letters out to loved ones before leaving for the unknown.

The *Resolution* hauled out late in the day and has ridden the afternoon westerlies for much of the afternoon and evening.

With some blustery winds and an open sea, the crew revels in their raised sails, full of nature's fuel.

Eli even tests the ship and its steering himself. He spins the wheel one way, then twists it in the opposite direction. He calls out for some tacking exercises, which has the crew adjusting the sails with each turn of the ship.

"Other ships are going to wonder what is going on out here," says Mosely. "They might think we've gotten into the rum."

With each attempt at finding a weakness in the steering, the vessel meets Eli's challenge. It moves rightly and steers as well as ever. His doubt in it and its repairs are quickly dispelled.

And with the crew primed for action from the tacking exercises, Eli has been sailing hard into the night. He expects a long and arduous crossing to England, utilizing a good breeze as best he can.

He's making great progress with relatively subtle seas. That is, until he spots a vessel in the distance. As dusk hovers over the horizon, he watches it sail past in the faint light of the evening sky.

Mosely rushes to the wheel, but never has a chance to say a word.

"I see it," says Eli. "What do you say, how about we get us a prize?"

He looks at his mate and gets a simple nod. Then comes the order: "Clear for action" shouts Mosely.

Some of the crew have already spotted the vessel, but many others are caught unaware when the call comes. The men rush into action. The vessel and weaponry are battle ready in a matter of minutes.

Eli steers the boat away from its course and begins pursuit. With a burst of wind, the *Resolution* rides across its heading in pursuit of the other vessel, now struggling to sail into the breeze.

Mosely gives the signal that the cannons are loaded and ready for attack.

As the *Resolution* bears down on the ship with reckless abandon, the crew of the other vessel scrambles to prepare itself. Eli has too much speed for them. He makes a diagonal pass across her bow and down her larboard side. With the one quick barrage of cannon fire, the *Wanderer* is quickly disabled.

Eli tacks back after his first passage and prepares for another attack, but there is no need. The cannon fire has destroyed the rudder and numerous crew have been killed. The survivors of the vessel immediately surrender.

Eli prepares a raiding party and the *Wanderer* is quickly captured and looted.

As his crew returns to the *Resolution* with prisoners and prizes, Eli watches the smoldering *Wanderer* left afloat in the Atlantic. It appears too damaged to bother towing back to port.

As the *Wanderer* smokes and smolders en route to a watery grave, Eli and his crew bask in the glow of another victory.

Off in the distance, the HMS *Everlast* has a fleet of British vessels around her, ready for their own maneuver. The flame of the burning *Wanderer* betrays the *Resolution* in the darkening night.

CHAPTER THIRTY-SEVEN
Aboard the *Resolution*, 1777

The smoke from what is left of the *Wanderer* blends into the blackness. The afterglow of the fire barely lingers as the defeated ship slowly sinks below the surface and disappears.

Eli watches it burn and begin its descent into the depths of the ocean. He's mesmerized as he watches the sea rise up and swallow it whole. All that is left are the waves that wash over the place where it floated moments before. There are a few pieces of debris that broke off or became dislodged and now linger atop the waves in its place. Otherwise, the *Wanderer* is gone.

He remembers that moment watching his father desperately trying to stay afloat. It is a memory that remains as fresh in his mind as the day it happened. He sees his father flailing in the angry seas. A wave of his hands and a last fleeting moment above water. Then in an instant, he sinks. A wave washes over. And he is gone.

Eli's unsure what bothers him most about that memory now. He still grieves the loss of his father and is still haunted from watching it happen. But now the memory not only overwhelms him with guilt, but also fear that he could suffer the same fate.

Eli hears the joyous noise of the crew on the deck. They're celebrating the capture of another prize and likely counting the abundance of riches they are accumulating.

Eli is pleased at the sound of their joy. He hears laughing and singing and the celebration of another victory. He hates to halt their revelry, but their journey must continue.

"Mate, let's get things settled and prepare to move," he suggests to Mosely.

The first mate nods and steps forward of the crew to hear him. He shouts out his orders but is interrupted.

From out of the black of night comes a flash. It's a quick and explosive noise that illuminates the darkness. But the sudden burst catches the crew of the *Resolution* by surprise.

The flash gets their immediate attention, but the aftermath is what alerts them to what is truly happening.

A cannon ball tears through the side of the ship, sending debris flying and crew members dodging shards of wood. Then comes another blast and another blow to the vessel.

Eli and Mosely are knocked over, back aft. The *Resolution* lurches as the vessel's progress is halted. Rather than stay low and sprawled on the deck, the captain and mate jump to their feet and try to rally the crew.

Both reach for weapons, but it may be too late. From his spot at the wheel, Eli can see his own crew being overwhelmed. With one ship making a pass to fire upon them, another has come alongside to board. There is a smattering of resistance, but it takes mere seconds for the British swarm to squelch any thoughts of a courageous stand.

He watches one crew member rush to challenge a British invader only to have a pistol fired into his face at point-blank range. The man's head blows apart and splatters on men all around him. That quickly ends much of the fighting spirit of his crew. With Eli looking on, those members of his crew who do offer resistance are beaten, maimed, or killed.

Before he can do anything, a half-dozen invaders are rushing aft to seize him and control of the ship. Mosely steps forward to protect his captain, but takes the butt end of a rifle across his head for his efforts.

Eli attempts to surrender peacefully, but is gouged in the stomach by one musket end and takes a similar whack across his brow.

As quickly as the *Wanderer* was taken by Eli and his men, the *Resolution* is consumed and captured by the British.

Eli and the *Resolution* are now someone's else's prize.

CHAPTER THIRTY-EIGHT
Aboard the HMS *Thunder*, 1777

As Eli awakens, he reaches to clear the dust from his eyes. His eyesight is still blurry and his head throbs with pain and a wooziness that swirls from one temple to the other.

He shakes his head once, but it does little to clear the fog. As it slowly lifts, the view before him emerges. It is the dark and dank recess of a ship. The smell hits him with an overwhelming stench, like nothing he has ever drawn into his nostrils. It makes him cough and shake his head all the more. It is the smell of death, he concludes, or something just shy of it.

As he is able to identify the stench, his eyes begin to make out the picture before him. Other men lie together in a small room. Only the faintest of light shines through, deep in the hull of whatever vessel he is on. The men are shackled. Some are confined together; others are chained to posts or to the ship itself. Some appear dead already, or close to it.

They are men he doesn't recognize. They've obviously been here for some time. They lie still, barely breathing or moving. One might bat an eye or heave his chest enough to show signs of life. Another might moan softly and let out a groan that announces his consciousness. They all look as though they're just waiting, existing, as if death is coming for them and they welcome its arrival.

As he examines the others around the small cell, Eli sees fresher faces. Some are still asleep, but they look in significantly better condition. Maybe they haven't been here as long. One or two are bleeding badly, as they appear to have been beaten severely. A couple are awake enough to gaze back at him. They just peer blankly, barely acknowledging his existence. Their eyes look at him with curiosity, but the faces show defeat and apathy. They may wonder who he is, but know there's no sense in learning the answer.

In another corner are faces he actually recognizes. There's Mosely, his first mate. He sports a nasty gash over his right eye and appears knocked out cold. Beside him are Nigel Squig, Ambrose Taylor, and Jackson Montsweag. All are members of his crew. They all look dazed, confused, and battered, but alive. Squig and Taylor appear asleep or unconscious, as well, but Montsweag stirs enough to hint that he's coherent.

"Jack, you all right?" he asks, whispering softly, not knowing how discreet he must be.

His words are loud enough to spark movement around the room. The other prisoners gaze over at him as his voice breaks the silence around them.

Montsweag stirs a little and spots his captain sitting with the rest of the prisoners. He's as startled to hear the words as he is to see whose mouth they emanate from.

He nods at first and tries to smile slightly, but his face cringes instead. Pain flashes across his cheek with the movement. He tastes blood seeping into his mouth as it drips down the side of his face. He blows air out to spit off the blood on his lips.

"Yeah, I'm all right," he replies. "Been beat pretty bad."

He and the captain both look over the rest of their men and watch them slowly begin to stir. When Squig comes to, he is near enough to Mosely to nudge him awake. Mosely shakes his head and grimaces as he tries to move. He lets out a groan that seems to rumble from the depths of his soul. Other men answer with moans of their own, as if the first were a signal for all others to answer a roll call of the battered and bruised.

Mosely glances at his captain. He is taken aback at the sight of him sitting there, shackled and ruffled. His clothes are torn and his body appears defeated. His face shows a fear and uncertainty Mosely has never seen from Eli Miller.

Above them all, a loud rumble seems to shake through the core wooden fibers of the ship. They don't know whether it is just weather or some kind of action on board.

The movement above Eli sounds too much like the decking of ship. Outside the room, there stirs more action that hints at the movement of sailors. He hears the barking of orders and talk of sails and rigging, all with thick British accents. He didn't notice at first but can sense the rocking motion of the ship, as well.

How, and what vessel, remain the questions. Eli doesn't recall what happened or how he and his crew ended up here. What he does understand is that he and his men are imprisoned and there's no telling what might happen to them.

Surrounding his own men are a variety of other prisoners. Many have obviously been captive for a long period of time. Eli catches the gaze of one man slumped in the corner. He appears emaciated, wasting away as time and malnutrition leave him to decay. He's pale and sickly, with a yellowish hue that makes him look like he is at the precipice of death. Eli has never seen a man so thin that he looks more like a skeleton than a human.

"The HMS *Thunder*," comes a scratchy and weak voice across from him. Eli looks over at a face staring at him. The man looks frail and appears to have been here for quite some time. His ribcage is prevalent beneath the sickly skin that veils it. The man barely moves, with little strength or energy to make his frail and weary muscles react.

"You're on the HMS *Thunder*," he repeats, straining to muster a voice.

Eli nods with gratitude for the information. He looks around the room a little more, getting acquainted with the surroundings, coming to grips with his appalling circumstances. He looks back across at the man, still watching him intently.

"Can you tell me, friend," he begins, "where might we be going?"

The man's face is sullen and dismayed. He takes a deep sigh, barely summoning up enough breath to answer. "To die," he says. "We're going to die."

CHAPTER THIRTY-NINE
Aboard the HMS *Thunder*, 1777

The events of the night before return in painful flashes.

Eli commanded his vessel in a quick strike against a British cargo vessel. The lumbering ship was no match for the speed and deft handling of Eli and his sleek privateer, *Resolution*.

Eli and his crew chased down the HMS *Wanderer* amidst the cover of darkness. Before the captain and crew of the British vessel knew what was coming, Eli was cocked and loaded to unleash a barrage of cannon fire.

Eli's guns didn't miss, either. One hurling ball of lead demolished the rudder with a thunderous crash. Another shot toppled a mast with a direct blow that reduced the towering mass of wood to smithereens.

In a matter of moments, one ear-splitting volley of cannon fire had crippled the *Wanderer* and left it dead in the water. Eli and his men were quickly aboard, taking prisoners and reaping the benefits of a captured cargo ship.

Eli had left the burning hulk of the *Wanderer* smoldering. The remaining flames lit up the night as the *Resolution* slipped away.

Not far from the wreckage, however, unbeknownst to Eli and his men, the HMS *Everlast* awaited its chance. Before its prey got up to any kind of speed, the *Everlast* emerged from the darkness and struck with a mighty attack of its own.

Eli's mind throbs at the memory of it all. He shakes his head in frustration that he could be so careless. So preoccupied with his latest capture, he'd let his guard down just enough to give the *Everlast* the chance to pounce.

He recalls the cannon fire, the boarding by the British and the whacks he took to his body and to his skull.

That is the last memory that lingers in his aching head. Now, he finds himself stuffed away in the hull of a British vessel. Around him are bruised and battered bodies. Some are his men, but others are obviously previous captures whose end may be rapidly approaching.

These men appear accepting of their fate. They lay helpless and hopeless, waiting for death to come.

The British came down to the bowels of the ship earlier to see if any prisoners had died. Sure enough, they found a motionless pair who showed no signs of life. They were removed, taken topside and likely tossed overboard into a watery grave.

The captors also brought food down for the prisoners, if you could call it that. It was some kind of gruel that consisted of oatmeal as well as some worms, living and dead.

Eli isn't sure what was worse, the sight of it or the smell of it. The weaker of the men wasted no time receiving their food offering for the morning. Some picked out the worms and tossed them aside. Others devoured their gruel like it was a delicacy, worms and all.

It turned Eli's stomach and made him retch just thinking of eating something so disgusting, though he's eaten grub onboard vessels in the past that didn't appear too appetizing.

"Heck fire, Ezra Budwick's cooking was enough to repulse one's stomach on occasion," Eli thought to himself.

Eli was tempted to pass on his allotment of gruel. He even liked the idea that it might help someone hungrier than he, even though this food obviously had not been that nutritionally beneficial for these men.

Still, Eli knows for his own sake, he needs to feed himself and maintain his strength as much as possible. To do otherwise would be to surrender, just as many of these men have.

It is an ending that Eli can't bring himself to accept. He looks over at his first mate. Mosely returns an angry and defiant look. Eli just nods his head slowly. His own fury burns inside him.

He dips into his bowl of gruel and begins to consume it, grimacing as each mouthful goes down. At first, it feels as though his body will reject it, but it suddenly settles in as his stomach accepts whatever is given.

He just might find death aboard this vessel, he concludes, because he intends to escape or die trying.

CHAPTER FORTY
Aboard the HMS *Thunder, 1777*

The sound of the latches on the door breaks the silence inside their own cramped, steam-box replica of hell. Many of the prisoners barely move; when the creak of the doors brings a slight glimmer of light into the darkness, they begin to stir.

Eli is wide awake and peers out through the open door. It is tempting to make a run for freedom, but he knows it would get him nowhere. Being stuck inside such tight quarters, he's not sure his body is limber enough to move with much swiftness.

"Miller," calls the voice of the sentry at the door. "Miller, come out here."

Eli wonders why his name is being called. Is he being freed? Or is he being executed? It could be either.

He slowly rises and stretches his achy, weakened body. It is a slow process for him to move. At least they've discontinued use of the shackles he'd been chained with. As he reaches the doorway, the guard reaches in to grab him by the arms and pull him forward

"Let's go, we don't have all day," the guard grumbles as he shoves Eli forward and then closes the door with a slam. "Captain Kane wishes to see you."

He points toward a companionway not far from the cell and pushes Eli forward. Eli stumbles along wondering, "Who the hell is Captain Kane?"

Eli takes in the ship's layout as he slowly works his way up the steps to the deck. As he arrives topside, he is nearly blinded by the brightness of the blue sky and shimmering sea. He shields his eyes with his hand but struggles to see through the glare.

Eli doesn't know any Captain Kane. He wonders if he should. The name doesn't register, which makes him all the more curious as to why the captain would wish to speak to him.

As Eli shuffles slowly away from the companionway, a large figure stands before him. He seems familiar, but Eli doesn't know why.

Kane has stepped down from the quarterdeck and stands mid-ship with his prisoner before him. He can't help but enjoy watching the weakened man cowering from the sun while struggling to move his weary body.

Kane has been patrolling the coastline to help curtail the smuggling that continued in various small ports and harbors. As the war has escalated, he's assumed a new role. His fleet continues to police the coastline from Boston to Halifax, but now he's chasing smugglers as well as privateers. He's collecting prisoners. Some are shipped off to prison; others are impressed into service.

"Captain Miller," Kane says, grabbing his prisoner by the arm. He tightens his grip until he sees Eli's grimace. He leads the prisoner toward the rail and lets him view the bright blue sky and sparkling water that seems endless from their view upon the deck.

"I thought you might like to get out of your cell and see the outside again," Kane says. "Would you like something to eat or drink? There's some fresh bread here. I'm sure a drink would do you wonders."

Eli's stomach grumbles at the offer. Its hunger echoes so loudly that he's sure Kane can hear his weakness. Eli is starving and the thought of something to eat, almost anything, makes him long for it. His thirst is even worse. The mere mention of a drink makes his throat dry and prompts a desperate need for relief.

Yet, Eli isn't swayed by Kane's offer. As hard as it is to resist, he does just that.

"No, thank you," Eli says firmly. "I prefer to eat and drink with my men."

Kane chuckles at Eli's fortitude. He's amused that Eli would so sacrifice for his men, many of whom would likely not balk at such an offer, even if it meant that others went without.

"Fair enough," Kane replies. "What I actually want to discuss with you can be about you and your men. That is, if you are smart enough to accept such an opportunity."

Kane pauses for a moment and takes in the view himself. He lets his words sink in and allows Eli to understand that a proposition is forth-coming that could affect not only himself but also his crew.

"Many a prisoner has switched allegiances upon their capture," Kane says. "It is a much better means of existing than rotting away in some prison camp or being sent to the gallows at somebody's whim in parliament. We could use a man of your skills and experience, and we could use some of your crew as well. It actually might be of benefit to you."

Kane pauses for a moment to let the idea sink in, allowing Eli time to mull over such an opportunity. Eli was a target as soon as Kane learned of his capture. A privateer captain is just the kind of example the British want to turn to their side.

"You'll make some money and, who knows, a man of your skills could work his way up the hierarchy quite swiftly," Kane suggests slyly. "You could become as powerful as I, in good time."

He stops speaking again. He turns and looks at Eli. He can see the thoughts running through his prisoner's mind. Eli glances back at Kane. He sees a smile, a grin from a face he doesn't trust. The offer sounds too good to be true. But regardless of whether the British captain could deliver on such a promise, to take him up on it would still be an act of betrayal. Eli, in good conscience, could never become a traitor.

"I'm sorry, Captain," Eli says. "The offer is certainly intriguing but I have a loyalty to the colonies and to the cause of liberty. I cannot and will not betray that."

Kane answers with a condescending laugh, as if what Eli has stated are the most outlandish words anyone has ever spoken.

"You are not as wise as I thought you were," Kane replies. "A good soldier, a good sailor, belongs to no colonies. What do those rabble-rous-ers do for you? What are they doing for your family right now? Nothing. Just as you are doing nothing."

Kane walks away from Eli and then stops and turns quickly. He looks at the colonist with a glare of contempt and frustration.

"You can go to prison and rot," Kane says with a growl. "You can leave your family to fend for themselves in your precious colonies. You can let your crew rot in prison with you. Or you can be a true sailor and align your allegiance to the sea, where it has always been. You can earn for yourself and earn for your family. You can give your crew, men who have been devoted to you, a future."

He approaches Eli and looks him in the face earnestly, his expression suddenly one of understanding and compassion.

"You have the power to be who you want to be, and make yourself a future while you do the same for those around you," Kane says with a smile. "This is your liberty."

Eli looks over the gorgeous sea and takes in the beauty of its vastness. He takes deep breath after deep breath, filling his lungs with the salty air that he loves. He feels the breath of life soothe his weary body and give him energy. The temptation of Kane's offer cannot be denied.

"Your liberty is different than mine," Eli says as he walks away from the rail and past Kane. He stops just above the companionway. "Your offer sounds tempting, Captain. I'm afraid it comes with too steep a price."

Eli looks at the guard and at Kane, as if their little meeting has been adjourned and he is ready to be escorted back to his cell. Kane glares at Eli and receives a look of resolve in return. He then looks at the guard and waves his hand, signaling Eli's return below.

CHAPTER FORTY-ONE
Henley Prison, Halifax, 1778

It is an image that still lingers deep in his mind.

As a young boy, Eli would often climb the trees in the yard in front of the family home. His father had purchased land just up the hill from the harbor. You could gaze down the street toward the cozy collection of ships, but it didn't take long for young Eli to realize he had an even more spectacular vantage point if he climbed one of the rugged maples trees in the front yard.

He could virtually disappear up there. He had every limb memorized and could scamper from ground to the top of the tree in a matter of seconds. He thought he could do it with his eyes closed… Until he tried it one day, and just missed a branch that was slightly further away than he'd thought. Rather than securing his foot on a branch that would vault him higher in his climb, he slipped. By the time he got his eyes open, it was too late. All he had a chance to see was the ground rising up to smack him in the face as he landed in a heap.

Another time, as an eleven-year-old, he climbed to the height of the tree to peer out over the harbor.

He can see ships in all their fully-rigged glory setting sail and hauling out for the sea. He often climbs up for a look to see if his father's vessel, Stardust, is fast approaching.

Though he maintains a vigilant watch for his father's ship, each day delivers disappointment. He sees plenty of ships come and go, but none of them have his father at the helm.

On this afternoon, his attention is diverted away from the ocean. He didn't see his father's ship, but he sees his father. He catches a glimpse of a man lumbering up the street slowly. Coming from the direction of the harbor, Eli doesn't recognize it as his father at first. The man looks like any other downtrodden sailor leaving the shores in search of lodging, drink, women, or all three.

It isn't until he gets close enough that Eli can see the man's face. He appears worn and weary, but he has the unmistakable wavy, tousled hair, a face leathered and tanned by the wind, and intense eyes of blue that only the clearest of skies could duplicate.

When the man spots his son perched high in the tree, like a hoot owl on the watch, his face wrinkles with a tired smile.

"You look like you're up in the crow's nest scouting out pirates," Luke calls out as he offers a wave of his hand. He pauses as he nears the tree and watches Eli slither down gracefully before taking a flying leap off the final branch. The boy lands with a solid thump on the ground and a bright grin.

Luke takes a few steps forward and wraps his tired arms around his son in an embrace.

"I didn't see your ship come in," Eli proclaims, disappointed that his father eluded his watchfulness.

Luke steps back from his embrace, but keeps a hand on his son's shoulder before patting him on the head. He smiles again as he glances down at the boy.

"You didn't miss me," he says. "I came in on another ship. You wouldn't have known it was me."

He begins to walk past his son and toward the house. He nudges the boy forward, and both walk up the hill toward the front porch that wraps around the entire front of the home. Eli calls out to his mother, brother Luke, and sister, Maddie. One by one, they all answer his call and come out onto the porch. They flash surprised expressions, one more startled than the other, as they realize that Father is home.

Eli continues to pester his father about his surprising arrival.

"On what other ship?" he persists.

But his father dismisses the questioning in short order.

"I'll explain later," he says, firmly suggesting that his boy discontinue the inquisition.

Eli can't help but wonder while his father greets the rest of his family with hugs and kisses.

That evening after dinner, which Hannah quickly throws together without expecting her husband's return, Luke tells the full story.

He was sailing Stardust to Barbados. Not too far into the tropical climate, his ship was pursued by a French vessel. Luke's merchant ship was a fast sloop, but still no match for the eight guns and crew of thirty-six on the other vessel, whose name Luke can't even recall, because it was French.

"La something-or-other," he says with a grin.

The French boarded the Stardust, commandeered the vessel, and imprisoned the crew.

"Hardly any of them spoke much English," Luke recounts. "Couldn't understand a blasted thing they said."

Luke tells his family he didn't know why they were captured or what their fate would be.

"We thought they were going to give us the guillotine," Luke tells his boys with a wink and a smile, slightly exaggerating his story. Of course, Eli doesn't even know what a guillotine is, but is wide-eyed anyway.

Luke says that he finally concluded that the French were claiming he and his ship had violated some act between the colonies and the French.

After four days, Luke was released and left ashore at St. Christopher. The French kept his vessel and its cargo and abandoned him and his crew. His men signed on with other vessels along the route home. Luke caught passage back to Portsmouth, but his shipping business was pretty near shy of ruin as a result.

Between the return trip home and replacing his ship, it took Luke the better part of two years to begin anew and sail again. By that time, his sons were nearly ready to come aboard.

Luke Jr., who quickly evolved into an even more rebellious and reckless version of himself, was captured and held prisoner a decade later.

As he thinks about his father and brother, Eli realizes he now faces a challenge similar to the one they once faced. The French and the Algerians may not have posed as great a threat as the all-powerful British Empire, but if Eli is to carry on his family tradition, he'll have to find his own means of escape.

He looks around the cramped and stench-filled prison cell he and his crew and others now share. He doesn't have any inkling of how he might produce a daring escape, but if his father and brother taught him anything, it is that there must be a way somehow.

CHAPTER FORTY-TWO
Henley Prison, 1778

There really is no time in prison. The days slowly drag on, one following the other at an agonizing snail's pace. The only means to feel the day moving forward is the scant daylight the prisoners see and the food that arrives. But between overcast and raining skies and a less-than-regular delivery of provisions, judging the passing of each day is unreliable.

What can be seen of daylight today slowly fades away. The building that serves as a prison is barren of much outside light, but there are just enough windows to offer a faint glimpse of the sun.

The prison is built on a small peninsula overlooking an inlet off a sizable body of water that flows in from the ocean. Eli surmises that it must be a deep-water river based on the large prison ships that come in on occasion.

The depot consists of multiple buildings. That number seems to grow continually, as does the number of prisoners. There is one main prison that houses most of the men. There is a small hospital, officer's quarters, various sentry boxes, and guard houses. Among the newer buildings are new prisoner quarters. They're smaller in size than the large brick building.

Eli was initially housed in the general prison quarters, but has since been moved to one of the recently built houses. It appears quickly constructed out of wood. It is colder here in the winter but less crowded and, hopefully, a little more sanitary.

As dusk creeps ever closer, prisoners lie sprawled around the room. It is devoid of anything but a handful of makeshift bedding tossed about the floor, the room overcrowded to make use of the space.

Eli recognized the area as Halifax as soon as the *Thunder* arrived and unloaded its collection of prisoners. He was in the harbor a few times before it became Britain's stronghold on this continent.

Conditions are minimally improved compared to what they experienced on the *Thunder*. The fellow prisoners are in slightly better health here. The food is somewhat more edible. They get a steady diet of stale bread and odd-tasting beef. They also get a soup-like mixture they call pea-water.

There's still the regular addition of worms and various bugs found in the food. Most any sailor is accustomed to that. No matter how much they complain about the beef, it still continues to taste a bit rancid.

They've shared their complaints with the master of the guards, a man they call Middlebrooks. He's a grouchy sort with sparse hair and even less compassion.

"You can eat it and like it or you can starve," he says at hearing all the complaints, which he gladly ignores.

Eli knows there are worse conditions for prisoners. They've heard the stories passed about from sailor to sailor. The prison ships are the worst. They're so overcrowded that the amount of food is sparse and the spread of disease continual. Most prisoner deaths come from those vessels.

Some of the prisons in Great Britain aren't much better. At least, that's what Eli has heard. One of the prisons there is made up of mostly sailors, he's been told. It makes Eli wonder if they might be transferred there eventually.

He doesn't know whether to believe the stories or not. Many a sailor has obviously survived and even escaped captivity in order to share the stories passed on from shipmate to shipmate. Many prisoners have been released in exchange for British sailors. They'd be able to tell a tale of prison life.

Eli expects the truth to lie somewhere in between. He's witnessed enough thus far to see some truth in what he's been told. He knows the prisons in the colonies aren't much better than the worst stories he's heard. That makes him believe that conditions are likely frightening on both sides.

Between prisoner exchanges and sailors with wealthy contacts able to buy their freedom, there are many prisoners who go free. Being an officer, Eli can't help but wonder if an exchange for him might be possible.

He'd hope that Lathrop would have the money and connections to secure his freedom, but he knows Lathrop likely doesn't have the wherewithal to make that happen.

In some places, prisoners are able to escape quite regularly. Between lackadaisical security and a whole lot of persistence and ingenuity, prisoners have found their way out. That doesn't seem to be the case here. Some have tried to sneak away, only to get caught. Some haven't even made it out of the compound. Those who have, at least those he knows about, have been quickly caught and returned. They barely got a look at the world beyond the compound walls to inform the rest about what lies out there.

The building they're in has a half-dozen rooms or so. Eli hasn't seen them all, but he can tell by the noise of various prisoners in other parts of the house. He and his fellow captives don't see many of the others beyond those in this room.

His room is emptied each day. The prisoners are led off to work around the compound and then sent back inside. Sometimes they are fed in the room, but other times they are given food outside before they return. He sees other prisoners when outside, but almost all contact is with only those in his room and the guards that run the house.

Once every two weeks or so, the house is emptied and given a good cleaning. The men stand in the compound while the rooms are washed down and cleaned. It helps combat the spread of disease but certainly doesn't eliminate it.

Men still get sick from the spread of a virus that can quickly wreak havoc through the prison, taking many a life if the disease spreads rapidly. The brutal winters here don't help matters. Eli thought it was cold in Portsmouth during the winter months, but the cold and blustery winter winds here freeze a weakened body like nothing he's ever experienced.

Tonight, the room is filled with weary men stretched out on their bedding. What little light that filters in from outside is starting to fade away, while the scant candlelight illuminates the faces around them.

Mosely is busily writing. He jots his thoughts down on occasion in a journal he stores inside his pocket. Eli wonders why he bothers.

"When I get out of here, I don't want any reminder of this place," Eli thinks to himself.

He watches his friend write intently, trying to scribble down every thought before the light of the evening disappears.

By now, Eli has spent enough time imprisoned with his first mate to know Mosely's story well. He grew up around soldiers. His father, Mattias Mosely, had migrated from Austria along with his brother, Hans. They soon became part of the French and Indian War, seeing heavy fighting in upstate New York. Hans was killed in an Indian ambush on the way toward Fort Johnson.

Mosely barely remembers his Uncle Hans. As a boy, he learned to shoot a rifle with the guidance of his father and a few lessons from Hans.

"I thought they just wanted to teach me to shoot, for fun," recalls Mosely. "But looking back now, they wanted me to be able to use a gun if ever I needed to."

When they went off to fight the Redcoats, Mosely was left home with his mother, younger brother, and sister, and told to practice his shooting.

"I shot so much that I started to run out of ammunition," he says. "I used to do shooting tricks with the rifle. I'd either earn money or get more ammunition or both."

As Mosely grew older and the war continued, he found other ways to get money or ammunition.

"I'd say I was going out to practice, which I was," he says slyly. "I was practicing on any British soldier that happened by on a trail not far from the town. I'd wait in ambush. Poor Redcoat never knew what hit him. Sometimes I'd get two of them. I'd hit the first. The second would be so surprised that I'd have time to reload and shoot him, too."

He'd bury the bodies in the woods somewhere and claim their money, ammunition, and weapons.

"So why go to sea?" asks Eli. "You could have easily joined a regiment and made a great soldier."

Mosely thinks about it for a moment. He hates to admit that it was primarily a financial decision. He joined up with a militia in his town, just north of Boston. He was part of a few skirmishes and could see what the fighting was leading to.

At first, defending his home and family was a priority, but with a major war on independence looming ever closer, the opportunity to be a soldier for hire was too tempting. He knew he could make more money with his skills on a privateer than fighting on some battlefield.

"I just needed somebody to hire me," he says with a laugh that can be heard but not seen in the darkened glow of their room.

Eli remembers them meeting. Mosely stopped by the vessel one morning inquiring about berths on the ship. Finding crew was becoming quite competitive among the many vessels fitting out for the fight.

Because Eli was late in agreeing to captain Lathrop's *Resolution*, filling out the crew was an even more challenging task with little money to offer and not many qualified candidates to choose from.

"I remember asking you what action you had seen," Eli says. "Your answer was that you had been there at Lexington and Concord."

Mosely had explained that he had been a sharp shooter and was accustomed to hitting targets from long distance. That sounded promising to Eli, if the man could prove his skill.

Mosely gladly took a pistol that Eli had stored aboard the vessel. He took aim in the direction of a seagull poised on a post at the end of the wharf. Taking a moment to have the bird in his sights, he fired the pistol. The blast of the shot spooked the gull and it leapt off the post and into flight.

"You missed the sea gull," said Eli, a bit disappointed at the failed demonstration.

Mosely handed him the smoking pistol and smiled. "I wasn't aiming at the seagull. I was aiming at the rat."

Mosely pointed toward the post. When Eli took a second glance, he could see what looked like the furry carcass of a dead rat.

"They're a bit of a challenge," said Mosely. "They tend to hear the blast of the gun. That makes them scatter. So you have to kind of guess which way they're going to move."

A bit befuddled, but nonetheless impressed at the skill of this prospective sailor, Eli quickly offered him a job onboard.

"So what did you do at Lexington and Concord?" Eli asked.

Mosely looked at him slyly.

"Who do you think fired that first shot," he answered.

CHAPTER FORTY-THREE
Portsmouth, New Hampshire, 1778

With each passing week, the garden at the church dwindles. The cemetery adjacent to it continually grows. It has expanded in all directions, and the last resort is that the land for the garden be used for new graves.

There's a new cemetery being utilized across town, but there are some who still want their loved ones buried here. The garden's output has been limited recently, anyway. Faith's ability to maintain it has decreased and the once-consistent crop isn't what it used to be.

It has been sad for Faith. She put so much into that garden in an effort to keep alive something so cherished by her mother. It was a way for her to feel connected with her mother's hopes and dreams in this world.

But the world is changing, Faith admits. She understands the need for grave plots as more and more locals return home as casualties of the war. She's not sure she likes the idea of destroying something full of life and replacing it with something mired in death. But she knows she has no choice in the matter.

So, each week, she still tries to cultivate whatever crops remain, even trying to dig up some in hopes of replanting them somewhere. Sometimes life doesn't have to end, it just moves on, she says to herself.

She's taken some plants out to her Uncle Franklin's farm. It is a few miles out of town and well away from the harbor. She often dreams of owning a farm and living off the land there. She occasionally takes the boys there.

It is a very different environment on the farm compared to the village and life so close to the harbor. There is no hustle and bustle here. There are no sounds of the sea. No rough-and-tumble waterfront.

On the farm, all she hears is the breeze rustling through the trees. There is the wildlife that surrounds the property, filling it with sound: birds singing, chipmunks chirping, the screech of hawks above.

Then, of course, there is the noise of the boys playing. They enjoy the outdoors and the spacious yard and field. They even help out on the farm on occasion.

Faith has tried to generate some income through the crops she's replanted and nurtured, but she only gets out there occasionally.

She also continues seamstress work, and sometimes helps George Lathrop with his bookkeeping. He had a bookkeeper, but realized he could pay Faith to do the work and save some money at the same time.

Her work at the church has lessened a great deal, but she still helps her father at times. Juggling various jobs while caring for two boys makes it a struggle.

Now, the boys are playing vigorously in the yard in front of the church. They run and chase their dog through the tall grass of the nearby, rocky field out back. There are moments when the small boys disappear in the tall grass, but the frisky border collie named Max keeps an eye on them. He entices them to chase him, but when they don't follow, he is sure to come back and maintain watch over them.

Faith enjoys watching them play. They run and chase and laugh. They seem so free of all the problems in the world. Still, she knows they are hurt and missing their mother and their father.

Today, it is a warm summer morning with a faint breeze in the air. The sun is just starting to heat up. It might make for a good afternoon to take the boys to a small beach at the head of the harbor, where they like to run and splash in the water along the shore. After working steadily all morning, Faith can't help but think she'd enjoy a little splash of fresh salt water herself.

She's realized that the goal each day is to wear out the boys before they wear her down. After spending her time aiding her widowed father the minister, it is quite the change of pace to suddenly be responsible for two rambunctious boys.

Faith is watching Max chase them when the dog suddenly veers off to bark at an approaching figure. The boys stop and look themselves. Faith turns to take a glance, as well. At first, she can't comprehend who could be coming. Dressed in a sun hat that shadows her face, it takes a moment for her to recognize Maddie Lathrop.

Faith is pleased to see her old friend, and just as glad to note that her husband isn't with her. Faith has known Maddie for many years, and loves her like a sister. But she's never taken to George, and never quite understood what drew Maddie to him. She accepted Maddie's marriage, but she's never trusted the man or gotten past her dislike of him.

It has been a challenge living in the same house with them, but often times, George isn't home. It is just the two women and the children. Those times are nice.

The boys excitedly rush to greet their aunt, Faith close behind. She's glad to see Maddie, but wonders what brings her here.

"What a wonderful surprise," she says as Maddie bends to greet the boys and then approaches Faith with a smile and hug.

"I needed to talk with you and since it is such a beautiful day, I thought I'd walk this way," Maddie explains.

It immediately makes Faith apprehensive. It isn't a long walk for Maddie to take for a visit, and she likes to come over and see the boys on occasion. But, she could have just as easily waited until they were at home. Something about this sudden appearance and her demeanor makes Faith think Maddie isn't here to just gossip. Something important is obviously on her mind.

"Let's sit down over here," says Faith, who sends the boys off to play. The two women sit on the front steps of the church, with the boys well out of listening range.

She and Maddie chat for a few moments, but Faith's anticipation gets the best of her.

"You said you need to discuss something with me?" she asks.

Maddie nods her head. She explains that George was going to talk to her, but they decided it might be better if it were she that came out to visit. As much as Faith prefers Maddie's arrival than George's, that explanation doesn't make her feel any comfort.

"I'll just get to it," Maddie says. "The *Resolution* has been lost. It was captured by the British. We don't know much in the way of details. We just know that it was captured."

Faith sighs deeply. She has always prepared herself for such news, even expected it, while hoping it would never happen. Now that the moment has come, her preparation fails her. The uncertainty and fear overwhelm her. She shudders with emotion and struggles to hold back tears.

"We don't know anything about Eli," says Maddie. "We can only hope and pray for the best."

She gives Faith a hug and tries to comfort her. Faith takes a deep breath and holds in most of her tears.

"He very well could be in a prison somewhere," says Maddie, knowing that may not be that comforting. Both women know that a prison could very well mean a death sentence in and of itself. "George is trying to find out more and see what he can do."

Maddie doesn't mention that George's shipping business is now in dire circumstances. He was struggling before hearing this news. The *Resolution* is a significant loss for him. It makes Maddie nearly break out in tears herself just thinking about it.

"We just wanted to tell you," says Maddie. "George is hoping some people he knows can help get the ship back... and possibly Eli."

Faith notices that getting the ship returned is mentioned first. Regardless, she doubts George's ability to find someone with enough power to get either the ship or Eli returned.

"Thank you Maddie," says Faith. "I'm grateful for your concern. We'll be fine. We can just pray that Eli is safe."

They both sit in silence. Both women immerse themselves in thoughts of their own future. Faith fears for Eli's safety and his return. Maddie worries about her husband's business and financial well-being. Both know that their futures are in question, and fear the worst.

CHAPTER FORTY-FOUR
Henley Prison, 1779

The pouring rain has soaked his cold body to its deepest recesses. Eli feels numb through and through. What heat exists in his dank prison quarters does little to ease the chill that is so intense it is almost painful.

His shivers are violent, but men around him look far worse for the wear. After a work detail outside followed by a march back across the compound to their quarters, Eli and his fellow prisoners have been worn thin.

It is a daily slog for them, but this weather only heightens the discomfort. Many talk of escape, but have little know-how or physical strength left to succeed at such an attempt. Eli wonders if the continual talk of escape is merely a means of finding that slight glimmer of hope that things may change in time.

Back in their quarters, the men replace their wet clothes with dry ones. The dripping fabrics worn during the day are hung on flimsy lines around the room. It sometimes takes a day or two to dry them completely, depending on the weather and temperatures. It takes even longer for the damp odor to leave the room.

Between the discomfort, the smell of decay, and the lack of cleanliness, the house feels desperate. Eli encourages his fellow prisoners to push on and persevere. Some attempt to follow his lead. Others resent him and prefer to exist in misery, hoping an end will come soon.

Lying on his bed wrapped in a thin blanket, Eli attempts to warm himself. His fatigue is so strong that he barely has the strength to talk to those around him. Mosely has fallen asleep almost immediately. Montsweag is curled up on his bed, resembling a trembling mound more than a human being.

Just as Eli's weariness begins to lure him to sleep, the sound of guards awakens him. There's always a racket when they arrive. Whether it is the stomping of boots, banging of doors, or shouting, the guards invariably announce their presence with noise.

Eli can't imagine what is happening. Other than delivering rations for dinner, the guards rarely appear at this hour.

Before he can reach a conclusion or even hazard a guess, his door flies open. A trio of guards stand at the entrance.

"Miller, Mosely, Mountswag," they announce, mispronouncing Jackson's name as they always do. "Come with us. Pack your things. You're leaving."

Woken out of a deep sleep, Mosely and Montsweag barely know what is happening, let alone understand what it means for them.

"Let's go," Eli whispers to them. "We're being moved."

Eli doesn't really know himself what is happening. His mind races. Could it just mean a change of quarters? Could it mean execution? Maybe it is an exchange?

Whatever it is, a significant change is on the way. Something is happening.

They gather their belongings and quickly stuff them into their respective sacks. The rest of the prisoners look on with wonder. They don't understand, either, but they know it might likely be the last time they see these three prisoners. And whatever fate these three are about to encounter could be what is next for them.

"Let's go," shouts an anxious guard.

Eli, Mosely, and Montsweag quicken their movements. They offer a few waves, handshakes, and goodbyes as they walk past their fellow prisoners and parade out the door.

The first assumption is that they're just changing quarters. It has happened before. When they are put into a carriage and transported out of the prison gates and towards the harbor, that piques their interest as well as their excitement.

It is just a joy to be outside the prison and see other parts of the world again. Simple visions of the town nearby are a wonderful sight. The landscape, the view of the river, the ships at anchor, are a picturesque scene that pleases their eyes. They're far enough away to now smell the salty ocean air instead of the stench of the prison. It is heaven for their senses. They savor the slight taste of freedom they didn't have before.

As they reach the harbor, there is a small sloop tied to the dock. It is obviously their transport, but to where?

Different theories run through Eli's mind. He can't imagine his destination or his fate. He just knows something is changing.

As the three are escorted away from the carriage toward the docks where the sloop awaits, Eli notices a vessel anchored nearby. He gives it a quick glance and then returns his sight to its lines and details. He pauses for a moment to give it a more thorough look, but is shoved forward in an attempt to keep him moving.

He's led to the dock and onto the sloop. Before being sent down below, he gets one last glance at the ship nearby.

It is the same vessel he saw pass years ago. Then, it was towing a prized capture and had his snickering brother on its bow. Now, it rests in the possession of the British.

Descending down into the depths of the sloop, a knot tightens in Eli's stomach. He assumes the worst about his brother's fate and feels a greater uneasiness as he ponders his own.

CHAPTER FORTY-FIVE
Aboard the HMS *Thunder* 1779

E li and his men are not sure, but it feels and looks like the same prison ship they were on before.

They are transported from Henley Prison to the coast, where they are put upon this vessel. They were quite worse for wear when they were captive here before. They're rather emaciated now, but at least their wounds have healed.

They are returned to the dark recesses of the ship and locked away in the same cell-like section below. They can hear the sounds of ship movement and crew busywork. They can feel the motion of the vessel at sea, but they can see very little. They've heard nothing about where they are going or what is happening.

Still, there is a sense of optimism from Eli and his men. To be taken out of the prison and transported elsewhere makes them wonder if they might be part of a prisoner exchange. It may only be wishful thinking, but going to such lengths to move them must mean something.

"It has been so long, I struggle to recall my children's faces," Eli says. "I'm sure they've grown so. I can't imagine how they appear or what I've missed."

None of them are sure how long they've been prisoners. They've watched season after season change. They counted three winters, but the time feels even longer.

"I wonder what kind of world we're returning to," says Mosely. "The kind of change that can transpire over such time is unfathomable."

Though hopeful, Eli tries not to think about the possibility of a prisoner exchange. Maybe his assumption is wrong. Still, he can't help but think of home and what he might return to.

His little boys will have grown considerably. They might barely remember their father, let alone know what he looks like. He knows he certainly won't recognize them. They'll have changed so, and he wonders how surprising it will be for him. He's anxious for a reunion with them and can't help but feel the deep love of a parent.

There are so many questions. It has been so long. And there are so few answers, including where this ship is headed. It could be taking them to England for a lengthier stay in prison there. That thought crosses his mind, even though it makes little sense to him.

His mind focuses on Faith. What must she be feeling? She's devoted her life to his boys and committed her love to him and his family. But what if her feelings have changed? What will a reunion be like for them?

He attempts to dismiss such thoughts. He knows he can't doubt Faith's commitment to him. He trusts her feelings.

They've all made great sacrifices in his family. His absence has created a significant void that will take time to fill. Will his children understand?

"I remember missing my father when he was gone at sea," Eli says, thinking out loud. "I never quite understood it. I was told he had to be away. That's what his life was, but it didn't make it any easier."

His brother Luke especially resented it. Eli can't explain why one was affected so differently than the other, but his father's absence took its toll on both his brother and him. It strikes fear in his heart as to what it might mean for his own sons. They don't understand sacrifice or duty or the concept of liberty. All they know is that their father is gone, as well as their mother. She will never return. They know little of when their father may be back. Meanwhile, the absence looms larger and their life is shaped by its consequences.

"Eli," says Mosely, softly and reassuringly, as if he knows exactly what is running through the captain's mind. "They'll understand. Someday, they'll see what your sacrifice was for, just as you came to understand your own father."

Eli sits quietly and mulls over that thought. He thinks about his own father and how he was shaped by their relationship.

His thoughts are interrupted when the door is unlocked and swings open. Two guards stand outside, along with the sentry holding keys to the cell. The sternness of their expressions doesn't elicit a sense of optimism.

"Miller," one of the guards shouts out. The one with the key looks directly at Eli and motions him out.

Eli steps out of the cell, noticing he now has two escorts instead of just the one. As he's led away, he hears the door close and the locks latch behind him. He continues to make a mental note of the ship as he's led topside, but he can't help but wonder if his observations will be a wasted effort.

The guards lead him up the stairs of the quarterdeck and down the companionway toward the captain's quarters. As he steps inside, Eli is in awe of the luxurious accommodations. On his own ships, the captain's quarters were quite sparse. This space is decorated with various trinkets and antiques. There is the finest of fabrics on the chairs, and port holes as well as glass and dishware fit only for royalty.

"Greetings once again, Mr. Miller," says Thomas Kane, seated behind a large wooden desk. Eli can't help but notice the man doesn't offer him the respect of his title. "Please sit."

Eli tentatively takes a seat across the desk from Kane. Kane promptly stands and paces behind the desk while looking down at Eli.

"I asked to have you brought here to continue our discussion," Kane says. "You've had some time to spend in prison. You have fared better than most. I wanted to offer you once again the opportunity to sail for the Royal Navy."

He pauses for a moment and looks at the stone face of his prisoner. Seeing no hint of what Eli is thinking, Kane begins pacing some more.

"The war in the colonies is coming to a close," says Kane. "It will be a matter of time before the rebellion is squashed and the British rule is restored. I wanted to offer you that chance once again, before it is too late."

Eli smiles and is amused to think that Kane has come all the way to Nova Scotia in this vessel for this brief discussion. Eli knows there's more to this story than he's being told.

"I'll have you know that I've conquered quite a few vessels of various smugglers and pirates like yourself," Kane continues. "I've forced many of them into the service of England. I've also executed many who refused. I'm offering you a choice, one that could mean good things for you and your men."

Kane offers a smile, not one of kindness but almost more a dare, tempting Eli to take him up on his offer.

"What if I decline?" Eli asks with a sly grin.

Kane laughs at his prisoner's gumption. He remains quiet for a moment. He then places his hands on his desk and leans forward, looking Eli squarely in the eyes.

"I guarantee the result won't be a good one," Kane replies. "Because of the Pirate Act, I can have you executed for being a pirate on the spot. You'd make a fine example."

Eli's heart beats faster and uneasiness grows in his stomach. He wonders if Kane is being serious or bluffing. Either way, his answer remains the same.

"If the war is truly almost over, then what use do you have for a sailor who hasn't been at sea in years?" asks Eli. "I'm afraid I'll have to decline your offer once again."

Kane shakes his head in disgust. He looks at the two guards standing behind Eli at the ready. He nods at them, prompting them to grab the prisoner and begin leading him back to the cell.

"You'll be sorry," Kane says as he watches Eli be led away. "Fortunately for you, there isn't much time left for regret."

CHAPTER FORTY-SIX
Portsmouth, New Hampshire, 1779

Just picking up the letter prompts tears.

Hannah Gibson can barely compose herself to read it. She holds the worn paper in her trembling hands like it is the most precious possession. But as she struggles to fight back her tears, she also struggles to read the words.

Faith is tempted to stop her, but feels it would be insulting. Her friend wants to read the letter for her. She had suggested it upon Faith's arrival. Faith convinced herself that it might make Hannah feel better, but now she's not so sure.

Hannah takes a deep breath and sighs. She composes herself enough to begin.

"My Dearest Hannah," she reads before breaking down. She sets the letter down on the table and buries her face in her hands.

"I'm sorry," she says amidst her sobs. "It is so hard to read it any longer."

Faith places a hand on her friend and runs her hand over her back and shoulder. She looks at the letter lying on the table. She's drawn to it and is now curious about its words.

"Shall I read it instead?" she asks, wondering to herself if that would be too much of an intrusion. But deep down, she feels as though Hannah wants to hear those words.

Hannah doesn't even speak. She just nods. She leans forward and picks up the letter slowly. She hands it to Faith with gentleness.

It feels powerful in her hands. It makes Faith nervous to have something so fragile and meaningful in her grip. She gazes at the paper. She sees the worn wrinkles. There are blood stains upon it. There's even what she guesses may be tear stains. Some are fresh, but some may be from when it was written.

"*My Dearest Hannah,*" Faith begins. She clears her throat, feeling a tightness in her chest and a rasp in her vocals as she tries to speak.

"*My part in this war is soon to end. So is my presence in this life. We have been engaged in heavy fighting here in Pennsylvania. We have been encamped in Whitemarsh for six weeks now. We have been guarding the nearby supply cities while also eyeing the British movements in Philadelphia. The British attempted a surprise attack but our Continental Army repulsed them with great bravery and resolve. But in that action, I have been wounded. I'm told there is little to be done. I am in great pain as I live my final hours, but I am comforted with thoughts of your face and your love. I have missed you so much, but feel greater sadness today as I begin to pass without seeing you. I long to share the greatness of my love for you. I desire to see your face one last time. I wish to feel your hand and your touch. I have strived to be a good husband and a good soldier. I am sad to be leaving you but feel glory in the reward that God has for me. I will savor your love in these final hours and carry your beautiful smile with me to eternity. I will reserve a place for you. Until then, be strong and feel my love with you. Though I am passing from this life, I leave my love and my heart with you until we are reunited. Your loving husband, Daniel*

Hannah received the letter shortly after the new year; Faith learned of the news soon thereafter. She came by to visit her lifelong friend and to comfort her.

Faith sets the letter back on the table, relieved to let it out of her grasp. It feels deeply personal to her and like an intrusion for her to hold and read it.

Hannah sits beside her and continues to cry. Daniel was home for a short time last year. Initially he wasn't going to return to battle, at least not right away, but with the war going poorly and the Continental Army in need of experienced men, he felt drawn to go back.

"He couldn't stay away," Hannah reflects while choking back her sobs. "He was torn between his family and the cause. He wanted to stay here, but felt he had to go."

Her words sound eerily familiar to Faith. She thinks about Eli, and knows she is likely to never receive a letter should he not return. She may never know what happened.

She looks at her friend and sees the pain and the love she has for her fallen husband. She also sees her fear. Faith suddenly feels her own. She wraps her arms around her friend. Hannah is appreciative of the comfort. So is Faith.

CHAPTER FORTY-SEVEN
Aboard the HMS *Thunder* 1779

Eli has been mulling over the conversation in his head ever since he left Kane's quarters. He doesn't regret his refusal, but he can't help but hear Kane's words over and over again.

"There isn't much time left for regret," were the words Kane sent him away with.

Eli knows he may have said that only to scare him, one last attempt at swaying his allegiance. Still, it makes him wonder what fate holds for him and his crew.

Would Kane attempt to sway him if a prisoner exchange were to occur? Would it be more likely that an execution is planned? What about the Pirate Act? They were taken out of the prison and transferred to this vessel for a reason. Eli still contemplates why.

When the locks on their door begin to turn, the prisoners inside are alerted. Their attention turns immediately toward the noise. It slowly swings open to reveal a guard at the entryway. He has a tray with bowls on it. It looks like the same flat, tasteless porridge they've been given since being put aboard this vessel. The guard sets it down on the floor.

He stands and looks over the prisoners. It's a different guard than they've had before. Eli watches him intently and senses a familiarity. He notices a look of recognition on the guard's face as well, though he tries to hide it. The man immediately looks away and begins to close the door.

"Wait," Eli says. He crawls toward the door, while the other men grab the tray and divvy up the food. Eli peers out the small opening and still sees the guard through the small iron bars. "Do I know you?

Suddenly terse, the guard growls, "No." He begins to lock the door, his head down.

Eli continues to peer at the guard and twists and turns his head for a better view.

"Garrett?" he asks, wondering if he's stumbled upon the identity of the guard.

The guard scoffs as the key completes its turn. He returns it to his pocket while turning away. He begins to walk toward the companionway, but Eli becomes more convinced that he has recognized the guard.

"Garrett Brown," he says. "Is that you? You're Garrett Brown, aren't you?"

The guard stops and quickly turns back to face the door. He moves in closer and lowers his voice to a whisper.

"Quiet," he scolds Eli. "I don't need you causing me trouble."

Garrett Brown was a young crewman out of Portsmouth. He sailed with Ezra and Eli once, but most of the time he had berths on other vessels. His father, Atkinson Brown, was a pretty good sailor himself before losing a leg during a skirmish with pirates in the West Indies.

"What are you doing here?" Eli asks, almost in disbelief at the reality he's stumbled upon. "You traitor!"

He can see that his words sting. Young Brown is angry, but keeps it to himself. He glances around to see what other crew are within listening distance.

"I was captured," he explains, speaking softly. "It was either work for them or rot in prison, or worse."

Eli sees the predicament the young sailor faced. He nods as if he understands and reels back his judgment.

"I'm glad you are fine," Eli says, reassuring him.

Brown gives him a thankful look and glances around again. The fear for his continued well-being is clear in his manner. As he begins to move away from the cell door again, Eli calls him back.

"Do you know our destination?" he asks. "What is to become of us?"

Brown shakes his head. Already having a tenuous place on board, he is given a scarce amount of information. His focus has just been to earn his keep and stay safe.

He's reluctant to get himself too involved with the prisoners. He fears that knowledge of his familiarity with them just might create problems. But he's always had respect for Eli Miller. He was a fine man to serve under, even if it was just one voyage.

"I'll make some inquiries," he answers.

CHAPTER FORTY-EIGHT
Portsmouth, New Hampshire, 1779

Faith glances through the slight fog on the windows and sees the boys sitting at a table on the front porch. They're busily working on their studies. They're growing up so fast, she thinks to herself.

She feels a sense of joy as she watches them work studiously and independently. Their father would be so pleased. Though his learning came at sea as a boy, he wanted his sons to get a proper education.

"Maybe they'll be able to stop wars instead of fight them," he'd say.

Those words make her smile. It showed the good heart that Eli possesses. He believed in his boys and wanted the best for them, partly because he knew he didn't have that himself. He doesn't begrudge his upbringing, but Faith could always tell a different path then might have led to a different life now.

The smile fades as she recalls the great number of regrets that Eli lives with. She feels sadness for that burden, but realizes she has her own regrets.

She looks back out at the boys and feels an immense love for them, as if they are her own. They are hers at this moment, both her responsibility and her gift. She feels her own desire that they have a better life than she, yet she knows they've already faced great hardship and loss. Who knows what more is to come?

"Faith," says Maddie. "Faith, did you hear me?"

Faith refocuses her attention to Maddie. She sits across from her in the parlor. The cloudy and overcast day makes it dark and dreary inside. It is fitting of the mood.

Maddie has been discussing more discouraging news. Her husband's business is nearly lost. George is all but ruined by the war. He's sold off his wharf and whatever else is left of his business. It has become so dire that it seems likely that they may even lose their house to pay his debts.

"He had such great hope that this war would bring great profits," she says. "So many others have made a lifetime's worth of money. I never thought we'd lose everything."

The capture of *Resolution* was a significant loss. It meant profits were not coming in and now the significant investment he put into the ship is not being paid. His attempt to build another vessel only failed when he ran out of money during its building. He sold it off, as well as the rest of his business to repay his debts.

"He's a broken man," says Maddie. "I worry about him so. He had such great dreams of being successful and providing for us all. He was going to be one of the pillars of the community. Now he has nothing."

Faith feels sorrow for her friend. She sees the worry for her husband and understands the fear that Maddie has for herself.

"He isn't left with nothing," says Faith. "He has you and the boys."

Maddie acknowledges the point. She realizes that she and their sons should be what matters most to George. But she also knows he is burdened by a great sense of failure, not only as a businessman but also as a husband and father.

Selling off their house will likely mean a lengthier stay in Eli's home.

"We hope it isn't for long," she says. "We will likely seek long-term shelter with his family. His parents may allow for us to live with them outside of Boston. It may be our best solution as we sell and relocate our possessions."

All of them living in Eli's house has been a good arrangement. Though it can be awkward around George, he has been so preoccupied with the war, business, and his failures, that he's hardly been an issue. Having both Faith and Maddie there to care for the boys has been beneficial to all the boys as well as the two women.

The war has been a struggle for many a family. The loss of life has been great, but so has the damage to family finances. Many still feel the strain as the war continues.

The British have vacated Philadelphia, but have relocated to New Jersey and have cleared much of the Continental Army from Rhode Island. The war is making its way farther south it seems, yet it still has its impact close to home.

More men and boys have left to join the fight. Businesses have closed. Faith's own work has suffered. People have less money to hire her and less need for her seamstress work. Even the church has struggled. Her father has regular services that are full, but little money is coming in.

Those who are financing the war are profiting, but so few others are seeing any benefits from the conflict.

It only makes Faith more concerned for her future with the boys. She doesn't face the debt that so many do, but with little to no money coming in, she knows drastic measures may be needed at some point as the conflict drags on. She knows selling off Eli's boat and wharf would be one solution. She's had offers for it but could not go so far as to sell it. She knows she may not have a choice. The selling of the house would be an act of desperation, but one that conceivably could happen, she fears.

She tries not to worry about such things, but can't help herself. She's a caretaker of Eli's home and family. The thought of failing to care for either terrifies her. And with George in such financial trouble, how soon might he suggest that Eli's boat and wharf be sold off, much like he has already been forced to do?

Faith sees a sad and distraught woman in Maddie. She is almost as broken as her husband, who is wallowing in his failure. The discussion has proven too much for Maddie. She rises from her seat and gives Faith a hug before leaving the house to walk away her sorrows.

Faith feels fortunate that by the grace of God she isn't suffering such a fate, but she knows life changes in cruel twists, without warning.

She sits back on the sofa and breaks down in tears. She feels such a weight and such a fear. She knows she accepted a heavy burden, but she increasingly wonders whether it is one she can truly embrace. It scares her, but she also knows she has no choice.

As she sits quietly and sobs to herself, the boys peek into the room and notice that Maddie has left. They see Faith consumed by sorrow and can feel her heart aching.

Joseph and Eligood leave their books on the table and rush in from the porch.

"What is the matter, Momma?" asks Joseph.

They enter the room and sit beside her on the sofa. She tries to wipe away her tears and hide her emotions. She knows it is of little use.

"There is no need to cry," says Eligood.

She suddenly feels the comfort of the boys. She wraps her arms around them. They lean into her and create one large embrace.

"I'm so thankful for you boys," she says. "You are my most prized possessions."

The boys hold her tight. Their lives and fates are as interwined as their arms around each other.

"We are the blessed ones," says Eligood.

CHAPTER FORTY-NINE
Aboard HMS *Thunder*, 1779

It has been a few days since Eli recognized Garrett Brown, now dressed in the red royalty of the British. It is a sight that still burns at his own loyalty. He can't help but wonder what the young man's father, Atkinson Brown, might think of his boy trading in his allegiance to revolution for a reasonably safe berth on a British prison ship.

It happens quite often, Eli acknowledges. Many a young sailor has been captured by the British and forced or voluntarily switched loyalties. Sometimes their loyalties don't truly change, but saving their own hides dictates their allegiance.

He wonders if something has happened to Brown. Maybe the British learned he was familiar with one of the prisoners. Maybe he's just protecting himself by staying away. Maybe he's told his superiors everything he knows about Eli. Whatever the scenario, there's still no hint of what is happening or where the ship is bound.

"It feels like we've anchored somewhere," says Mosely.

The ship has been on the move steadily since leaving Nova Scotia. Despite being locked away deep inside the hull, the ship and crew typically make enough noise to reveal that the ship is under sail and making headway toward some destination.

"Maybe we've arrived," said Eli. "Maybe an exchange is looming."

They've tried not to dwell on the idea of gaining freedom. They're fully aware that such a trade may not be imminent, but the thought of being set free and returned home is too enticing an option for them to not consider. Just the optimism of such a possibility lifts their spirits.

"The waiting is tedious," says Montsweag. "Especially when we don't know for which we wait."

What little light has seeped below decks to their cell is dwindling. It's a sign that the day is drawing to a close; nightfall is setting in. It also means for a long, dark existence ahead. The prisoners are often brought food and then left in the darkness until some small rays of morning lessen the dreariness.

The damp cell can go from stifling hot when men are jam-packed in the steamy confines of the ship's bowels. But its leaky walls and timbers above can make it chilly, as well. The almost constant darkness makes it feel even more extreme, and the mind seeks to cope with such miserable surroundings.

At this time of day, every approaching footstep might mean food being delivered. But the only movement they hear is topside as the crew scrambles to do whatever tasks are required.

When they do hear the approaching sound of boots on the nearby wooden planking, they not only anxiously await the food but also the brief warmth of light that comes with the opening of the door. Sometimes it is almost blinding, if the sun hasn't already set.

Sometimes the prisoners are so adrift in their own thoughts, they don't hear the approaching guard and are startled to attention only at the tumbling of the locks that signal the door opening.

"Here comes somebody," Montsweag says as he hears the footsteps getting closer.

They hear the jingling of keys and the echo of the locks being turned. The door opens slowly and the tray is set on the floor before them.

It is Garrett Brown who brings them the food.

"We thought something had happened to you," says Eli, glad to see that Brown isn't harmed.

Brown looks around behind to see that there is no other British officer within earshot.

"We're back in the colonies," he explains. "We're anchored. Looks like not far from Portsmouth. I can see the mouth of the river."

The prisoners are excited at the news. It seems as though they're being returned home. An exchange very well might be imminent. They grab their bowls of food, glad to eat the bland porridge they've endured for days.

"Tell us, Garrett," begins Eli, more interested in answers than feeding his appetite. "Are we being exchanged for other prisoners? When will it happen?"

Brown looks at Eli in surprise. He's startled by the prisoners' misconception, and reluctant to tell them the truth.

"There is no prisoner exchange," he says. "I've been told we're headed for New York. The war is over. Britain has crushed the revolution. You are being taken there for execution."

The hungry slurping of food ceases. The prisoners in the cell sit motionless. Eli is stunned, as are his men.

Brown backs away from the open door and swings it shut. He looks back in through the iron bars.

"I'm sorry," he says as he walks away.

Eli remains in stunned silence. He can't quite get over the heartbreak of knowing that instead of going home, he's going to his death.

The silence in the cell is disturbing, a deafening absence of sound as the men contemplate their imminent demise. Eli hears nothing, not even the locks clicking to shut the door.

CHAPTER FIFTY
Aboard the HMS *Thunder*, 1779

The night has increased in darkness and in anticipation.

It has been hours since dinner was delivered. It is impossible to tell just how long it has been. But as the darkness has set in below deck and the quiet of the ship has followed, the evening has progressed into night.

This is the time Eli has been waiting for. He nudges Mosely, who is slumped over beside him. He reaches across and pokes Montsweag as well. They both perk up and glance at Eli.

"It's time," he tells them.

Both look perplexed. "Time for what?" Mosely asks, speaking louder than a whisper, which prompts Eli to glare at him.

Eli raises a finger to his lips and offers a quiet, "Shhh." He looks around the cell to see who else might be awake. He leans in closer to his two friends.

"Time to escape," he says softly.

Both look surprised. They'd both likely ask audibly if Eli has lost his mind, but don't want to make any noise. They just look at Eli with wonder.

"This is the only chance we may get," he says.

Mosely looks around the cell and can't help but point out the obvious. "Escape? From a locked cell? How?"

Before either Mosely and Montsweag can say anything, Eli begins to move. He crawls toward the door, trying not to wake any other prisoners and also hoping to avoid arousing the attention of any guards.

"Let's go," he says quietly, looking back at his confused cellmates.

He gently pushes on the cell door. It doesn't move. He reaches up and slides the latch up. The click of the latch echoes in the quiet night, but when he pushes on the door again, it slowly opens.

He looks back at Mosely and Montseag and smiles. They look on in amazement. They quickly begin crawling behind Eli.

As the door swings open, it creaks loudly. Eli is sure it will awaken some guard nearby. After all three men scramble out of the cell and close the door again, they pause for a moment. They listen for movement. There are the usual sounds of the night, voices from topside, the creaking of the ship, but nothing that sounds like a sentry has been alerted.

They slowly approach the companionway that leads topside. Again, they pause to listen. When all sounds quiet enough, Eli, Mosely, and Montsweag continue upward. With every step comes a faint creak of the planks, but it prompts no alert and no reaction from the British crew.

Eli's escape plan doesn't have much strategy at all. He hopes to sneak topside under the cover of darkness. The chance to sneak overboard is the goal. Eli doesn't even know how feasible a plan it may be. They could reach their destination only to find an army of guards awaiting them with muskets and bayonets at the ready.

Eli realizes they don't have a lot of choice; this might be the only chance they have.

The slats of the companionway creak with their steps, but light and quick movement limits the noise. The second level of the vessel has sailor's quarters. Many are asleep, but others are on watch or still awake. A gathering of soldiers can be heard, their conversation and laughter overwhelming whatever noise is made by the movement of prisoners.

They quickly ascend to the second tier and stealthily move up the next companionway, which takes them topside. Eli peers out from the opening. A few guards are pacing on watch. They are all forward; nobody seems to be back aft.

Eli signals to the men behind him that it is time to move. He quickly emerges from the companionway and scurries back aft into the darker shadows of the quarterdeck. Mosely and Montsweag follow one at a time.

Their movement has gone undetected. While most of the guards are forward of the vessel, the time is right for their escape. Eli makes the first rush for the gunwale. Dashing for the security of the aft deck, he quietly scurries up the steps and races to the darkened corner to the left of the wheel. He's a bit surprised that nobody is at watch, but knows he'd have no chance if there were.

He leans against the rail and slides his body over as if he is part of it. As he goes over the other side, he holds on and extends his body lengthwise. He tries to lower himself as best he can but ultimately just lets go and tries to make a compact splash into the water.

While he is headed over the rail, Mosely rushes into position behind him, ready to follow. When he hears Eli hit the water, he wastes no time in seeing whether the sound has aroused any suspicion. He is up and over the gunwale himself and into the icy waters in a matter of moments.

Montsweag hesitates, however. The splashes, he fears, might alarm the guard, but they seem to be oblivious to it. He rises from his crouch and makes a run back aft. With his potential freedom in sight and his body full of excitement, his weary legs can't match the movement of his mind. His foot catches one of the steps as he darts back aft. It trips him up and sends him falling forward in a heap. Between his heavy thud on the floor and the "Oomph" from the exhale as his body lands hard, the guards hear the sound and quickly respond.

"Stop!" one of the guards shouts.

The others move aft. Some aim their rifles. Others draw their pistols. Montsweag sees them in pursuit. He gets up off the deck, frozen with panic, and then he makes a last desperate effort. He races for the nearest rail and jumps. He plummets and splashes awkwardly, but he is free.

He sees no signs of Eli and Mosely. Both have likely started the long swim to shore. Dazed and disoriented in the chilly water, Montsweag begins his own swim toward the faint light he sees in the distance.

On board the vessel, guards rush into action. When some reach the rail with their weapons aimed at the water, they can see little to shoot at. When one spots Montsweag's movement in the water, he opens fire.

His shot misses. So does that of another British guard. But the musket shots bring more officers to the deck. A pair of longboats are lowered into the water. Both are filled with armed British guards in hot pursuit.

They begin rowing hard in hopes of cutting the distance between them and the prisoners. One of the soldiers spots movement in the water ahead. He draws his pistol and fires.

The sound of agony can be heard in the quiet of the night. Montsweag is struck in the leg and struggles to swim. His progress is hampered and his hopes of getting away decrease with each heavy stroke by the rowers in the longboats.

He continues to slice his way through the water with the kick of one leg and the pull of his arms, but the weariness catches up with him. So does the longboat.

As hard as he swims, the British pull alongside him. With a pistol firmly aimed at his head, he realizes he has no chance of escape. He stops his swim and reaches for the longboat. Two British soldiers reach down and haul him aboard.

Montsweag lands on the floor of the longboat in a weary and wet heap. He takes a whack across the back of the head with the butt of a pistol for good measure, leaving him crumpled and captured, mourning his brief taste of freedom.

The rowing begins again. The longboat returns to the vessel, bringing a tired and bleeding Montsweag back to captivity.

CHAPTER FIFTY-ONE
Aboard the HMS *Thunder* 1779

A s Montsweag makes his way up the side of the vessel, his leg bleeds and aches from his wound. It was only a glancing blow. A bandage and some healing might be all it needs.

Still, it stings fiercely. Even more painful is his return to the *Thunder*. Only a lengthy swim away from safety, his escape attempt has failed. Not only is he a captive again and the brief feeling of freedom is gone, he now faces an even more uncertain fate.

When back on the deck, his hands and feet are bound. He's made to kneel, his bleeding leg pressed hard against the deck boards. He winces in pain, but takes a deep breath and sighs.

Still a bit dazed and full of adrenaline from the excitement, he kneels there trying to clear his head and settle in to his new circumstances. He hears commotion topside and wonders whether Eli and Mosely have been recaptured, too.

Then, he hears the hard steps of boots stalking across the deck. He senses a figure approaching behind and then watches a man pass along his left side. He's a tall imposing figure, especially with Montsweag bound and on his knees. Montsweag looks up to see the stare of a British captain, full of anger.

Kane looks down at Montsweag with contempt. Having been awoken from his sleep, he is even more infuriated than he'd normally be. He's also enraged that he had three prisoners escape under the noses of his crew.

"Where are the others?" he asks.

Montsweag is relieved at the question. It means Eli and Skandar must have gotten away. He knows he can answer the question honestly.

"I don't know," he replies.

Kane isn't satisfied with the response. He draws his pistol and aims it directly at Montsweag's face.

"I said, where are the others?" he repeats.

Montsweag fully knows his answer could be greeted with a pistol shot to his head then and there. But he knows no other answer to give.

"They got away before me," he says. "I lost them."

Kane lowers his pistol slightly and gazes intently into the eyes of his prisoner.

"Look at him, who has already helped them escape," says Kane. With his pistol aimed at Montsweag's chest, he points with his other hand toward the yardarm up forward.

Montsweag strains to turn his head to see. He sees a lifeless body hanging, swinging from a noose. It is Garrett Brown.

"If you don't want to be next, tell me where they are and where they are going?"

Montsweag's body begins to shake. "I know they were swimming to shore," he replies. "Where they were going, I don't know. We don't even know where we are."

Kane smiles back at Montsweag. He seems convinced that his prisoner has no further information. He lowers the pistol and holds it there for a moment. He then slips it back into its holster. Montsweag feels relief that Kane isn't going to shoot him there on the spot.

Kane turns for a moment as if walking away. But then in the glimmer of moonlight, the shimmer of Kane's blade whips around as the captain spins with a mighty swing. The guards standing beside Montsweag desperately step backward to be out of the way. Montsweag only sees the blur of light and Kane's movement before the sword makes a clean cut.

Montsweag's body slumps over and hits the floor while his head rolls forward, stopping just at Kane's feet.

Kane slips his sword back into place. He looks at his guards, somewhat surprised themselves at what just occurred.

"Take care of the bodies," he says. "Find the other two prisoners."

CHAPTER FIFTY-TWO
Portsmouth, New Hampshire, 1779

The once-expansive and blossoming garden is now a lesser version of itself. What hasn't been overtaken by the growing number of graves in the adjacent cemetery has been consumed by the early frosts of the season.

Faith has had little time to tend to the garden recently. It has been overrun by weeds and weather, as well as desperate people helping themselves to whatever they can scrounge.

She's never seen the garden in such a state of neglect. It saddens her. She feels the guilt of letting it go, but knows she's had little choice. Life just gets in the way sometimes.

She's hoping to find a few crops still worth picking and perhaps some plants worth saving and relocating. She might even try and grow some in the house in hopes of replanting them in the spring.

She fully expects there to be no room for a garden at the church by the time spring comes around.

As she works diligently through the plants and weeds, she notices her father arriving to the church. She waves and he approaches to observe her work.

"This garden has seen better days," he says. "I wish I had more time to tend to it. It is so easy to take such growth for granted. We get so preoccupied with other things, we neglect such responsibilities."

Faith pauses for a moment and looks over the plot of land. She remembers when it was full of green leafy plants, full of life. She's so disappointed to see it in such a state now. It makes her just want to leave it for good and let it wither away. But she knows she can't.

"Your mother would be so proud of all that you have done for this garden," says the pastor. "This was something she truly loved. Your care for it has meant a great deal to me, as it would to her."

Faith is glad to hear that, but it also makes her feel worse for letting it be reduced to such a state. Fully expecting it to be gone by spring only makes her feel worse, though she knows there's little she can do to prevent it from being overrun by the growing cemetery.

Pastor Hamilton walks over and gives his daughter a hug. He holds her close for a moment as he feels the sadness in her heart.

"Sometimes all we can do in life is plant the seeds, work our hardest, and have faith that the harvest will come," he says. "Having faith is like being a farmer. You trust in your diligence and in the results that will follow. If you work hard and do those things you need to do, you will reap what you sow."

He stands with his arm around his daughter. They look out over the garden and think about the glorious life it once had.

"This garden was a sign of great beauty and a source of great love," he says. "But sometimes love moves on. It is needed elsewhere. So, we take that love and begin growing new and wondrous things. And we have faith that our work and dedication will bear something bountiful."

He acknowledges how important the garden was after the passing of his wife. It was a great source of his attention and that of Faith's. It was a means of coping with their grief and carrying on what his wife loved.

"What she began here wasn't about vegetables," he says. "It was her way of making something beautiful and seeking a way to help others. She nursed it and made it grow. With it, her love grew and was shared through the community."

He pauses for a moment and smiles at the thought. He recalls his wife and the love and pride he had for her. It is so much greater than the grief that still lingers from her passing.

"You didn't just carry this garden forward," he adds. "You continued that expression of her love. You continued to nurture it and share it."

"But now there is nothing left," says a tearful Faith, feeling the grief from the loss of her mother as well as the garden. Her father thinks about his own grief. He tells his daughter how he felt when his wife died. She had been too young and too vibrant to be lost. She was too loved and too special to him to be taken away. "At first, I didn't want to continue the garden," he recalls painfully. "I didn't even want to continue the ministry.

I began thinking of running away somehow. I wanted to seek a new life, do something different. I just wanted to get away from my pain."

He explains that he couldn't do that. He had two young daughters. He had a responsibility to them. It helped him realize he had a responsibility to his wife, as well, and even to the ministry. God had called him there. He couldn't abandon it all, especially when he'd advise his parishioners against doing such a thing.

"I knew I had to carry my love of your mother forward," he says. "She had blessed my life in so many ways. I needed to take that with me, nurture it and share it with the world. Doing that began with you and your sister."

As he holds his daughter close, he feels the love and joy that he shared with his wife. It is as strong as ever, and he feels the same abundance of love for his daughter.

"Love doesn't go away," he says. "We hold it in our hearts and find new ways to share it. As our lives evolve, the places in which we need to show our love grow with it. We must carry that love to different places and express it in different ways."

He steps forward and leans down to pull a carrot out of the ground. It is a small one. He holds it up. He wipes it clean of the dirt around it.

"This carrot likely wouldn't have lasted the winter," he says. "All of this won't last. But the love you put into it and the passion that kept it going still exists. It just has a new garden to grow."

He looks at his daughter and smiles. She returns an appreciative glance and grabs her father for an intense hug.

It makes her feel better, not only about the garden but about her place in her life. Filling the role of others doesn't seem so burdensome any longer.

As she pulls away, her father looks at her and holds out his hand.

"Want a bite?" he says, offering the carrot.

She just laughs and declines. Her father pats her on the shoulder as he begins to walk toward the church. She hears the snap of him biting into the carrot.

"Mmm," he says with satisfaction. "Good carrot."

CHAPTER FIFTY-THREE
Atlantic Ocean, 1779

There's only a flicker of light on the horizon, but it is enough for Eli to navigate by.

He flails one desperate arm ahead of the other while his feet kick frantically to propel him in the cold ocean waters.

The frigid waters were enough to elicit a shriek of pain when he was first immersed, yet he kept it muffled. As he's continued to swim, the activity has warmed his body but the exertion is wearing him down.

He can't tell how much longer he has till he reaches shore. He just knows he must keep swimming. The splash of water around him limits what he can hear. He can't even tell that Mosely is a few yards away from him.

Both are pressing on, knowing full well that a longboat could be in pursuit. Eli has been tempted to stop and listen, but knows he must continue forward. His freedom is before him now. If the British catch up to him, he'll know it quick enough.

With the waves washing over him, it is difficult to see. He navigates by the sparkle of light ahead and keeps a steady course for it. He feels a drag in his arms and weariness in his legs, but knows he can't stop.

For a moment, he thinks of his father, washed away and desperately staying above water until the inevitable consumed him. It's the same fate Eli would have had if he'd tried to save him.

He's never liked swimming since then, and has always feared the idea of drowning. And yet, he always assumed that it would be how he would die.

As much as he tries to remove such thoughts from his mind, they seem to help. Whether it be fear or determination, he summons every bit of energy he has to pull him closer to shore. There are moments he wonders whether he can make it, but keeps pressing on despite his fatigue.

When his quick glance forward reveals more light ahead than ever, he knows his destination is close. His strokes take every last ounce of energy. But he's a bit revitalized as he feels himself getting closer. Before he knows it, he's close enough to shore to set foot on the ocean floor.

He feels rocks and sand beneath him. He stumbles, tripping on the uneven surface, and struggles to find the strength and balance to stand again. When he does and finds the water just up to his chest, he's able to look about. There, standing just twenty-five feet away, is Mosely.

Both men try to speak, but are out of breath. They can barely see the exhausted smiles on each other's faces. They continue to wade through the water until they emerge from the ocean blue, only to feel the sudden chill of the night air. It prompts immediate shivering from both as they each step out of the water and onto the sandy beach. They grab each other and hug at their freedom.

They look out over the dark ocean to see or hear whether Montsweag is close behind. There is no sign of him.

Instead, the quiet of the night reveals the sounds of the longboats coming. The creak of the oars and the splashing of their movement warn of their close proximity.

"We've got to keep moving," says a shivering Mosely.

Eli glances around the shoreline. It's a small sandy beach with some scattered rocks. A few houses lie at the top, but they're all dark. He has no idea where they are, but there's a sense of familiarity about it.

He believes this patch of sand and beach is just around the shoreline from the larger beach he has walked regularly for years. The area all looks different in the darkness of night.

"We might be best off if we separate, my friend," he says.

He doesn't know how many soldiers are in pursuit. But if they go opposite directions, there's a better chance at least one of them will escape.

Mosely agrees. That means there's little time to linger.

"Take care, Captain," he says to Eli.

They give a parting hug, knowing they've been through a great ordeal together and thankful for this chance to escape. But neither knows of the other's fate.

"Be safe," says Eli.

The two men part. Mosely immediately turns and runs up the beach, disappearing into the darkness.

Eli looks back out to the ocean. No sign of Montsweag. He can't help but fear for his friend. The sound of the longboats is closer. He knows he must hasten his escape.

He sees Mosely's footprints in the sand leading away from the beach. So, he steps back into the water and runs along the waterline. It is hard slogging through with his tired legs, but at least he leaves no trail. He reaches a part of the beach to the far right where ledges and rocks are at the water's edge.

He steps out of the sea and onto a ledge, then scampers his way up the beach, stepping only across what stones he can and leaving little trace of himself behind.

He reaches the top of the beach. There are houses and fishing shacks along the shore, but none look occupied. The glow of light comes from further inland. That's the direction he must take.

He glances back to the beach one last time. He sees nothing of Mosely and nothing of Montsweag. What he does see is a British long-boat hitting the sand, British troops jumping ashore.

CHAPTER FIFTY-FOUR
Portsmouth, New Hampshire, 1779

With each step, Eli feels a little stronger on his feet and closer to his freedom.

His body still shakes from the night air chilling his soaked body. He knows he needs to find shelter and get warm.

He doesn't know where he is, but the houses and roads begin to look familiar. His guess is that he's in a little town that settled at the mouth of the river. It's a short ways from the harbor, but sits just southwest of it.

He tries to recall someone he might know who lives in these parts, but can't think of anyone. The only person he knew with a home anywhere close to here was Ezra Budwick.

Ezra had a small home and wharf here. Who knows what has happened to it now? Someone else might own it. Eli is not even sure he can find it. It's been a few years since he's been anywhere near here.

He skulks through the streets, staying in the darkness. There's very little sign of life, but he expects sunrise will change that. He just doesn't know how soon it will come.

His only hope is to find some helpful stranger who might be awake and willing to hide him, or at least point him in the right direction. But there's no one like that out on the streets at this hour. Eli is not sure someone would be willing to help a water-logged stranger like himself in this condition.

His name might mean something to some, but he also realizes that it has been a long time. His weariness is catching up to him, leaving him stumbling and disoriented. He stops and sits on a block of wood tucked out of sight. He could curl up and sleep for days. He also knows he could be awoken by a bayonet pointed at him.

As he rests momentarily, he can hear the sounds from down the road. It is a primary road with a few houses along each side. A few roads branch off from it. It makes it difficult to disappear into the town when there isn't a whole lot of town to hide away in.

He gets up and peeks around the corner of an abandoned building he is hiding behind. He can see two British soldiers, one on each side of the street, progressing up the row of buildings. They're glancing at every space and place to hide along the way, surely looking for any sign of their escaped prisoners.

That spurs Eli back into motion. He ducks into the shadows and detours around a building or two. He returns to the main road further ahead of the soldiers and moves at a quickened pace in the darkness.

As he continues, the town expands and the roads branch off in greater number. There are more houses and buildings. He hopes this will give him greater opportunity to sneak away from his pursuers for good.

He unexpectedly sees a street that looks familiar, though Eli doesn't quite know why. He follows it down, hoping to come across a house he knows. He fails. In fact, he reaches a dead end. It forces him back out onto the primary road. As he continues up the road and away from the shore, he can see the British soldiers coming his way.

Before he has a chance to duck and hide, one of the soldiers spots him. They both take off running in his direction with their guns pointed. Eli sees no recourse but to run himself.

His legs are tired and he knows he doesn't have much energy, let alone strength to carry him much further. As he darts up the road, he quickly tries to cut in and out around different houses, looking for a place to hide or escape through.

When he steps out onto another side street and looks over his options, he sees a dark, old battered house at the end of the street. It is Ezra's house. He's sure of it. It still looks as ramshackle as ever, especially in comparison to those around it.

He glances around hastily to see if the soldiers are close enough to see him. He doesn't spot them nearby. So, he dashes quickly toward the house that looks not much different than he remembers it. He questions whether anyone has even been in it since Ezra was killed. He had no family or children.

Eli reaches the door, uncertain whether it is locked. Could someone be inside? Ezra never locked doors. He always said if someone was dumb enough to come into his house, they better be prepared for a welcome of guns blazing.

Sure enough, the door is unlocked. Eli opens it, slips inside, and closes it tightly. He secures the lock and even moves a table to barricade the door.

He then ducks down in the dark corner of the room and sits silently. He waits anxiously, hoping the soldiers have lost sight of him and will keep on their way. He figures he can sleep inside here for a while in the hope that the search is called off or moved elsewhere.

He takes a few deep breaths to try to relax. He huddles himself up in hopes of keeping warm. He finds a rug on the floor to wrap himself in.

His movement ceases quickly when he hears voices outside.

"In here?" he hears someone say.

He doesn't hear the response, but hears the front door rattle. It stays secure. All is silent for a moment. Then, he hears a sizeable crashing sound. A soldier bursts through the door and the push from the other makes it open that much more. The table Eli had set in front of it proved to be a mere nuisance. The two soldiers storm the entrance and force the door open enough to shove the table out of the way.

They both step inside. Though dark, the little bit of light coming in off the street and through the door illuminates things in the room just slightly.

As they peruse the room, one of them spots Eli cowering in the corner.

In an instant, two guns with bayonets attached are pointed at him.

Eli has vowed that he will never be taken alive and returned to that ship. It seems obvious to him that he would just be executed eventually anyway.

So, now his option is to find an opportunity to escape or die trying.

"We're taking you back to the ship, dead or alive," says one of the soldiers. "Your choice."

Eli slowly gets up from the floor, his body stiff. He tosses aside the rug. He stands there hesitantly, unsure whether he should rush the soldiers now or try to find some means of escape later.

"Let's go," says one of the guards.

Eli doesn't move. He still mulls over his options, wondering if this is his best chance or just the right moment to die and get it over with.

"Now!" shouts a frustrated and impatient guard.

Eli still doesn't move. He is about to, reluctantly, when he is distracted by something. It's a subtle smell. He can't identify it, but it seems familiar.

Suddenly, there's a creaking of the stairs to his right. Eli has been up there before, but it was years ago.

He hears the sound again. Then, a flurry of creaks and groans from the wood are accompanied by a pistol shot. The flash and the noise create confusion. When the smoke clears, one of the British soldiers is dead on the floor. The other soldier is just as surprised. Before he can turn and offer a volley of his own, another pistol shot rings out. The other soldier is knocked backward and onto the floor, bleeding profusely from his chest.

And there standing on the stairway, with two smoking pistols in his hands, is Ezra Budwick.

Eli can't believe his eyes. Or his nose. It was the whiff of Budwick's musty old clothes, a distinctive smell that always accompanied his friend. Eli stands there as speechless as he is stunned.

"Lucky for you I only got two pistols," Budwick says as he descends the stairs.

As he reaches the bottom step and gets a closer look at Eli, he realizes who he is.

"Godfrey mighty, is that you, Eli Miller?" he asks. "What the hell are you doing here? And why you bringing two Redcoats in here with ya?"

Eli still doesn't know what to say. Budwick simply stands there, perplexed.

"I thought you were dead," Eli finally says.

Budwick scoffs as he looks over the two soldiers to make sure they are dead and that their guns are secured.

"Do I look dead to you?" Ezra says.

CHAPTER FIFTY-FIVE
Portsmouth, New Hampshire, 1779

In the glow of the faint candlelight and the impending dawn, Eli can see that Ezra looks a little older. His hair and beard are grayer. He looks thinner.

And having believed his friend was dead for a few years, Eli can't help but feel like he's looking at a ghost.

"Quit looking at me like that," barks Budwick.

Eli smiles, embarrassed. He struggles to come to grips with Budwick still being alive.

"How did you escape?" Eli asks. "I heard you were captured, executed, even."

Budwick laughs boisterously at the thought.

He tells Eli that he had been captured and roughed up pretty good. His ship was lost, either set afire or commandeered. He never saw it again. After that, he spent a few months in captivity. Much of his crew died from illness and disease.

"Damn tropicals with their viruses," said Budwick, "Wiped out most of the island."

The illness spread so rapidly that many of his captors became ill, as well. They all started dying off quickly.

"They was so afraid of the fever, they just abandoned everything and everyone," says Budwick.

Budwick and a few survivors were left behind. They snuck away from their captors unnoticed. The captors were too focused on fleeing themselves to pay them any mind. Budwick then had to find transport home.

"We found an abandoned tender," says Budwick. "Me and two others rowed it. It took some hearty work with the oars to get us anywhere, but we got to another island with a small cove. We got transport to another harbor and hitched passage out of there."

"George told me you were dead," explains Eli. "He said you were captured and executed. He even told me they chopped you up and fed you to the hogs."

Budwick chuckles so hard it leads to a coughing fit. "That good for nothing son of a bitch is full of it," he says.

Eli explains Lathrop might have been feeding him false information with the intent of luring him into his privateering adventure. What irks Eli most is that it actually worked.

"I should have known better than to believe what he says," says Eli.

"Well, he ain't talking a whole lot these days," says Budwick.

Budwick explains that Lathrop's shipping business has been ruined. Between the losses from his vessels that were captured or destroyed, he's got very little left. He's sold off whatever remained of his business, including the wharf he had in the harbor. He's since moved out of town.

"His hopes of getting rich during the war didn't go as he planned," says Budwick. "Many have profited from the war but not George."

The reality of being free and being near home suddenly sinks in. Eli realizes his family is not far away.

"What about Faith?" he asks Budwick, fearing some unexpected fate may have befallen them in his absence. "What about the boys?"

"They're all fine," Budwick answers, shaking his head as he glances over the British soldiers bleeding out across his floor. "It ain't been easy on them, but they're all right."

He gets close enough to see Eli in the light. His friend is weary and withered looking.

"Well, look at you," he says. "Looks like you've been to hell and back."

CHAPTER FIFTY-SIX
Aboard the HMS *Thunder*, 1779

Kane storms into his cabin and begins pacing.

It is his way to wind himself down, get control of his emotions. With each pace, his anger lessens. He walks his way from rage to calm and collected. At least that's what Kane thinks, though sometimes it works just the opposite and stirs him up like a pot approaching a boil.

After a few moments, he finds control of himself when he sets himself down. He sits on a chair by a window. It overlooks the stern of the ship. Out there somewhere are his escaped prisoners. Above deck are a dead captive and an executed traitor.

The thought of it all still makes Kane's blood boil. He tries to simmer any frustration rising within.

He pulls out his sword and grabs the cloth he uses to clean it. There is fresh blood still coating the blade. It sticks to the sword like the shame that Kane now feels in his heart. He swipes the cloth over the blade, wiping off the blood. It takes a few attempts to completely clean the steel and restore its shine. He pauses to examine it. He admires the pristine sheen, but also realizes the evil that it possesses. It is a powerful weapon, fueled by anger and rage and wielded with a furious heart.

He acknowledges that he is that man. He doesn't like the realization. He thinks about the execution of his soldier. He was a traitor. He failed in his duty. He warranted discipline. As for the enemy who tried to escape, he was going to be executed anyway. There are two prisoners still at large. They've escaped and are being hunted. Kane hopes they'll be captured and knows he'll have retribution for them.

He slips his blade back into its sheath and then tosses it aside.

There is a conflict between his angry heart and the loving soul he seeks within. Justice can be a hard objective.

He leans forward and places his face into his hands, weary and pained by the life he leads. He feels his sense of duty and his allegiance to it. He is determined to serve it well. Part of him enjoys it: He relishes his command of the law and the opportunity to uphold it. He welcomes the ability to unleash his rage on those who forsake it. He has honor for his role in serving his homeland and its interests. Punishing those so reckless in their actions and disrespectful of the laws is his duty.

That calling drives him. Yet, he feels guilt. He feels he has forsaken his own heart and the person he wants to be. Can he serve both? He finds it increasingly difficult. Each time he tries, he feels he has betrayed one or the other.

His anger subsides. Instead, now he finds himself attempting to suppress tears, consumed by emotion and desperate for release, something to purge his system and cleanse his soul. But a man of his stature just can't let himself break down and cry.

He wipes away a tear or two that slips down his cheek and buries his face in his hands.

Then comes a knock at his door. Before he even has a chance to compose himself completely, Clive Henstridge walks in.

"Captain," he begins, a bit taken back at Kane's state. "One of the longboats has not returned. There's no sign of the men or the prisoners. Shall we deploy more men ashore?"

Kane glances out the window. All he sees is darkness, but he senses a coming dawn. He ponders his options. Should he continue the search, or move on from what has happened?

"Send a unit ashore," he says. "Have them look for the prisoners and the two missing soldiers. They have till mid-morning. Be sure they return in time. Otherwise, we haul out without them."

Henstridge nods in agreement. He slips out of the captain's quarters and closes the door behind him.

Kane rises to his feet and begins pacing again. He looks out the window once more. His prisoners are out there somewhere. There are two missing soldiers, as well. He doesn't like the thought of either.

One betrayal and one moment of inattentiveness has led to this and created more havoc. It infuriates Kane and insults his command.

His vessel will have to leave in the morning. He knows a new day brings a new course. This night will have to be left behind. He looks over at his sword, lying discarded on the floor. He picks it up and attaches it to his waist.

He longs for the capture of those prisoners. He imagines what retribution he might deliver upon their return. And he smiles, a devilish grin, at the thought.

CHAPTER FIFTY-SEVEN
Portsmouth, New Hampshire, 1779

As one step slowly follows the other, Eli's legs weaken. His body is weary after being imprisoned for so long. He could just collapse right here and rest his bones.

But as he looks up the hill, his eyes are filled with a glorious sight. He is almost in disbelief as he stops and fixes his gaze to the end of the road. It is the picture he's had in his memory for years. Now, it comes to life again before him.

His house looks similar to when he left it, though perhaps a little older and a little worse for wear. But it still stands just as it was imprinted on his heart and mind.

As he draws closer, he smiles as he looks at the tree that towers over the front lawn. It was his personal perch as a child. He recalls climbing as high as he'd dare to look down over the town. He'd watch for his father and wonder if he might spot him arriving home.

He remembers once more that glorious time he did see him return, a battered and worn shadow of himself. That was after his father had been captured and held prisoner by the French. Between losing his ship and being held captive, Luke Miller returned home a broken man.

As Eli makes his own walk towards his home, he fears he likely looks even worse than his father did. And his future appears equally bleak. He feels a sense of shame to be returning in such a state, but he is thankful to see his home again. His weariness is overcome by the anticipation in his heart.

He's longed to see his family for ages now. He doesn't even know how long it has been. He's struggled to keep track of the months and even the years. The air felt like fall to him when he first came ashore. The color of the trees confirmed his suspicion that summer has passed and winter is closing in.

As he approaches the front of the house, he sees movement on the porch. He's startled, because he hadn't seen someone there. The figure comes down the steps and stands before him.

A child gazes up at Eli with a puzzled stare, but a sense of familiarity. He squints his eyes just a bit and tilts his head, seemingly looking past the ragged beard and worn face.

"Father?" asks Eligood.

Eli can't believe his eyes. The toddler he left a few years ago has grown into a handsome young boy with Eli's golden blonde hair. His own deep blue eyes stare back at him. His long frame reminds Eli of his own body when he was a boy. He can barely speak at the sight of his son, a small version of himself.

"My beloved Eligood," he says with a voice weakened by emotion. "My, how you've grown into a wonderful young boy."

He steps forward and opens his arms. Eligood rushes to meet him. He's quickly enveloped in the arms of his father. Eli can barely contain his joy and his tears as he holds his son close. How long he has waited for such a moment.

He slowly releases his embrace, hating to let his son slip from his arms. Awkward and unsure of what to say, he is overwhelmed by the pride, love, and joy of seeing his son.

"Where is your brother?" he asks. "And Faith?"

Eligood still appears stunned at the sudden appearance of his father. He mulls over the question for a moment and simply points toward the house. He gives a quick wave of his hand and then rushes up the front steps toward the door.

"Mother!!" he shouts at the top of his lungs. "Joseph!!"

Before Eli can even get to the steps to follow his boy, Eligood has opened the door and rushed inside.

Eli is excited to see his other son and Faith again. His thoughts suddenly are consumed by the long journey he has endured. There were many times he wondered whether he'd ever live to see this moment. He feared he would never have the chance; his hopes to fulfill his promise would never materialize. He had faced the fact and was ready to accept that he had failed once again.

He tried to be faithful. He tried to seek God's plan and will for him. Sometimes it was all he had to cling to, but his fear was a burden that often crushed his faith under its weight.

Now, he stands at the steps of his home. His long journey is nearly complete. His promise is about to be fulfilled.

He falls to his knees, weeping. He tries to get to his feet but just hunches over as his hands prevent a full fall to the ground. He pushes himself up, still resting on his knees. He lowers his head and buries them in his hands. He tries to wipe away his tears, overwhelmed by the blessing he's been given.

There is commotion inside the house. Steps approach and the front door swings open. Out steps Faith, wondering what Eligood is so excited to show her. As she steps out the door, she is amazed at what she sees.

Her legs wobble for a moment. She steps back and places her hand against the house to hold her balance. Her heart beats with joy she feared it would never feel again. Then, she rushes down the steps and throws herself into Eli's arms.

"Eli," she says. "I feared I'd never see you again."

They topple into a heap, wrapped in each other's arms. Joseph scampers down the steps and throws his arms around his father. Eligood does the same, sharing in the excitement of the reunion.

The four of them laugh amidst their tears of joy. Faith simply grabs Eli and holds him tight. She's overwhelmed by the reality of his return.

It is the greatest gift, pure joy and pleasure. A feeling they all feared would elude them. God's gift handed down. The ultimate reward of such tested faith.

"I heard you had been captured," she says, recalling the fear that came with such news. "I feared you would die there."

Eli knows he had the same thoughts, but he also knew he had reason to live. He had faith. Now he is consumed by the love of his family, something he has missed for years and been afraid he would never feel again.

"I promised I'd return," he says. "I promised to marry you."

He lies on his back staring up at the blue skies above. Faith lies to his side with her head on his chest. She holds him close. Her body quivers as she sobs. His dream has been realized. His life feels right. His burden feels lifted, he thinks to himself. He could lie in this moment forever.

CHAPTER FIFTY-EIGHT
Portsmouth, New Hampshire 1779

Eli watches his boys gaze back at him with amazement. He sees not only the awe in their eyes but also the love as they listen intently to the retelling of his experiences.

It is difficult to recall that time spent in prison, especially now that he has escaped it all and returned to the comforts of his home.

He sits in the parlor basking in the coziness of his house and the warmth of his adoring family. The home smells of joy. The aroma of Faith's cooking has filled the rooms and become a heaven for his senses.

It is the most lovely smell he has relished in a long time. The last few years have been filled with death and decay. It all lingered in Eli's mind until Faith's cooking overwhelmed the stench with something beautiful.

The meal she cooks is the grandest collection of food he's ever tasted. Though she just reheats some leftovers and quickly prepares a meal, it is ecstasy to a palate that has tasted nothing but stale rations and gruel for the longest time.

"You've made me want to eat again," Eli says with a mouthful of warm bread smothered in creamy fresh butter. He can't recall the last time he actually ate real food.

Faith is overjoyed at seeing him before her, but also glad to see him eat. He is pale and very thin. He looks as though he's aged twice as many years than the time he's been away.

The boys wait anxiously for him to finish eating and continue with the storytelling. They are engrossed in his tales of chasing down British ships and avoiding capture with a few risky but nifty maneuvers.

As much as he's been informing Faith and the boys about his experiences, they have been updating him on the latest news around home.

George and Maddie have moved outside of Boston. They're living with his brother in hopes that George may recoup his financial losses somehow. Maddie has been working as a teacher while George has settled for a job mending shoes.

"That must be hard for Maddie," says Eli, somewhat relishing the hardship that has befallen George while feeling bad for his sister.

Things haven't quite reached such a financial state in Eli's household, but that time is nearing.

Faith reluctantly informs him that his fishing sloop and wharf have been sold. She had the opportunity to part with it and needed the money.

"I felt I had little choice," she says, still sad about doing so.

Eli understands. He knows how difficult times have been and money has been sparse. Another few months or so and it might have been necessary for Faith to sell the house.

It is distressing for Eli to learn that Faith faced so much hardship in his absence. The financial losses also concern him for the future. He'll have to generate income and he knows the best way for him to do that is to go back to sea.

"We'll figure things out," he says, not having the heart to bring up the subject of leaving again. He's not sure he even wants to think of the idea himself.

As they're gathered together in the parlor enjoying a comfortable day as a family, a sudden hard knock beckons at the door. It startles them all.

Knowing he may still be pursued by the British, both Eli and Faith are concerned about who it might be.

"Eligood," Faith says. "See who it is."

The boy quietly approaches the window and peers out through the curtains. Before he has a chance to inform his parents, another knock raps against the wooden door.

"I ain't no British sentry," comes a loud, raspy voice. "Hurry up and let me in."

Eli laughs as he recognizes Ezra's voice. How he's missed that man, he thinks to himself. He never did have time to truly mourn him when he thought he was gone.

Young Eligood opens the door and Budwick steps inside.

"Something smells good," Budwick says upon entry, hinting at his interest in a bite to eat. Budwick's keen senses have also always allowed him a whiff of any meal that's cooking.

Faith gets up and greets him with a hug and a promise of food. That brings a smile to his weather-worn face.

"The least you can do is feed me," he says. "I've spent the morning cleaning up the mess in my house."

Budwick disposed of the two bodies of the British soldiers he had shot earlier that morning. He dragged the men to a field out behind his home and buried the bodies in the soil there.

"Pretty near took most of my morning," he grumbles, wondering what is holding up the arrival of food.

Faith arrives with a warm plateful. That brings a smile to Budwick's face.

"Like that's the first time you've had to dispose of two bodies you had shot from the night before," Eli says in jest.

Budwick, with a mouthful of bread and a dab of butter on his lips, flashes a devious look with upraised eyebrows.

"You may have a point there," he mumbles between bites.

Faith brings Eli a plate with more food on it as well, seemingly knowing that watching Ezra eat will only make Eli hungry again.

"I actually came by to tell you that that fleet of British ships has moved on," Budwick reports. "Guess they gave up on their own men and decided you weren't worth huntin' down any longer."

That's a relief to Eli, and Faith, too. He has been concerned about how much hiding he would need to do. He has already contemplated the need to relocate somewhere temporarily.

"I hear they've moved on down the coast," Budwick says. "That's the direction the war is moving. I'm thinking we could go chasing them. Get us a fleet of our own. I'll show you my ship."

The idea of jumping aboard another vessel and sailing with Budwick in pursuit of the British doesn't appeal to Eli. He's not even sure if his old friend is serious, but he fears that he might be.

Eli doesn't have to say a word. Faith sits down next to him and wraps her arms around him. She looks at Ezra and offers up her answer.

"He's staying right here," she says with a smile and a serious tone.

Eli is glad for that respite and opportunity to stay put, but he knows it is inevitable that he'll be boarding another ship in pursuit of a living one day soon. It is a moment he doesn't look forward to, but one he surely knows is coming sooner rather than later.

CHAPTER FIFTY-NINE
Aboard the HMS *Thunder*, 1779

Kane stands anxiously just before the aft deck. He paces nervously, blood still staining the boards beneath his feet from the execution of Montsweag just two nights before.

He watches as his men escort five men topside. They appear bedraggled and beaten down. Their time below has worn them significantly.

They shake their heads and shield their eyes as they face the brightness of the sun for the first time in weeks. They grimace as if it is almost painful. Two of them stumble into each other, walking blindly and wearily.

They are paraded toward the aft deck where they face Kane. Still, barely able to see, they are presented to him with no idea why they have been summoned.

"These are the best we could find," says one of the guards.

Kane glances at them. His first thought is that they're certainly not as healthy or formidable looking as the group that escaped. The thought of them getting away only eats at him more as he thinks about it.

He tried to coerce Captain Miller to the side of the British. He would have been a good seaman for the Royal Navy. Recruiting the captain of a privateer from the colonies would have been well received by his superiors.

It still irks him that he couldn't do it. Making it worse is that the man may have escaped. Kane tries to convince himself that he probably drowned. That would have served him right. But he still wonders if he got away.

Perhaps he shouldn't have killed Montsweag. He was a better option than any of these men. Kane could have probably spared Brown's life, as well, and used him.

What's done is done, he says to himself. If they weren't expendable, he wouldn't have disposed of them. Still, he wishes for better options to deliver to his superiors.

His orders are to send these men ashore. They'll be used for some sort of propaganda purposes. They might be swayed to switch sides, or forced into service. They'll likely just be executed, another show of Britain's brutality to strike fear into the locals.

"We recently sent a few of your fellow sailors ashore," says Kane, showing no sign of the blatant lies he's about to tell. "They've all chosen to join England's cause. They've been pressed into new service, assigned new opportunities on other vessels, with some decent pay, I might add."

He studies the faces of the men before him. He doesn't get much of a reaction. He thinks they look skeptical, but even if they believe their fellow prisoners managed to escape overboard, they don't know whether the escapees were captured later.

"We want to give you the same opportunity," he tells the prisoners. "We'll ferry you ashore and hand you off to the commanders there. They'll gladly arrange a new start for you."

The prisoners look puzzled and confused. One of them defiantly speaks up, shaking his fist as he shouts at Kane.

"I will never fight for England," he says. "I'll die in that cell if I have to."

Kane has been expecting such a reaction, and is ready for it. He is also ready with his response.

He nods to his men, who have no idea what their captain is about to do, but know Kane well enough. They step away from the rebellious prisoner. Even his fellow captives follow suit and move away from him, leaving him alone.

Kane swiftly pulls his pistol from its holster. He barely takes a moment to aim before firing a shot into the man's forehead. The prisoner's head snaps back. His body goes limp and crumples to the floor, bouncing slightly off the rail before he lands with a thump on the wooden deck.

Kane looks at his guards and points to the dead prisoner. His crew rushes into action, lifting the man's body and tossing him overboard. As the prisoner splashes into his watery grave, a crew member tosses a bucket of sea water that washes the blood off the deck and through the scuppers.

Kane stands before the remaining prisoners with smoking pistol still in hand. He sees the shock on their faces and the fear in their eyes.

"So, where were we?" he asks with a devilish grin. "We'll be running a tender ashore later. You can either be ferried ashore or you can hope to float there," he tells them.

All four men raise their hands and shyly agree. They look embarrassed and ashamed as they commit themselves. Kane just looks back at them and smiles, victorious. He holsters his pistol and looks toward his crew.

"Take these men to the galley," he says. "Give them a taste of some real food and help them get cleaned up. They'll be leaving us shortly."

The crew rushes the prisoners away while Kane turns and leaves in the other direction. He walks across the aft deck and ducks below.

In his quarters, he pours himself a glass of rum. It is a habit that has taken hold during his time at sea. He sits down and let's go with a sigh of relief. He glances at the cross he has hanging on the wall of his quarters. He can't bear to look at it and turns away. He drops his head as if to pray, but finds himself unable to do so.

He raises the glass and gulps a mouthful of rum. He sets the glass aside and grabs the bottle. The cross attracts his gaze a second time. Kane just stares at it and tips the bottle.

CHAPTER SIXTY
Portsmouth, New Hampshire 1780

Pastor Hamilton appears unusually nervous. He's presided over a multitude of services including quite a few weddings, but he's never been as anxious as he is on this day.

He's playing the part of pastor as well as father as he watches his daughter get married. He has thought of this day, the chance to marry his daughter away to another man. He has wished for such an opportunity, but realizes the trepidation that comes with it. He's nervous about the service and being able to conduct it with his daughter before him with wedding vows on her lips.

He's also struggling with the reality of his daughter starting a life with someone new. It isn't something he didn't see coming. It still is a helpless feeling for him to see her married off, but being the one performing the ceremony makes it that much more difficult.

He watched his other daughter marry and then move away. She lives down in Virginia now, where he hardly sees or hears from her.

The church has a small gathering of friends and family of Faith and Eli, including Faith's distant cousins and uncles. She has various friends in attendance.

George Lathrop and Maddie are here with their boys. George has the appearance of a humbled man. It is hard to say whether it is his business failure that has ruined him or if it is his pride. While Maddie appears cheerful and earnestly excited for her brother, George is disheveled and sullen. Watching Eli wed and continue on with his life in a positive way can't make Lathrop feel better about himself.

Standing among Eli's friends is Budwick. He's dressed nattily with a suit and tie. He's obviously uncomfortable in formal attire. In fact, his suit looks as though it has been resting in a cedar trunk for some time. He twists and contorts his neck as if to create some breathing space between his skin and collar. When that doesn't work, he gives the collar a tug and a grumble in hopes of letting some air and breathing room seep in between.

He likens it to wearing a noose, something Budwick is not unfamiliar with. It seemingly explains why Budwick remains unwed, especially when he likens marriage to an execution.

Eli watches his friend's antics and gets a good chuckle out of them, only to realize watching Ezra makes him feel a bit conspicuous and uncomfortable in formal wear himself. Fortunately for him, he hasn't gained all his weight back quite yet after returning from his time as a prisoner. So, it actually makes his clothes fit loosely on him. Initially, his clothes were far too baggy, but Faith's cooking has filled him out a little more. He's still about twenty pounds under his normal weight.

When Pastor Hamilton gives the nod to organist June Presby, the sanctuary fills with music. That quiets the small crowd and gets Maddie's young boys to stand at attention quite quickly.

The crowd turns their heads to the back of the sanctuary as Eligood and Joseph begin the walk down the center aisle. They approach the front of the church and stand to the side of Pastor Hamilton.

Following them is a beautiful Faith, looking radiant in her wedding dress. She smiles as her eyes meet Eli's. She can't help but break out into a happy girlish giggle as she sees the delighted twinkle in his eye. She's thrilled to see him standing there, living up to his promise. It is one she wondered whether she'd ever see while he was held captive.

As she walks down the aisle under the gaze of friends and family, Faith relishes the moment, the powerful sound of the music, the smiles on the faces and the joy in her heart. For all that fear and worry, she finally feels blessed by the happiness she has sought. She sees it in Eli as well.

As she reaches the front of the church, she takes her place beside Eli. They pause for a moment to glance at each other and smile before turning to face Pastor Hamilton.

It feels awkward for Faith to look at her father now. She's seen him conduct many a service and thought nothing of it, but now her father is the pastor standing before them. She's pleased to see him there and is excited to have him marry her.

As he begins to speak, he chokes back a tear. He tries to hide his emotion and clears his throat. Budwick helps his cause by deciding it might be an appropriate time to clear his own, but Budwick does so in a slightly more obvious way, enough to lure attention away from Pastor Hamilton.

"I want to share a story of love's extravagance," begins the pastor.

He tells the story of Jesus being a guest in the home of Mary, Martha, and Lazarus. Martha was in charge of the serving in the kitchen. On impulse, she broke open an expensive ointment and anointed the feet of Jesus.

"Judas recoiled in surprise and criticized Martha for being so wasteful," the pastor says. "Selling that perfume could have raised funds to give to the poor, Judas said.

"Jesus corrected Judas, saying that what Martha had done was an expression of love. 'She has done a beautiful thing. Let her keep the remainder for my burial,' Jesus said. His point was that such love is never wasted.

"Simple gifts of loving and caring often carry a meaning that goes far beyond the event itself," the pastor continues. "Jesus needed a healing touch to help refresh him for the last steps of his Holy Week journey."

He explains that love doesn't solely exist in the large gestures and extravagance. The true power of love is in the devotion and commitment to carry it forward.

"There is a time and place for the impulsive gift, but the real mission of Christ is accomplished by the ongoing and continual giving of ourselves day after day, week after week," the pastor says. "It is the serving in the kitchen kind of continuous expression of love and caring that counts most. This is much harder than the impulsive, occasional show of devotion."

The pastor looks at Faith and Eli. He notes their time apart and their continuous devotion for each other, even amidst the hardships of war and distance.

Though the day-to-day commitment to one's love is vital, the pastor says that it can't exist alone. There is the devotion and continuing parts of love, but the passion of impulsive giving must join with the intentional giving in expressing our genuine love.

"Love continues to give because love is giving," says the pastor.

With those words, Eli looks at Faith and thinks about all he's struggled with in order to reach this moment. It was a promise he vowed and one he was able to deliver. He feels blessed himself to feel such joy and contentment, in addition to achieving this moment he had promised.

As he looks into his love's eyes, he feels her commitment to him and is thrilled about their future. Still, he feels a twinge of fear, fully knowing that a time at sea appears inevitable.

Budwick is preparing to haul out in a few months. He's already brought Skandar Mosely aboard. Eli's former mate made a safe escape that morning when he and Eli parted. Mosely came across a fisherman who had just arrived at his wharf, not too far from the beach. He took Mosely in and hid him for a day, until he saw that the British fleet moved on. The fisherman happened to be friends with Budwick. He introduced the two, and helped Mosely and Eli reconnect.

Eli hasn't given a final commitment to the journey, but knows financially, it is an opportunity he can't let pass. The idea of telling Faith and leaving the boys again pains him deeply. So much so that he's hesitated mentioning it, hoping some other recourse will appear.

As he loses himself in the grandeur of Faith's beauty, he is overwhelmed by his love for her and the fulfillment that has finally returned to his heart.

He takes her face in his hands. Her cheeks are warm against his palms. He leans in and kisses her, overwhelmed by the strength of their bond and their kindred hearts.

He pulls his lips away slowly, savoring that moment. She looks at him and smiles.

"I love you," he whispers to her.

Her eyes sparkle and she fights to contain a slight giggle as a response. She just beams with an approving grin.

"I love you, too," she says.

She leans in and kisses him.

As she pulls away, she leans toward his ear and whispers.

"So much so, I know I have to let you go again," she says. "But my love will be here upon your return. That's my promise."

CHAPTER SIXTY-ONE
Aboard the *Wicked*, 1780

Eli gazes around the harbor with awe. It has been a great while since he has sailed in these parts. He searches his mind for recollection of his last anchorage here, but he can't recall. Too much has passed since then. Too much clutter has buried many of the thoughts that existed prior to the war.

From his vantage point aboard the *Wicked*, life seems the same. They've sailed up from the Caribbean and stocked up on cargo. They arrived in New York and unloaded, replacing the cargo with more items to transport.

The vessel is named *Wicked* as a play on Budwick's name. It was his idea. He thinks it humorous, even though nobody else seems to get the joke.

Life aboard ship feels no different. New York looks no different to Eli, either. There's a constant flow of vessels coming in and out. Some are of British origin, some of French, and some from the colonies.

After the British left the Boston blockade, they moved south to commandeer New York City. That proved a challenge, as the Continental Army continued to secure positions in New Jersey and Pennsylvania. As time went on, the supply lines for the British in New York dwindled. It made it difficult for General Howe to maintain his presence there, especially with the war slipping away further south. Eventually, Howe retreated from New York harbor, leaving the fight for the state in General Burgoyne's hands. He didn't succeed, either.

Burgoyne's failure opened the harbor up again to the merchants, though it is uncertain how safe it might be to sail in and out of the area now. There is still a British presence, but it is minimal and with little influence. If anything, the British vessels just come and go like all the others.

Still, Budwick and Eli have kept a sharp eye out. The last thing they want is any kind of trouble. So, Budwick makes sure he creeps into the harbor under the cover of darkness, something he's well accustomed to doing.

"Hell, I can see as good at night as I can during the day," he often says. "Less crazies out here at night. I'm usually the only one."

They blend in with the other vessels in the harbor. It doesn't take long for them to empty their cargo over the course of a day. They spend the better part of a night reloading and haul out first thing in the morning. It seems as though hardly anyone has noticed, which is just how they prefer it.

As Budwick and his crew ease their way toward the mouth of the harbor, the sight of a large vessel catches their attention. The immense size of it makes it clear that it is a British ship. They don't even bother looking at its colors.

"She's just anchored out there," Mosely says as he returns from the bow, where he gave the ship a good, suspicious once-over.

"Well, let's get a little closer and see what we can find," Budwick says, with little concern about inviting trouble.

As the ship gets closer, Eli's eyes widen. His mouth drops for a moment and he feels a tension inside. It is no ordinary British vessel, he concludes. It is one he's seen before and knows well.

"It's the *Thunder*," he says, disbelieving his own sight.

The name doesn't seem to register with Budwick, but as he watches the ship and notes the reaction of both Eli and Mosely, he figures it out.

"Ain't that the ship you escaped from?" he asks, knowing the answer already.

Budwick spins the wheel to turn away, yet Eli stops him.

"No, let's sail by," he says. "I want to look."

Mosely seems in agreement with that plan, but grabs his musket. He proceeds to load it and has it at the ready in a matter of moments.

Eli glances his way. He sees the anger and hatred in the eyes of his friend. He can sense the same feelings rising himself. He feared he might die on that ship at one time. He knows many good men suffered that fate aboard her.

He can picture Kane's face in his mind's eye, mocking him and tempting him. The sense of evil he felt back then begins to consume him again. He knows fear lingers inside, but so does a need for vengeance and a release of the rage that still runs deep.

"I wonder if Kane is aboard," he says to himself, loud enough for both Budwick and Mosely to hear.

The three look intently, searching for that tall, intimidating figure that could only be him.

"I hope he is," Mosely says. "I want nothing more than a shot at him."

He stands there with gun in hand, looking anxious and eager for the opportunity. Eli looks at him and feels his anger. He glances at Budwick, who steers a little closer toward the vessel, obviously enjoying the thrill of such an opportunity.

"But he won't see it coming," Budwick says. "Might be fun to pluck us a Redcoat. Leave town with a bang."

Budwick gives the command for the crew to be at the ready for anything. They all look confused, but they prepare themselves regardless. They watch as the hulking British vessel looms closer.

Budwick tries to stay off and away from them, only to steer back at the last moment, getting them closer without appearing to be closing in on the other ship.

There is little to no movement on the deck of the hulking British vessel. Most of its crew are standing around or doing chores topside. But, as Eli scans the deck for the one figure they search for, the man suddenly appears.

"There, in the stern, by the wheel," Eli says, almost a shout in his excitement.

It is unmistakable that the figure standing tall above the wheel is Kane. For a moment, he is turned away, but as the *Wicked* steers closer for a quick pass to its stern, he looks their way.

"I'm going behind them and then off to their starboard," Budwick says. "That should give you a clean shot of him. And a good getaway for us."

Mosely picks up his musket and aims. He waits as the *Wicked* slowly moves closer and the pass behind the stern of the *Thunder* begins. Kane is completely aware of them now and watches intently as they draw closer. He makes no sudden movement. He just stands there and watches.

"Got him in your sights?" Budwick asks.

For a moment, there's no answer. Mosely is focused intently on his target.

"Yep," he says.

Suddenly, there's a sense of quiet; the anticipation of the blast. It seems to take forever. They wait. Mosely focuses on the right moment and the right view of his target. As the *Wicked* bobs on the small waves, Mosely fixes his aim on Kane. He's got the sway of his vessel in his mind and anticipates the moment in which he can't miss.

"Stop," says Eli. "Skandar, don't."

Mosely doesn't move. He maintains his focus. He's intent on getting his shot off.

"Stop," Eli shouts again. Not waiting for a reaction, he leans toward Budwick and gives the wheel a quick pull. The *Wicked* suddenly jerks in a different direction and Mosely's concentration is broken. He lowers the musket and glares back at Eli.

"Sorry," he says. "We're better than this."

Mosely looks at his friends and realizes that Eli might be right. Killing for revenge is only answering Kane's evil with something similar. He is suddenly ashamed of his own weakness and thirst for vengeance.

Budwick turns the wheel some more and turns off and away from the *Thunder*. Eli looks up at the stern and sees Kane staring back at him. He can't tell whether the man recognizes him, but they're close enough that Eli can clearly see Kane's intense glare.

Eli is tempted to yell out something, or even give some sort of gesture. Instead, he lets the moment pass. What was done is done. Kane is nothing to him now. He just stands and watches. He returns Kane's glare with a deep intense look of his own. His mind is clear. His anger gone. His need for vengeance is no more. All he feels inside is peace.

CHAPTER SIXTY-TWO
Aboard the HMS *Thunder*, 1780

Kane has read the letter over and over again. Each time he digests the latest update from home, his heart aches and the conflict in his soul stirs.

His wife has been feeling poorly but has seemingly recovered. His children continue to grow in his absence. He can only read about their progress and think about the things he's missing in their lives.

It might not be so bad if the war effort wasn't so prolonged and frustrating. It has been years since he's been home. He's wanted to return to England, but never felt he could afford to leave the cause to do so. It has tugged at his allegiances and been a constant ache in his heart.

Life goes on without him while the war continues with him in tow.

This conflict was supposed to be over by now. This rebellion was to be squashed and order returned to the sovereignty of Great Britain. Yet, here he is and here is the Royal Navy, continuing this slog of a grueling war.

Most of the ships have headed south. The British are in pursuit of Washington there. As many times as they think they're putting down the Continental Army, Washington and his troops manage to escape and continue to frustrate Howe and his pursuit.

Kane and the *Thunder* are lagging behind. It has been converted into a full-time prison vessel, at least until it is so full that a trip to Nova Scotia to transfer the captured is warranted. Kane has already made that trip once this year, and is tired of being a simple prison warden. It wasn't what he agreed to, even though he is fully aware that once he joined the fight, his orders came from others. And his say meant little.

His misses his wife and misses his children. It leaves a void inside that the conflicts of war can't fulfill. He feels a hardened heart and an anger that grows as the war continues. He believes in the cause, but the injustice of a rebellion that won't end and won't surrender to proper authority only fuels the ire inside.

Part of him wants to silence such rebellion with all his might, while another part grows weary from the conflict. Doubt creeps into his mind on occasion. Is it really a cause worth this kind of fight and sacrifice? Every time he reads a letter from home, that doubt only grows. It makes him feel weak.

It's been a few years now since he's been there. He recalls sitting in the backyard, enjoying the calm and quiet. The only noise was the delightful glee he'd hear from his children as they ran and shrieked and played.

The thought brings a smile to his face but an ache in his heart. His children must be growing fast. His wife must have her hands full raising them alone.

"For what?" he asks himself, muttering under his breath. "I sacrifice so much. For what?"

He was devoted to the cause. He believed in upholding Britain's supremacy and enforcing its laws. He saw a duty in serving and a commitment to halting any rebellion to England.

He hasn't been privy to all decisions made, but he's heard plenty of grumbling about the leadership in the British ranks. This rag-tag, ungrateful throng of rebels should have been squashed immediately. England had superior power and numbers. Yet, the conflict has been prolonged through poor planning and even worse execution.

Kane was sent to the colonial shores to patrol the harbors, especially with the blockade of Boston. He was there to limit the smuggling and combat the privateers.

Things have changed since then. Many of the privateer attacks are happening elsewhere; the British shores face threats from them regularly. Many supply ships have been lost, and a great deal of British firepower has had to be repositioned to protect the British shores and valued channels.

Kane has expected a call for his return home. He could be part of that defense and help rid England of the threat off its shores. Instead, he's sailing a prison ship, following on the heels of the Royal Navy.

He takes a deep breath and composes himself. He is consumed with frustration. He folds the letter and slides it back into the pocket of his overcoat.

He glances over the deck of his vessel. All is quiet. The crew is milling about. Some are swabbing the deck while others catch up on repairs. He's expecting to haul out in a day or two and follow the rest of the fleet south, unless new orders arrive.

As he turns to look out over the New York City harbor, he spots a ship cutting a path toward his stern. It's a suspicious maneuver. It's a concerning one as well, especially with the smaller vessels among his fleet having already moved south.

He hears the first mate call to the crew to rush them into action, in case any kind of attack materializes. Kane just stands quietly and watches it approach.

He sees nothing alarming. Most of the crew on the vessel are just standing there, looking at him as he gazes toward them.

Then, he spots the raised musket. He sees it aimed right at him and expects to see the instant flash. When he doesn't, he realizes he has a moment to duck or hide, but he does no such thing. He remains still and watches. He stares back at the pointed musket, almost daring it to fire.

Yet, it never does. Instead, he sees it lowered. A man beside the gunman gestures as if to halt any assault. He spots the other man staring up at him. He fixes his gaze upon him and senses a familiarity. He watches as they sail past, his stare meeting that of the other man.

He doesn't remember the name, but recognizes the foe. It is the privateer captain he attempted to sway to the British side. He recalls the man's face, a determined, deep-set stare of intensity. It was full of scorn and contempt when he tried tempting him. The conviction was strong in him. It was one of the reasons he was chosen for execution. And then he escaped.

Kane can feel his anger inside. It was bad enough that he got away once. Here he is again, sailing on past, as if to taunt him. Kane thinks about reaching for his pistol. He's not sure he could reach them now, but he'd love to take the shot they didn't dare to take.

He realizes his thinking about it was enough hesitation to let the vessel slip too far out of range. He has no smaller ship to pursue them with now. A barrage of cannon fire would take too long. He concludes there's little he can muster now. He takes a deep breath and sighs. All he can do is watch them sail off. Kane has been left behind.

After being forced to let them go, he descends the rear companionway. He enters the small meeting room adjacent to his quarters. There's food left there that some of the officers have been eating. Captain McCruddy still sits enjoying a bowl of soup when Kane storms in.

He takes a sip and begins to speak, but his words are halted as Kane walks directly to the table and tosses it over with one swift, violent motion. McCruddy sits there stunned until Kane leers at him. He drops his spoon on the floor with the rest of the broken dishware and food and rushes to the door.

Kane slams the door behind him. The destruction down below continues as Kane's fury is unleashed in solitude..

The *Wicked* sails away. Eli Miller is at peace. For Kane, the war goes on.

CHAPTER SIXTY-THREE
Aboard the *Wicked*, 1781

The harbor is full of constant motion. Ships sail in and drop anchor while many other vessels are bustling in an attempt to haul out before the day slips into night.

Despite all the coming and going, the harbor still doesn't seem to change. Anchored ships are scattered across the waters. There's a hum of activity, both in the sights and sounds of the harbor. It is constant. Maybe it will quiet down as evening sets in, but for now there's a steady flow of movement and sound.

Eli observes it all. He maintains watch on the deck. The crew is busily handling chores aboard the vessel. Some are fixing rigging while others are swabbing the deck. Budwick is ashore. He's there to secure a new load of cargo, but he's been gone most of the day. Eli oversees everything happening in the harbor around them, but there's no sign of Budwick.

There's no reason to be concerned, he tells himself. Certainly, Budwick could be delayed on shore. Maybe finding cargo hasn't gone as smoothly as he had hoped. Yet, it doesn't usually take this long. That's what worries Eli, that and the bad feeling that stirs deep inside.

He had concerns about coming back to this port. Budwick has made his share of enemies here. Of course, you could say that about many a harbor.

Being a merchant mariner is as challenging as ever as the war evolves. With less ships coming out of the colonies, an American vessel is easier to spot. Between pirates, privateers, and the British fleets patrolling just about everywhere, it can be an even more tenuous existence out at sea. If a ship isn't getting halted and harassed by British ships, it is running the risk of attack from a variety of nefarious foes.

To Eli, he feels as much in danger now as he did on his own privateer. The only difference was that he was better armed and he was the ship seeking to initiate conflict. Budwick has been fortunate to avoid anything in the way of trouble so far.

With the vessels from the colonies no longer under the arm of the British, it has allowed for visits to a variety of new ports around the world. It has also meant that ships don't have the protection that British vessels once provided. Instead, now the British are as much the enemy as anyone else.

Budwick managed to be a little creative on their first voyage. He had developed some new business in various ports in recent years. So, France, Spain, and Africa all offered promising ports of call for him. They spent a sizeable portion of the year sailing to Europe and visiting ports there.

This time out, Budwick wanted to return to some more familiar places, but it also made it more dangerous. The British presence in the south has increased as the war has moved in that direction. It makes it a challenge to be inconspicuous in a place like Charleston. Mexico was relatively quiet, but the Indies is fraught with trouble. Eli can't help but wonder if Budwick wanted to sail here to test his own iron.

When Mosely comes topside and realizes that Budwick has not returned, he is worried as well.

"I don't like the looks of this," he says.

Mosely had meant to go along with Budwick. He often joins him on such visits to shore but on this day, a painful stomach had sidelined him to his quarters for much of the day. He still feels weak, but the rest has done him good.

"We'll give him a little more time," Eli says, knowing that he'll have to make some sort of decision should Budwick not return. That might mean making a quick escape or going ashore to attempt to find him.

"But we should begin preparing for some sort of action. If he doesn't arrive soon, a counter on our part may be inevitable."

CHAPTER SIXTY-FOUR
West Indies, 1781

Staring at the barrel of a gun is nothing new.

Budwick has faced many a musket or pistol aimed in his direction. This time it is no different. What he never thought he'd see is a confident and cocky Buddy Bush staring back at him. One of his subservients has a pistol cocked and pointed at him. Bush has his own pistol in hand. But it is the look on the other man's face that surprises Budwick most.

He's always seen Bush as a bit of a boob. No more competent than he was intelligent. Budwick has always said if Bush wasn't such a nitwit, he wouldn't have any wits about him at all.

But here the nitwit is with the upper hand on his old nemesis. Now backed by the British, Bush has a little more backbone and competency. He's emerged as quite the force in the West Indies. Not much happens there without Bush knowing about it or being involved in it.

Budwick is actually surprised that some up-and-coming businessman hasn't already moved in on him and ushered him aside or left him at the bottom of the sea somewhere.

Though he knew Bush would be out for him if he ever showed his face on the island again, Budwick thought nothing of it. He'd outsmarted him before, it wouldn't be so hard to do now.

But when he inquired with some locals about someone looking to move cargo, he was steered to a name he'd never heard before. Budwick can't believe he was so careless. He went in pursuit of this potential cargo only to walk into the man's office and discover it was a well-armed and waiting Bush.

"So glad to see you, Captain Budwick," Bush said with delight. "I believe the time has come to settle some business."

Budwick looks back with a bit of contempt for Bush and some annoyance at himself. But as he sits with a pistol aimed at him and an almost giddy Bush delighting in his capture, Budwick wonders how to escape this predicament. Or whether Bush's intent is to gain revenge and get money. It could be both. Budwick knows that Bush certainly could choose to execute him then and there and still attempt to claim his cargo.

"I ought to shoot right here and now," Bush says with a devilish grin. "That would certainly be a judgment against your previous actions."

As Budwick mulls over the likely offenses for which Bush seeks vindication, he grimaces at the thought. He's swindled Bush on a number of occasions. He's used him to barter for a better price. He's shortchanged him on deals. He's smuggled cargo that he assumed Bush never knew about. He's even made a mockery of him by avoiding Bush's capture and also escaping from his grasp a few years ago. He concludes that there may be no easy answer for how to get himself out of this situation.

"I'll gladly compensate you," Budwick says with a smile, trying to look sincere even though his grin is as phony as they come. "I'm a reasonable man and I'm willing to make amends with you, Mr. Bush."

Bush laughs, with an awkward grunt of a chuckle. It makes Budwick think of a groundhog he beat with a stick once. The men around him all join in the laughter. Apparently, Budwick's offer of reparation isn't well received.

"You'll make amends, Budwick," Bush says in a serious tone. "You'll make amends indeed. With your cargo. With your ship. And maybe even with your life."

CHAPTER SIXTY-FIVE
West Indies, 1781

Budwick realizes he's left with nothing but desperate measures. It may mean the unthinkable, but he knows he has no choice.

With Bush seeking redemption and a little vengeance, Budwick understands that drastic measures are needed to potentially save himself. He does so by offering up his ship and his crew.

"You know my first mate is an escapee from the British," Budwick mentions, looking and sounding as smarmy as possible. "So is another member of my crew. I can be sure your British counterparts would be pleased with their capture and return."

He can see that he has Bush's attention and interest. He suggests that rather than an attack on the vessel that would lead to great bloodshed, another option is possible. It would not only save the ship but also surrender him the crew without much fight.

"If I escort you out there and lead you aboard, I can simply hand you over the ship and the men," Budwick suggests. "You'll calmly commandeer the vessel and the crew. You'll have everything you want, with little resistance."

He can see Bush mulling over such an option. Could Budwick be so unscrupulous as to give up his ship and his crew to save himself? Of course he would, Bush concludes.

Moments later, Bush has rounded up a group of armed men and the loaded longboats are underway. The *Wicked* is their destination. Two boats full of armed men with pistols. A gleeful Buddy Bush sits in the stern of one. Budwick has been placed in the bow. He may be equally gleeful, but doesn't show it.

The intent is to board Budwick's vessel, where Bush and his men will seize it. The cargo and crew will be taken. The ship will be comman-deered. What happens to Budwick and his men, who knows?

Budwick is ecstatic. He's not completely sure this plan will work, but he thinks it just might. He wasn't sure Bush could be sold on it. He feared that maybe he had smartened up and couldn't be outwitted as eas-ily as before. Budwick is pleased that maybe Bush is still just as dimwitted as ever.

As the longboats draw closer to the *Wicked*, Budwick waves to the men onboard. He spots Eli gazing down upon them. There's Mosely, as well. He looks at them and waves.

"We come in peace," he shouts, providing a few more waves to get their attention. They wave back, both at the same time. Budwick strains to hide his smile.

He turns to look at Bush. It is as if he's eyeing his new vessel al-ready.

"I have plenty of gold coins I've collected on board," Budwick says. "That should make up for much of the money I've cost you."

Bush is pleased and grins, flashing a mouthful of broken teeth and spaces in between. He's thrilled to have reduced Ezra Budwick to a sorry sailor that would stoop to such measures to save himself.

"You have seen the error of your ..."

Before Bush can finish his sentence, a musket shot rings out and echoes across the harbor. It stuns Bush momentarily. Then he notices the hole that has ripped open his chest. He puts his hand to the wound as warm blood gushes from his body. Before he can think or do anything more, he slumps over dead into the surprised arms of the man seated beside him.

The other men in the boat stop moving. They're stunned at the sight of a dead Buddy Bush and are suddenly terrified of where the next shot might go. Sure enough, more shots ring out. The men in the other longboat have little time to react. In a spray of gunfire, three men are hit. Their toppled and slumped bodies upset the balance of the boat. It cap-sizes, leaving the others even more helpless as they splash in the water.

In the other boat, Budwick takes advantage of a stunned oarsman. He's stopped rowing and is rendered helpless as he watches the chaos around him. Budwick grabs one of the stout wooden oars from him and delivers a blow to the back of his head.

The man in the stern with Bush bleeding all over him realizes the next swing is likely for him. He shoves the dead Bush from his lap and dives over the stern, hoping for a watery escape.

With the paddle-end of his oar cracked severely after the blow to a man's head, Budwick drops it and picks up the other. He stands in the boat and guides it toward his own vessel, where a rope ladder has been lowered for his use.

It was all a plan that Budwick had put in place long ago. He warned his crew that if ever he were being escorted back to his ship by another party, he was likely being held captive. He knew Eli would recognize Bush and with the words, "We come in peace" and a wave, he had signaled that a defense of the vessel needed to be underway.

He knew Mosely would be able to incapacitate Bush, and that the suddenness of that shot might be enough to render the rest of them useless. Just in case, other members of the crew would be armed and ready to fire if needed.

As Budwick climbs aboard his vessel, he gets a rousing cheer from his crew.

"No cargo here, men," he shouts. "Let's haul out and try elsewhere."

He glances over at Eli and smiles.

"Now we're even," he says.

CHAPTER SIXTY-SIX
Atlantic Ocean, 1781

Out in the open ocean, where the sky is blue and the sea reflects a deeper shade, is what Eli appreciates most about being at sea.

It comes with the hard memories of his father, but even something as tragic as that can't overwhelm the intense beauty and peacefulness of the water.

As he mans the wheel, he takes deep breaths and savors each taste of the fresh, salty air. He loves the smell and the taste of the pure sea breeze.

He's always been aware of the conflict this creates for him. As much as he has grown up following the sea and loving so many aspects of it, he also loathes many things about it.

He's always been torn about following the path chosen for him as a child or forsaking it. He's never been able to solve that conflict, in his life or in his mind. He reckons that sometimes life dictates a man's path, but sometimes he does get to choose which direction to go.

That is finally what Eli has concluded. Growing up at his father's side, he developed an appreciation for following the sea. He also developed a dedication to that legacy. He was groomed a sailor. That's what he was.

But as life moved on, he became more than a sailor, and responsibilities were greater than just those things contained on a sailing vessel. He was a merchant mariner by duty and by life's circumstances. But he wasn't sure if it was by choice.

It was always a safe haven for him, even with all the dangers that come with it. He was carrying on his father's legacy and making that family sailing tradition his own. He loved the satisfaction in that. He enjoyed having the skills and experience to be so successful at sea at such a young age.

But the rigors of the sea and the challenges of being away wore at him, especially as life expanded beyond the shores. He was more than just a sailor, but the sea was where he was best.

He doesn't feel tied to that trade any longer, and he doesn't feel obligated to pursue it any further. He knows he's tried to leave the sea before but now, more than ever, he believes the time is right.

He's made some money over the last few trips with Budwick. He's hoping to settle down with his family and begin anew. They've looked into buying farmland and starting another life there.

He's excited about the future and has come to grips with his past.

"Quit yer daydreaming," says Budwick as he emerges from the cabin below. "I see ya staring off into the blue. I hope yer paying attention to where we're going."

Eli laughs and explains to Budwick that he was just about to summon him from below.

"I thought you might like to see this," he says. He points off the bow toward the horizon. As far away as the eye can see, is a collection of ships. They're coming from the east and sailing pretty hard. Budwick grabs the spyglass and takes a look.

"I'll be a friggin' French pastry," he exclaims. "It's a whole fleet. Looks like an invading force."

"French?" Eli asks, assuming he knows the answer already.

"Yep," replies Budwick. "Looks like they're joinin' the party."

The colonies have been in negotiations with the French for the longest time. Limited progress had been made, but the aid of the French, especially with a fleet of fighting forces, just might help turn the tide of the war.

"Let's just stay out of their way, shall we?" says Budwick.

Eli turns the wheel and begins to steer the *Wicked* east. His intention is to sail on past them well to their stern, far enough away that they barely notice them.

Budwick calls to Mosely on the forward deck and instructs the crew to be at the ready, just in case a threat poses itself.

"So maybe we'll have some excitement on the way home," says Budwick. "Been about a week now since I nearly been shot last."

"Don't worry," replies Eli. "I'm sure another chance will present itself soon. I don't think there's any shortage of people who would gladly put a musket ball in you."

Ezra laughs at the suggestion, but realizes maybe he shouldn't think it that funny.

"Well, maybe a peaceful trip home ain't such a bad thing, either," he says.

The two friends stand and watch the fleet of ships sailing off in the distance. It is a sign of more conflict to come, but both are thankful to be avoiding it.

"You know, Ezra," begins Eli. "This is my last trip."

Budwick says nothing for a moment. Normally he'd joke about the numerous times Eli has said that before.

"I know it is," he replies. "I knew someday you'd say it and would mean it."

"I'm sorry, my friend," Eli says. "But it is what I have to do. My life is elsewhere now."

"I'll miss you," Budwick says. "You're a pain in the ass, but you're a good sailor and a good friend."

The two laugh like two young schoolboys poking fun at the other.

"You know, you're a lucky man," Budwick says. "I think following the sea is a choice you make when you got nothing else to follow. You've found that. I'm still looking for the life that's better than the one I got."

"You've got a pretty good life yourself there, Captain Budwick," says Eli. "Never a dull moment, is there?"

"Not if I can help it," says Budwick with a smile.

CHAPTER SIXTY-SEVEN
Massabesick Plantation, 1782

Young Eligood tosses the ball toward his waiting brother. His older sibling watches intently and eyes the ball wobbling toward him. He twitches his arms and shoulders in anticipation and as his eyes widen, he lets go a mighty swing. And misses.

"I ain't felt a breeze like that since Cape Horn," shouts Budwick with a boisterous laugh.

Farmhand Buddy Grimmel picks up the ball and tosses it back to Joseph. He winds up and offers his brother another chance.

This time, he connects with a mighty wallop. It flies on the wind well over Joseph's head and past the reach of another farmhand, Isaac Dent. Isaac goes in pursuit of the ball while Eligood runs around the field, gleeful from his mighty hit.

The boys have lured the two farmhands away from their chores and enticed them into playing a game of rounders. It's a game that Budwick has taught the boys. He saw it played in England and brought back the notion to teach the boys. He even provided them some sticks and balls he found overseas for use in the game.

It's a game in which one player tosses the ball to a hitter. He tries to hit the ball and run around the field while the opposing team fields the ball. It is a simple version when the two brothers split up the farmhands to field a pair of two-man teams.

"I taught that boy to hit pretty well," Budwick says.

Eli chuckles at Budwick's boasting. He finds it ironic that after a prolonged war with the British, his friend has been teaching the boys a game he took from England. Budwick perfected his hitting skills by swinging those same bats at the stale and hardened biscuits left over in the galley. He'd smack them and watch them sail out into the deep blue ocean, breaking apart as they plummeted to the water.

He'd raise his arms following a particularly good hit, something Eligood currently mimics as he runs around the field.

"You might be a bad influence on them," Eli says to his friend.

Budwick, his face showing the grayness of age, flashes a wrinkly smile, taking pride in his influence on the rebels of the next generation.

Eli and Faith have lived in Massabesik Plantation for over a year. With a life at sea finally behind him, Eli began to develop the land inherited from Elizabeth's ancestors. It is 165 acres of woods and farmland. It is a short trip from Portsmouth and the ocean, but it feels like miles away.

The British surrendered in Yorktown, and the colonies are finally rid of the Redcoats and British rule that threatened for so long. Instead, Great Britain is now trying to maintain its rule in the rest of the world, fighting more battles as their hold on their dynasty continues to slip away.

Eli certainly doesn't miss the war, and he doesn't miss the sea. There's a quiet and peacefulness about the land that Eli only ever felt when being well out at sea. The distance from the rest of the world has created solitude and a calmness that Eli relishes after the hustle and bustle of harbor life and the chaos of war.

The nearest neighbor is only a mile or so away, but it feels like a complete escape from the rest of the world.

As the colonies begin to rebuild and expand and families resettle in new frontiers, lands like this are being claimed.

For many years, there were no permanent settlers in this area. Much of the land has been divided in parcels and sold off. Some assumed they could claim the land and subsequently inherit it for service in the war, but that proved a faulty assumption. Settling on land that wasn't owned by the government led to a tax so high that many of the people couldn't afford it.

That's how Elizabeth's ancestors came to own the property. They purchased it years before and continued to develop it. When Eli chose to no longer follow the sea, he sold his property in the harbor and purchased this land from the Douglass clan.

He's continued to farm the land with some success and has expanded the house into a sizeable dwelling for his family.

He watches his friend Budwick playing with the boys. He realizes he never really expected his longtime friend to still be here. His life at sea, his reckless abandonment and his penchant for getting himself in and out of trouble would surely catch up to him, Eli assumed.

As much as he hated the thought of it, he always wondered if that was Budwick's destiny. Budwick has always been a hot spark who ignited a lot of flames, but it seemed inevitable that he'd burn out eventually.

But there he is, swinging a bat like he is a boy, relishing any deep ball he hits while ignoring any aches and pains that accompany the groans from his body when he runs and jumps around the field.

Eli never wanted the life that Budwick seems to thrive in. He saw his father engaged in something similar. Luke certainly wasn't the rebel that Budwick is, but he sailed the seas with the same disregard for danger.

Eli can understand it with Budwick. What did he have to live for? He had no family, no responsibilities at home. He was free of what he calls 'life's baggage.' He was a scoundrel with no attachments, other than his ship and whatever he called home.

As for Eli's father, he had those commitments at home. He had a wife and family. It wasn't that he wanted to be away from them. He often hated leaving for long voyages. It was hard on him and on the family. Eli's brother was likely a sorry example of that cost.

It was hard for Eli's father to escape the lure of the sea, especially with the money that came with it. In the early settlement of the colonies, especially in Portsmouth, the sea was the means for survival and building a future.

Eli has faced that same choice. It has been a difficult decision, one fraught with pain and guilt that he feared would never cease.

As he watches his boys gleefully play with Budwick, he glances over at his wife. Faith stands and watches and laughs at the sight. She's expecting a child in a few months. He sees a happiness and contentment in her.

It is the same sense of peace he now feels within himself. For years, he's been tormented by his past. The tragic losses, the hurt and the guilt, the difficult choices, the imprisonment, the thoughts of never seeing his family again, the seeming inevitability of his own death… They all created an incredible amount of fear and a sense of failure. He feels free from all that now.

The spaciousness of his farm feels like an abundance of freedom after all his time on confined ships and prison cells. The joy and laughter he experiences with his family is something he missed when being so far away. Their love fills his heart and replaces the longing and regret that was there and so constant.

His mind suddenly flashes back to that moment at sea. That vision of his father flailing helplessly in the stormy waves replays itself yet again. He feels that sense of helplessness all over again. He wishes the sea had delivered his father home instead of devouring him like so many others.

His father never had the chance to live as Eli is living now. His brother likely didn't either. The younger Luke has not been seen or heard from since being spotted on that privateer. It is assumed he was another casualty of war.

While the knowledge saddens him, it also makes him realize the true blessing of what life has brought him. It took years, heartbreak, too much conflict and an abundance of fear, but Eli smiles as he realizes that he's finally found peace. He's broken free from a life in which he'd been trapped for too long.

He rises from his chair and walks toward Budwick. He extends his hand, waiting for his friend to relinquish possession of the bat.

"Let me show you how it is done, old man," he says.

He sends Budwick out to the field to offer him a pitch. The boys scatter in the field in hopes of catching the ball.

Budwick stands a short distance away, eyeing his friend and the practice swings he takes. When Eli nods, Budwick knows he's ready.

Eli watches as Budwick prepares to throw him the ball. He grips the stick tightly and leans backwards just a touch before stepping forward with all his might. His timing is off, however. Eli's swing flails at the air as the ball harmlessly sails on by and lands in the dirt behind him.

"A gale force breeze comes off that swing," boasts Budwick.

Eli groans. Budwick and the boys cheer with delight.

"I'll have to slow it down fer ya," Budwick taunts, looking back and smiling at the boys.

Budwick gets the ball back and dusts it off. He smirks at Eli. He nods, acknowledging that another offering is on the way. This offering is a little faster, as Budwick attempts to throw off his friend with a different velocity.

Eli watches it leave his friend's hand. On this attempt, his timing is just right. His swing connects and follows through, twisting and contorting Eli's body for a moment. His blast sails high above Budwick's head and soars well past the boys. They initially don't chase, simply stand and watch as it rises into the sky and then slowly comes down, landing deep in the grass of the field. The boys race each other for the ball while Eli stands still grinning. He flips the wooden stick into the air and raises his hands high.

He grins at his friend, now frowning in frustration, who had his heart set on blazing a pitch past him. Eli slowly turns and winks at Faith as she looks on and smiles.

With victory claimed, Eli relishes the feeling and walks away.

ABOUT THE AUTHOR

His ancestors were privateers, shipbuilders, merchant mariners, and lighthouse keepers. Kevin C. Mills is a product of his own rich maritime history. A love of the ocean and its history has been passed down through numerous Mills generations.

Sea of Liberty completes a trilogy of historical novels based upon that storied history. It is loosely based on the life of his privateer ancestor, Eligood Mills. According to family legend, Eligood was aboard the privateer *Grand Turk* and captured by the British. After years in prison, Eligood made a daring escape and returned to life in Portsmouth, New Hampshire. He then retired in Waterborough, Maine and is buried there.

His first novel, *Sons and Daughters of the Ocean,* was loosely based on the maritime history of his Brooksville, Maine ancestors. Many of the characters were rooted in true life experiences. *Sons and Daughters of the Ocean* offers an accurate portrayal of life in the age of sail.

Historical Novel Review wrote this about *Sons and Daughters of the Ocean*:

"While the opening portion of this book builds gradually, readers should be encouraged to know that there are genuinely tense scenes later on, as well as some powerfully descriptive and detailed passages about ocean storms and sailing. Kevin C. Mills confidently guides his readers through this nautical tale with an unfailing knowledge of his subject."

The Bangor Daily News said this about *Sons and Daughters of the Ocean*:

"Great efforts are made here to bring the world of 19th century seagoing Maine to life."

The follow-up novel is called *Breakwater*. It is a story based on the life of his grandfather. The novel chronicles the life of Hal Miller, who struggles to find purpose in the pain of his life. He is challenge by his wife's declining health, which tests his strength and shakes his faith. Clark Miller barely knew his grandfather. Still, he learns from Hal Miller's life as Clark struggles to understand his own happiness.

Bushnell on Books wrote this about *Breakwater*:

"Mills vividly and convincingly describes the emotions of love, happiness, missed opportunities, sadness and loss both men experience. They are good men confronting life as best they can, trying to do the right thing no matter their sacrifice."

TCM reviews had this to say about *Breakwater*:

"I sometimes wonder if we've become a society of comfort seekers. We shy away from anything that could be uncomfortable or the least bit difficult. Somehow we feel entitled to an easy and carefree life filled only with good things. (In Breakwater), our grandparents knew differently. Life was filled with hardship and heartache. Yet, there were these treasured moments too. More than that though, there was trust, and faith that things were exactly as they should be."

Mills also wrote *Sidelined*, a nonfiction account of his journalism career. It looks at sports journalism in a unique way. Reliving his own experiences and adventures with some of New England's top newspapers, Mills presents strange but true episodes from his life as a sports writer.

The Kennebec Journal and Waterville Sentinel wrote this about *Sidelined*:

"Sidelined is Maine sports reporter Kevin Mills' funny and perceptive memoir of his more than 20 years experience on the sports beat, covering everything from football, basketball and hockey, to skiing, auto racing, soccer and sailing."